FOR LAMB

LESA CLINE-RANSOME

HOLIDAY HOUSE   NEW YORK

Copyright © 2023 by Lesa Cline-Ransome
All Rights Reserved
HOLİDAY HOUSE is registered in the U.S. Patent and Trademark Office.
Printed and bound in November 2022 at Maple Press, York, PA, USA.
www.holidayhouse.com
First Edition
1 3 5 7 9 10 8 6 4 2

Library of Congress Cataloging-in-Publication Data is available.

ISBN: 978-0-8234-50152 (hardcover)

For Lamb Whittle and those whose stories call to us to write, speak up, fight on

PROLOGUE

And then, there, there in the torchlight, I see her. Pressed in close against the others. Her face red as a fever sweat. Hair bright as a flame. *My friend.*

When the men let her go, I hear branches snapping and watch the crowd move closer. I search again for my friend, but I can't hardly tell one from the other in this crowd. Pressed in tight, each one of those white faces looks just like the next. Smiling through shiny white teeth like a pack of hungry dogs.

Simeon is long gone now, I suspect.

Far.

North.

Safe.

From this. From them. From all of it.

A branch cracks as loud as a gunshot and the crowd cheers. I stay hidden behind the bush, just past the fence, and look up through the leaves at the dark. Not a star in the sky tonight. But the flickers of gold from the embers light up the sky in what looks like fireflies. Pretty almost.

LAMB

"**THE** choir will lead us in our devotional hymn," Reverend Greer said, and sat down behind the pulpit.

Soon as I heard the first note on the piano, the sweat started under my arms. In the back row of the youth choir during rehearsal every Saturday morning with everyone's voice singing on top of mine, I didn't know Miss Twyman even knew I could carry a tune. But one Sunday, after service, Miss Twyman told Momma I had a "lovely voice," and Momma told Miss Twyman she already knew that but was surprised Miss Twyman was just finding out. And now, since she knew, my momma said, couldn't Miss Twyman find a way to let me lead next week's devotional hymn? Momma has a way of asking that lets you know she's not asking at all. And now, here I was leading, when all I wanted was to follow, singing along quiet, in the back, with the rest of the choir. There were days, listening to Momma, I could make my ownself believe near anything she believed about me. Not today.

At breakfast this morning, when she was braiding up my hair, she could tell I was getting the scared feeling I always get when I have to be up in front of people.

"Now Miss Twyman wouldn't have you up there looking like a fool if you couldn't sing. You know that," Momma said, pulling my braid tight.

1

"Miss Twyman says everybody has a lovely voice," I told her. "Not just me."

"I don't know about everybody. She was just talking 'bout you."

In the back was where I felt I belonged, looking at Juanita Handy's curly ponytail, swaying from side to side while she sang all the youth choir solos. Every once in a while her voice would crack when she tried to reach too high for a note, and Earvent would hit my hand or one of the boys in back would laugh, but I kept looking straight ahead, wishing I was brave enough to stand up every time like Juanita, not caring if my voice cracked or not, but knowing, like Juanita always did, that up front was just where I was meant to be.

Now standing alone with the choir behind me, I was too scared to be mad at Momma. Just needed to get through one song and be done. Let Momma see I ain't never been and never would be a soloist. I could almost feel Juanita Handy's eyes staring in the back of my head. I could hear her sweet voice hitting those notes right and know she was wondering what I was doing in her spot. I wished I could tell her to go ask my momma. The blood was pounding in my ears, louder than the piano, but I came in,

> *Would you be free from the burden of sin?*
> *There's pow'r in the blood, pow'r in the blood.*

Too soft, too shaky, I could tell. I looked over at Miss Twyman and she pinched up her face. I closed my eyes tight.

"Sing it, child," Reverend Greer said beside me. I opened my eyes and looked out into the pews. Staring back at me was Simeon, grin stretched from one end of his face to the other. He saw me looking and nodded his head, telling me to go on ahead, give it some more. So I did. Now the front pew chimed in.

"Yes, yes, Lord" and "That's right" mixed in with the song, and I looked over at Miss Twyman, watching her hands tell my mouth what to do. She smiled up at me.

There is pow'r, pow'r, wonder-working pow'r
In the blood of the lamb...

I looked over at Momma swaying, quiet, her head bowed low, one hand raised just above her head. The sweat dripped down my back now. In the pews together, when we sang this song from the hymnal, Momma would squeeze my hand, remembering.

I closed my eyes again.

Would you o'er evil a victory win?
There's wonderful pow'r in the blood.

After the second verse, Miss Twyman was circling her hand, telling me and the choir to sing the chorus one more time, and this time, my voice got a little louder, a little deeper too.

Let God move you, Miss Twyman reminded me after yesterday's rehearsal. And I think I did let God in, and he helped me move from side to side, with the music making my voice stronger as I swayed. I hoped it was God, because Simeon and Momma weren't gonna be enough to make me sing the song the way it sounded it my head. Just when I was finding my way, the song ended, and the reverend stepped up again to the pulpit.

"Amen, Sister." He nodded at me. "A-men..."

I walked to the back row of the choir stand, not looking at Juanita, not hearing any of Reverend Greer's sermon. Not even Earvent said anything as I made my way over her legs and back to my seat. I just made my lips move along to the rest of the hymns we sang in service, hoping Momma would let me alone now but knowing she never would.

"You sang that song today, Sister Lamb," Reverend Greer said after service as I stepped down from the choir stand.

"Thank you, Reverend Greer," I said. My momma stepped up beside me, smiling. Simeon stood behind her, grin still on his face.

"This girl can sing, can't she, Reverend?" my momma said. *Too bold*, I thought. My momma is always too bold.

"She sure can," said Simeon, his head nodding. I hit his hand.

"Why didn't I see you up there in the choir, Brother Simeon?" the reverend said, his hand slapping down hard on Simeon's shoulder.

"Well, uh...God has blessed each one of us with our own special gifts." Simeon smiled. "Sadly, singing is not mine."

Momma looked at Simeon, trying, I could tell, to keep smiling and not say what she wanted to say in the House of God and in front of Reverend Greer.

Reverend nodded his head at Simeon, smiling back. "You are right there, son. Lord knows, some folks sitting in that choir have talents that should be put to use elsewhere in the church. Can I get an Amen, Brother Simeon?"

"Amen!" Simeon laughed.

Me and Momma stood watching them. No matter who Simeon talked to, it wasn't long before he said something to win them over. Everyone except Momma, who stood watching him and smiling for Reverend Greer but not Simeon.

When we left church and headed home, Momma turned to Simeon. "You can't let her shine for just one day?"

"What?"

"Don't you *what* me. You always gotta take away her shine?" she said.

"Momma, I—" I started.

"You know she was only up there because you made her do it, right? That wasn't nothing about Lamb. That was about trying to make *you* shine," he said.

"Boy, I—"

"Can we please not do this today?" I asked. "On a Sunday? After church? Please?"

They were both quiet.

"Well, Amen to that," Simeon said.

LAMB

I ain't never seen my momma as someone who was saved. More like she sees God as the insurance man who comes round once a month collecting and you pay up because if you don't, you die without a halfway-decent burial, laid out in some pitiful pine box. For my momma, Sunday service is like paying the insurance man. She don't like paying up, but knows it could be worse if she don't. I think for both of us the best part of church is the music. Me singing in the choir and the two of us singing loud to the one hymn they play nearly every week that makes my momma reach over and touch my hand, like just hearing it brings her right back to the day I was born.

"You wasn't nothing like your brother, screaming to be seen the minute he came into this world. Nope, you just looked at me, real quiet, with those big old eyes of yours. Miss Ruby helped deliver you and I said to her, soon as you were in my arms, not making a sound, but watching me close, 'She's as quiet as a lamb.' By the time your daddy came home, you hadn't even moved and that's when I knew.

"He said to me, 'Thinking we can name her Cora, for my momma.' I looked him right in his eyes, tired as I was, and said, 'Her name is Lamb.' He laughed some. Everybody did. 'You can't name her no

Lamb. You out your mind, Marion?' But I knew. I knew your name the minute I saw you. *My Lamb.*

"You had me worried, though, quiet as you were. When I took you back home for my daddy's burial, you spent the whole time hiding behind me. And with Simeon 'bout talking you to death, even my momma said, 'She ain't never gonna speak if that boy don't stop talking for her. My momma wasn't right about much, but she was right about that.

"Your daddy used to ask me twice a day—morning and night—'That Lamb sure favors me and my people, don't she?' And I'd have to tell him 'Yes she do, Chester.' But he was just asking because he could see you up under me all the time. He wanted a little piece of you too."

You can't get my momma to talk much about the past. Ask her about where she grew up or anything about my daddy, she barely has two words to say. But the one thing she can talk about all day long is naming me Lamb. Like it was the one thing she did right in her life.

"But Daddy picked Simeon's name, right?" I made the mistake of asking her once in the middle of her storytelling. She stopped me right there.

"Simeon is from the Bible. I picked his name too. Wasn't going to let no one name *my* children."

It's always *my children* with my momma, like she made us all by herself. My momma prides herself on not needing nobody to take care of hers. I suppose if there was a way to make us on her own, she would have done that too.

After that, I never interrupted when she was talking about the past. She needed to tell it her way.

LAMB

I remember my daddy in pieces, but not enough to make him whole. Simeon says he remembers him living with us one day and packing his bags the next. Come the next week, here he comes back again, unpacking the suitcase he just packed. I don't remember a lot of fighting, just the quiet of my momma and daddy. Sitting at a table not speaking.

Working on a railroad. Traveling to see his family. Working all kinds of hours. Simeon and Momma told me all kinds of stories until we all knew I knew the truth of it. He was gone for good.

One thing I remember about my daddy is the smell of him. Like the smell of fresh-cut wood and smoke, like the cigars I remember him smoking. And he was big. I'm expecting one day to be tall like him, but for now I just took on being big-boned and "bright," my momma calls me, with skin as light as my daddy's. Not sure I'll ever be anywhere near as tall as Simeon or my momma, so I'm sure never going to be as tall as I remember my daddy. One day Momma stopped talking about Daddy altogether. And when she did, me and Simeon did too.

I had just started school. And I was happy to finally not be away from Simeon for so much of the day when he was gone. Now Momma walked us both to school. Soon she said I'd walk with just Simeon. Didn't matter much to me. Walking in between the two of them was all

I really needed. Momma told me I'd need to start speaking for myself once I got to school.

"Won't be no Simeon to tell the teacher what you need," she said to me.

But I already knew that. I knew too I could find the words when I needed, but Simeon always had the right ones when I didn't. His words were pretty and he could find a way to make them funny or mean or serious or smart anytime he wanted, without thinking much about it. I couldn't do all that with mine but I knew I could get by fine until the school day was out and he'd be waiting for me by the door.

"What did you teach the class today?" he used to ask me every day that first year. And I would laugh.

"I'm not the teacher, Simeon."

"No? But I bet you're the smartest one in that class." I shook my head no, hung it low. Simeon always made me look at him. "You are the smartest one in that class, Lamb. Don't you forget that."

"But Simeon—I'm not…"

"You are what you say you are." Even young, Simeon always talked old. Like he was born knowing what to say.

So when the kids would make "baaa baaa" sounds like a lamb when I walked past, I tried to remember what Simeon told me about being smart and being the best even when I didn't always feel it.

From what I remembered, Momma wasn't much different after Daddy left. Maybe a little happier. Or as happy as Momma can be. Not long after Daddy left is when the Saturday parties started up. Momma would start cooking early in the day. A pot of neck bones and greens, corn bread. She'd fix us a cold supper early and draw our baths. Get us into bed. And then she'd put on one of her nice, flowery dresses, some lipstick, put music on the record player in the front room. And then we'd hear folks come in loud and laughing. Couldn't call them her friends because Momma didn't have people she saw regular outside of those Saturday night parties. We opened up the door from Simeon's room just enough to get a peek to see who they were and so Simeon could make up names for everyone, like Big-Boobied Bertha and Lil' Marge, that'd make me laugh till I cried. Sometimes the floor would shake, and the records would skip with all the dancing they were doing. We always knew when my momma's younger brother, Uncle Chime, came in. We could hear his voice above everyone else's. And before the night was over, he'd make his way into Simeon's room and check on us.

"I know y'all ain't asleep, so don't even play," he'd say, leaning in the doorway. I would run to hug him even though I hated the smell of drink and sweat on his clothes. I'd hear some woman shouting behind him, "What you doin' in there, Chime? C'mon back out here and dance with me," or "Chime, it's your hand." But I loved that he always took a minute to check in on us.

LAMB

I don't know when Momma started letting us come out to see what was going on. Probably Simeon just said he was gonna do it and did. Or maybe it was when I would sing along to the records, standing on Simeon's bedspread in my bare feet, and Simeon would practice all his dances. And Momma, who never checked in on us, one night did. She was just standing in the doorway, leaning the same way Uncle Chime did. A little smile on her face listening to me. When I finished singing "A-tisket, a-tasket, a brown and yellow basket," she clapped real slow.

"C'mere, baby," she said. I hated her drinking voice, which was deeper and slower than her regular voice. I stepped down thinking I was gonna be in trouble for being out of bed. But Momma took hold of my hand and pulled me into the front room, where all her Saturday night friends were sitting and talking or dancing.

"Listen to my baby," she said to everyone, and they got quiet and looked over at me. Then she walked over to the record player and played the song again. "Sing like you just did," she said to me, leaning up against her friend Myrtle, and everyone was looking, even Simeon. But I didn't want to sing in front of her Saturday night friends, just Simeon, and burst out crying.

Momma leaned down and whispered in my ear, "You got to stop being so scared of everything. Now go on and sing."

Simeon stepped in front of Momma, looked at me, and said soft, "Pretend it's just us, in my room. I'll stand in front of you and dance." He smiled down at me. And that was how I did it, with Simeon in front of me, swooping low and shaking his shoulders back and forth, and me singing loud as I could behind him, while everyone yelled, "Go on now," and "Git it!" I don't know if it was for me or Simeon and I didn't care. It felt a little bit good to be a part of the party with Momma and her friends. Uncle Chime walked in and watched too, yelling, "That's my Chop!"

When the song ended, Momma scooped me up, swaying a little bit. Told me I could go on back to the room if I wanted. But me and Simeon stayed in the front room, walking around trying to match the faces to the voices of the folks we'd been hearing. After that, when Momma didn't yell or make us go back into the room, we stayed every Saturday night there was a party until Momma's friends started expecting us to be there. I never liked the parties the way Simeon did. I said hello to the people I knew. Turned out Big-Boobied Bertha was the woman who worked at the Alamo Theater ticket counter.

When I was old enough, Momma would have me help with the food, stirring a pot or making a pan of cornbread. If it was warm, I'd fix two plates and bring them outside for me and Simeon. I liked to sit out back where it was quiet, unless Momma pulled me onto the floor with her.

"C'mon and dance with me, baby," Momma would ask, moving her hips in that way that made me feel like I was seeing something I shouldn't be.

"Nah, Momma, you know I hate dancing. Ask Simeon," I'd say, backing away.

"But I wanna dance with my baby. Simeon ain't my baby."

"Momma…" I had to do a little two-step to get her to stop.

"Bend your knees, baby," Momma told me. "Like this," she'd say, squatting low and laughing.

I bent my knees, but I still wasn't doing much of nothing. Finally she'd stop fussing with me, knowing that was the most she was gonna get.

But Simeon always stepped in for me. "C'mon, Momma," he said. He dropped his tall, skinny self down deep and spun around. Held out his hand. Momma rolled her eyes but laughed. Everybody watched the two of them together. His dancing was more like floating across the floor. Just about every part of his body moved together—arms, legs, head, and shoulders—and he sang along with the words.

"Do it, Simeon!" someone shouted. I could see Simeon soaking up that attention like bread to gravy, getting every last drop of it. When the song ended his face was shiny with sweat. I went out to the back porch to sit and a few minutes later I heard the screen door bang behind me. Simeon sat down next to me with two cups of Myrtle's punch.

"This ain't got nothing in it, right?" I asked him before taking it from him.

"Only one way to find out," Simeon said, swallowing his in one gulp. I sniffed and took a small sip.

"I think you're gonna have to teach me to dance," I said.

"I tried to, remember?" he said, taking a sip of my drink. "As I recall, you are a lost cause."

We laughed. "Tell Momma so she'll stop asking."

"That ain't her asking, it's the whiskey."

Sometimes Simeon stayed inside talking, sometimes playing cards or dancing with women old enough to know better but too drunk to care. Momma was different on Saturday nights. Laughing loud in a way she never did with just us during the week. And she even danced, something we never saw her do even when her favorite songs came on the radio. But on Saturdays she was pressed up close with her friend Myrtle, who was round and could have been called big-boobied for as much as she had in the front. Sometimes I watched them in the middle of the front room, laughing with Myrtle's arms around Momma's neck, swaying, and Momma's hands would rest on top of Myrtle's big wide behind to a slow song. Myrtle was the only one Momma let sleep overnight on Saturdays. Everyone else had to be gone by midnight. Momma's rules. "You heathens don't got Sunday service at nine in the morning, but I do," she'd tell them.

Saturday nights were the only times she'd let me sleep in the room with Simeon on a little cot next to his. I started looking forward to Saturday nights because there was nothing I hated more than sleeping alone. Even when I was little and scared and would go into my momma's room at night, she'd hold me a bit but bring me right on back to my own bed to sleep. My momma didn't like to share her bed with no one, scared or not. I asked her once, "You ever get scared sleeping alone in here?"

She laughed. "I been waiting my whole life to sleep in my own bed, without someone's elbows or stinkin' feet all up in my face. Last thing I am is scared."

There wasn't much that made my momma scared. After that, when I got scared, I went to Simeon. And he held my hand, sometimes he'd even move over, make room in his bed for me to lie down next to him. I'd have to leave before daylight, though, because Momma told Simeon it "wasn't natural" for a boy child to let his sister lie next to him like that when I had my own bed. She told him, "I had to share a bed with my brothers. Wasn't no choice." Most times whatever Momma said, Simeon was just contrary and did what he pleased, but when she told him that, he started sleeping on the floor if I had to stay in his room. I could tell she made him feel ashamed in a way he hadn't felt before.

SIMEON

To hear my momma tell it, I started complaining the first breath I took, and I haven't stopped since. But what she calls complaining, I call being impatient. Started crawling and wanted to run. I opened a book, read the first page, and flipped to the last. And now, all I want to do is get out of Mississippi and live in a place that lets me walk on two feet instead of crawling around on four. Problem is, that's not what my momma wants to hear. It's like I can always see what's next for me, a little bit further down the road.

Now, a lot of folks say Jackson has plenty to offer our people—good jobs, a section of town where Negroes can work for themselves, a pretty downtown, not like where my momma's people came from, where the only work they could do was farming and more farming. Here you even got a choice of schools that ain't too bad, with some of the teachers from colleges up north. This is what they call *opportunity*. What they never talk about, though, is that the best Jackson has to offer is for Whites Only. Those Whites Only signs ain't just for water spigots and buses, nah, they are for anything worth something in Ole Miss. If a Negro wants something more than some scraps, you best pack your bags and make your way over to the train depot, start heading north yesterday because you ain't going to find it here. The *Chicago Defender* posts jobs with good pay asking, no, begging, Negroes to make their way north. And what do they do? Stay right here, scraping and waiting for someone to treat them just a little bit better than a dog. This Jackson Negro is gonna be long gone come August.

When our daddy "took up lodging elsewhere"—that's what my momma told me first time I asked her when Daddy was coming back—Lamb was too young to remember much. My daddy was in and out so much, I'm not even sure Lamb understood much of who he was. Momma told her he worked out of town and she believed it. But I knew better.

"What's that mean, 'lodging elsewhere'?" I asked my momma. She was folding laundry from the line out back and I must have already knew what she meant because I remember watching to see if any of the clothes she was folding was Daddy's.

"It means he ain't living here no more," she said.

"Why's that?" I asked her. "Why isn't Daddy living here anymore?"

She stopped folding. Leaned down and looked at me. "I already told you. Because he took up lodging elsewhere." I waited, watching her fold some more, and then I went on in the house. I waited awhile before I told Lamb. By then I had a story for her better than the one Momma told me.

"Daddy got a job on the railroad," I told her at first. She just nodded. I showed her a picture in a book of a train. Pointed to it. She put her finger on the picture next to mine. "Yup, that's right, the train. He travels everywhere so we ain't gonna see him like we used to." She nodded again. Lamb wasn't much of a talker, but she understood everything I said. "But when he comes back, he's gonna tell us about all the places he visited." Sometimes I told her Daddy came by when she was sleeping or that he told someone to tell us hello. I hated lying to Lamb, but I hated more what Momma might tell her. Momma ain't never been known for holding back on her words.

16

One thing I know is that if you want something in this world you gotta get out there and take it. My momma never had much schooling, but I give her credit, she makes sure we get ours. She is proud in her own way that I get good grades and all the teachers tell her I have a good head on my shoulders.

"Didn't get it from me," she tells them to their face, talking the way she thinks mothers do to teachers. But to me, she says, "I may not be book smart like you, Simeon, but I know one thing, can't no one call me a fool neither. There isn't nothing I can't do if I don't set my mind to it, book or no book."

"I know, Momma," I told her, not knowing why she was needing to tell me about herself every time the teachers told her something about me. To me, my momma does all right for someone who, according to her, "barely made it past grade school."

"Didn't you want to?" I asked her. "Didn't you like school?" Too young to know better than to ask my momma questions like that.

"You thinking I had a choice?" She laughed a mean laugh. "When I had to work in the fields every day? I was lucky I got the schooling I got. Don't you forget that, Simeon. You best thank God for what you got." I nodded, not knowing if I was supposed to be thanking God for not working in the fields, for going to school every day, or for the momma who was reminding me of both.

She went over my letters with me, best as she could. She was good with numbers, I could see that. She could add them quicker in her head than I could with pencil and paper. She sat next to me when I did my lessons. She didn't say much but she was checking on me to make sure my answers were right and everything was neat and on time to hand in in the morning to my teachers. When I finished up, she'd put her hand on my head, rub it quick, then get up and tell me to go on to bed. That's how she let me know I'd done a good job in her eyes. That was more than I could say for some people's mommas and daddies. Franklin Hall, my friend since third grade, had a momma who never even made him go to school if he wasn't in the mind to go. He ribbed me about my momma making me go, but I didn't let it bother me none. Franklin and every one of my friends knew that going to school didn't bother me one bit.

By the time I got to junior high school, Momma didn't sit with me anymore at the table or help me with my work, but Lamb was with me, and I started helping her with hers. When I started at Lanier High School, it was in a different direction than Jim Hill Junior High School, so I could only walk with Lamb partway. Lanier's building was tall and prettier than Jim Hill's with more steps heading up to the front door. On my first day, the principal was there at the front, in a fine white suit, with small little spectacles, almost like mine, shaking the hands of every student who came in. Most of the older ones he knew by name, the others he introduced himself to.

"Good morning, young man," he said to me when I reached him. I was tall enough so we were almost looking eye to eye. "I'm Dr. Atkins, the principal."

"Good morning, Dr. Atkins," I said back to him. And as I started to walk into the school, I thought of something and turned back to him. "If you're a doctor, why are you our principal?"

Dr. Atkins was reaching out to shake the hand of the boy behind me when he stopped. "What is your name, young man?" he asked.

"Simeon," I told him. "Simeon Clark."

"Well, Simeon, I do love a young person who asks the right questions, so we'll begin your first day of high school with a lesson about higher education. I have a doctoral degree in education—a PhD." He tapped his chest. "I am a proud graduate of Wilberforce University. All doctors do not practice medicine."

My mouth was just about hanging open. "Happy to have you with us this morning, Mr. Clark," he said.

"Nice to meet you, Principal—Dr. Atkins." He nodded his head at me and smiled. I went home thinking *A doctor of education?* Just when I thought I knew just about everything, I found out I knew next to nothing.

That night at dinner, I said to Momma, "Did you know you could be a doctor and not ever see a patient?" She looked at me and kept right on eating.

Lamb spoke up. "Is this a riddle, Simeon?"

"Nope." I looked at Momma.

"You know I don't like you playing at the table, Simeon," she said.

I turned to Lamb. "My principal is Dr. Atkins but he isn't a doctor doctor with a stethoscope and all who sees patients. He says he's a doctor of education. He's a PhD."

"A PhD?" Lamb asked me. Lamb was always interested in whatever I was saying but my momma said that most times my talking was a way of showing I knew more than everybody else. Momma kept eating and acted like I was telling her the sky was blue.

"I wanna be a doctor like that," I said, not knowing it was something I wanted until I said it, but after talking to Dr. Atkins it was all I wanted. Not just because of my name with the word "Doctor" in front of it, but because it sounded like it meant a lot more years of spending time learning all of the things I wanted to learn. Maybe even at the college Wilberforce he talked about.

I heard Momma laughing.

"Momma?" Lamb asked, both of us looking at her. Wasn't often we heard our momma laughing out loud.

"I think I heard just about everything now. My son gonna be a doctor and never see a patient." She shook her head. "Maybe you can be a lawyer, Lamb, and never try a case," she said, smiling.

"Well, it's true, Dr. Atkins—"

"Didn't say it wasn't true. I just said I heard everything is all," Momma said.

I saw something on her face I hadn't seen before. Something aside from her laughing. Momma looked proud.

"You think I could be a doctor?" I asked her.

"Don't see why not," she said, putting her head back down to eat. "But here's the thing—Dr. Atkins at your school paying for you to be a doctor just like him?"

"I don't think—"

"'Cause if he ain't, then I'm not sure who is," she said, finally looking at me.

"I'll figure out a way," I told her.

"You gonna have to. Last I checked, my paycheck is barely keeping food on the table and clothes on our backs. Not sure who is paying for people to become doctors." She stood up to clear her plate. "Lamb, wash up these dishes. I got to finish up this order before the morning."

I watched her back as she left the room.

"You *are* gonna be a doctor," Lamb said to me soft.

I nodded my head. "I know I will," I told her.

The next day, I went looking for a job. If I was going to be a doctor and go to a college named Wilberforce, my momma was right. I was gonna have to figure out a way to pay for it all by myself.

The day I got the letter from Wilberforce University saying I was accepted into the School of Education, it felt like I was reading the Emancipation Proclamation. I must have read it over five times. Even took off my glasses and cleaned them good, then read it again. Later, I took Lamb in my room and told her I needed to show her something. I could hardly stand still when I handed her that letter.

"Simeon, what's wrong with you? You can't hold your water?" Lamb asked, laughing.

She unfolded it and I watched her head go back and forth reading until I couldn't take no more. I snatched the letter back.

"I got accepted," I whispered hot into her face. "Into Wilberforce. With a full scholarship, Lamb! You know what that means?"

Lamb snatched the letter back and kept reading. When she finished she looked up at me and back again at the letter.

"Simeon!" she said. "You really—" She threw her arms around me. "I knew it, I knew it," she said. I could feel her tears on my neck.

"Now don't go and get me to crying," I said, and pulled her away so I could see her face.

"A full scholarship means they think you are one of the smartest students," she said, staring at me and smiling.

I nodded at her. "It must, right?"

"You already told Momma?" I knew she wasn't trying to kill my celebration, but she just about did. The one thing I knew was my momma would not be celebrating me going to college, Ohio, or any other place that meant I was trying to be my own kind of man. But I didn't tell Lamb all that. Didn't want to get her started up again on me and Momma. Not when I was in the middle of my celebration. There was a lot I couldn't say to Lamb about our momma. A lot she couldn't know. Not yet anyhow.

"Not yet," I said to Lamb. "I'm gonna surprise her later."

Lamb tilted her head to the side, looking at me.

"Well, you know how Momma is—" I started. "I gotta make sure I get her in the right mood. I'm gonna tell her soon, don't worry. But you have the distinction of being the very first to know that Simeon Clark is going into Wilberforce University's Class of 1944."

Lamb smiled then. "But you'll tell her soon, right?"

"I promise," I told her.

After Lamb left my room, I tucked that letter in my top drawer and knew I wasn't going to be able to sleep that night. I could already see myself graduating from Wilberforce. I could see myself in a suit just like Dr. Atkins with my diploma in my hand. Lamb sitting in the front row. I was going to have to tell Momma soon, I just needed to find a way to do it without her making a fuss. Without her muddying up my dreams. When I closed my eyes, tossing and turning, trying to make myself go to sleep, I went back again and again to the picture of me crossing the stage. I could see me in my white suit, see my hand reaching out for that diploma, hear Lamb shouting my name. But the funny thing was, even with that picture clear as day in my head, I couldn't see my momma anywhere.

LAMB

SIMEON kept newspaper articles he cut out tucked between the pages of his notebook, and every morning, before Momma came in, tired from being up late sewing, he'd tell me what he figured I ought to know. Simeon didn't care nothing about what was happening overseas or even who was getting married in town. Simeon was only interested in the stories that had something to do with Negroes. Now if a Negro was progressing or being held back from progressing while getting married or being overseas that was fine, but otherwise, he'd skip right past it.

This morning I sat down with my toast and Simeon let out a long whistle. "One of these days, one of these days…" I started chewing, waiting. I liked to start my mornings not hearing about Negroes fighting, dying, struggling, or surviving, but Simeon wasn't all that interested in how I wanted to start my mornings. He put down the paper and looked at me.

"Now look at this," he said, pointing to a small article on the front page of the *Clarion-Ledger*. "Seems it's time for the annual Daughters of the Confederacy meeting this weekend."

He shook his head. "Least we know where *not* to be," he said, whistling again. "May as well be 1840 instead of 1940.…"

"Fortunately for you, it's a *Daughters* of the Confederacy meeting. It's only for women," I said, trying to make him smile. When he didn't look up, I opened my math book. "Can I ask you something *not* in the newspaper?"

Simeon kept talking like he didn't hear me. "You would think white folks got other things to do aside from trying to make our lives harder." He shook his head one more time.

"So you won't help me with math?" I asked again.

He looked up. His little round glasses made me feel like I was looking at his eyes through a magnifying glass. "Aren't you just tired of it? Tired of being here?"

"Simeon, we barely see white folks. 'Side from your job, and when I go to the store with Momma, we wouldn't see them at all. And since I don't plan on going to any Confederacy teas anytime soon..."

"See, it's thinking like that that's setting us back," Simeon said to me.

I put my head in my hand. I liked math but that didn't mean it came easy. I had to go over my work two, sometimes three times to make sure I got things right. And even then I made Simeon check it. I knew Momma liked numbers, the way when I was young she sometimes watched me do my math schoolwork over my shoulder. I could hear her whispering numbers to herself. She told me once she did all the figuring for her daddy's books back on the farm. But Momma didn't do much talking about what she wished she'd done. She didn't talk about anything from her past.

"You listening, Lamb?" he said, trying to get me to look at him.

"Are you listening, Simeon? You want me to be better? Do better? Help me with these math problems!"

He was quiet, then started laughing. He snatched my book and paper with my homework. "Let me see what you got." He circled two of them with his pencil, shaking his head. "Good Lord, girl, you planning on spending your whole life in eleventh grade?"

"Shut up, Simeon. That's not even bad." I hit him on his head with my pencil. "Just show me what I did wrong."

He took out another piece of paper and went over my mistakes step by step. He wouldn't move to the next problem until he was sure I understood. Just as we finished the second one, Momma came in the kitchen, yawning.

"Y'all gonna be late you don't get a move on," she said.

"And good morning to you, Momma," Simeon said.

Momma stared at him. She hated when Simeon talked too loud or too happy too early in the morning.

"Lamb, c'mere, let me fix your braid," she said.

I stood up, and Momma had to bend down a little because she was so much taller than me. I loved the feel of her fingers in my hair. They moved light and quick, and it seemed like only Momma's hands could get through all the way to the scalp and make my hair do what it needed to.

We packed up and left Momma in the kitchen stirring her coffee.

Me and Simeon never minded when it was just the two of us walking to school together. I think we both liked being alone, out the house, away from Momma, though we never said it.

"As I was saying..." Simeon started up again, like we were still sitting having breakfast, "someone needs to teach these white folks a lesson."

I looked behind us, checking to make sure no one heard him. "Don't talk like that, Simeon. That kind of talk ain't helping no one."

"*Isn't* helping *anyone*," he corrected me. "What good is us staying quiet when every day things are getting worse and worse? You need to leave with me," he said.

25

"How am I gonna do that, Simeon, when I have to finish school here first? Besides, I can't leave Momma by herself."

"She has Uncle Chime. She won't be alone. Momma's never gonna leave here. Suppose I found a school for you near me? A better school than Lanier? Me and you got to make plans for our future, Lamb. A real future in a place with real opportunity for Negroes. People here can't see beyond their circumstances," Simeon said.

"You saying Momma's dumb for wanting to stay in Jackson? This is her home, Simeon."

"Not dumb, Lamb. Her world don't go much beyond Jackson. She's scared, like everybody else here. Just the way white folks like it," he said.

"Just because people stay don't make them scared, Simeon. Just because people quiet don't make them cowards neither. Sometimes that makes them smart. Makes them want to live and take care of their families. Maybe live to see another day."

Simeon stopped walking and pushed his glasses up again on his nose, sweating now the way it does when he gets worked up. "But that ain't really no way to live, now is it?"

LAMB

IN my English class, Miss Thompson takes her time handing back our last papers. You can always tell how just about everyone did by the look on her face when she hands back assignments. Sometimes she stops at a desk and shakes her head before she flips the paper over with the grade facedown. Other times she nods her head up and down and you can tell they did all right. Today, Miss Thompson stopped at my desk, looked me in my eyes, nodded her head two times, and said out loud, "See me after class." A couple of students looked over at me, knowing I musta done pretty bad for Miss Thompson to want to see me after class.

Simeon stayed up with me half the night working on my essay. I love Miss Thompson's class even though everyone says her class is the hardest of all the English classes at Lanier put together. She expects "excellence" and "diligence" in everything we write. She's not as old as some of the other teachers at Lanier, but she has old ways, asking us to sit up straight and to "enunciate" when we read out loud. She even dresses like someone's grandma, wearing shirts and dresses with high collars and long sleeves even when it's hot. It wouldn't be so bad if she wasn't about seven feet tall. I've heard the boys whisper "Tim-ber" when she turns her back to write on the chalkboard, because she does look like a black oak tree, still and straight. But even with her old-fashioned ways and hard lessons, the ways she talks about books and words make me feel smarter just sitting in her class.

"Every grade counts if you're going to get into college," Simeon told me when we were working on my essay, scratching out half of what I wrote and rewriting better sentences that Simeon suggested. Momma was up late too, sewing in the front room. When she came in the kitchen to pour coffee, she turned and looked back at us at the kitchen table.

"Time you all got to bed," she said, tired.

"I know, Momma, we're almost done," I told her.

"We? Whose paper is it? Yours or Simeon's?" I could feel Simeon's body get tight, but he kept right on scratching out words with his pencil.

"You just need to tighten up your conclusion, Lamb," he said, ignoring Momma.

"Your teacher know your brother's doing your papers? Seems to me that's cheating." Her head was tilted to the side, looking at me. Waiting.

"He's helping me, Momma…showing me how to make it better."

She smiled a smile that didn't mean she was happy. Just meant she knew she was right. "That's what you call cheating now? *Helping*?"

Now Simeon looked up. "Would you like to help her instead?"

A dark cloud passed over Momma's face. "I want her to help herself!"

I snatched the paper and stood up. "I will. He was just trying to help, Momma. Why are you—" I stopped and looked at her. She could see the tears starting in my eyes.

Her face settled some. "I'm just playing with you, Lamb," she said. "Sit on down and finish your schoolwork. Let Simeon *help* you." She stirred her coffee and went back to the front room.

"Good ole Momma. Always count on her for support…." Simeon mumbled, looking over his scratch marks and shaking his head.

I stayed up late copying over my work, making sure I had every word right but wondering if when Simeon left I could do it by myself. If I was smart enough on my own without him.

At my desk, I flipped over my paper and saw that Miss Thompson wrote with her red pen, *Nice work, Lamb! B+!* I couldn't stop myself from smiling. I looked up at Miss Thompson, but she was already three seats behind handing out more papers.

When the bell rang, I gathered up my books slow, waited till just about everybody left, and made my way to Miss Thompson's desk at the front of the class. I didn't see her, but when I leaned forward I saw she was filing more papers in a box under her desk.

She sat up. "Oh, hello, Lamb. I didn't see you there." She patted down her hair in the back where it was standing up straight. "I really wanted to tell you how nice it was to see such an improvement in your work. I thought your conclusion was especially insightful," she said. "I am hoping to see that level of work from you in the future. You are such a bright student, but I can't say I feel you always put in your best work." She tapped her desk.

"Yes ma'am," I said to her, wondering why teachers always feel they know better than you do when you are or are not doing your best work. Just suppose my best work isn't ever going to be good enough. And just suppose someone is barely trying but they're doing better than I am. For a minute I let myself think just like my momma standing in front of Miss Thompson, and say to myself, *Teachers don't know every damn thang.*

"Is that 'yes,' you don't put in your best work, or 'yes,' I will be seeing that improved level of work for the remainder of the school year?" she asked.

"Both, ma'am."

"Well, I'm glad to hear it," she said.

I had a hard time looking her in her eyes. Feeling like if I did, she'd know that Simeon helped me, and maybe if she felt I wasn't ever doing my best work, I wasn't smart enough to be in her class after all. Her desk was neat and organized, everything lined up in a row with stacks of papers in piles. On the corner of her desk, I looked down at a book lined up straight next to a stack of papers. She followed my eyes.

"You know this book?" she asked me, picking it up.

I could read the cover upside down. *The Good Earth* by Pearl S. Buck.

"No ma'am," I said.

She smiled a little. "Well, I've just about read it to death. It's a story about a farmer, Wang Lung, and his wife, O-lan, in China." She stared down at the book. "Just outstanding writing. Parts of it are quite… romantic, I think." She put her hand to her mouth for just a second. "They start out very poor but together they work hard on their farm, buying more and more land until… Well, I don't know why I'm telling you the story when you can just read it." She laughed a little. "I sent away for it, but I wouldn't mind loaning it to someone who would take extra-good care of it." Even though she was homely and too tall to be a woman, when she smiled, she had about the kindest face I'd ever seen. When I didn't reach for it, she said, "Don't worry, I won't test you on it!"

I smiled back then and took it from her desk. 'Side from the Bible, it was about the heaviest book I ever held. She must have seen my face.

"It's long but, trust me, once you start reading, you won't be able to stop. Well…at least that's how it was for me…I get a little excited about my books…" she said, looking 'shamed now like she had said too much. She smiled a shy smile one more time. In the classroom, Miss Thompson was one of those teachers who was so serious, we almost never saw her smile. She wasn't mean like some of the others. She was nicer to the students who were smart or who she thought were trying their best. I'm one of those she's nice to. But when Simeon was in her class, she was *very* nice to him. He told me she sometimes actually laughed out loud at his jokes. Gave him an A+ on every paper and always told him he was "going places."

He said once, "I think Miss Thompson may just be a little sweet on ole Simeon," strutting past me. I laughed at him, trying to imagine a teacher sweet on Simeon. It wasn't that Simeon wasn't good-looking. At least I thought he was. But even though he was taller than most boys in his grade, he looked like his arms and legs had grown faster than the rest of his body. He had a little sprouty patch of hair on his face, not even fully grown in yet. He sure didn't look like he could catch the eye of a full-grown woman.

But I did sometimes wonder if Miss Thompson had a sweetheart. Or if it'd be hard to find anyone who wanted to date a woman so tall.

She stood and patted the front of her dress. She made me feel so small standing in front of her. I had to stretch my neck just a little to look at her face. "You take your time and get it back to me when you can," she said, reaching for her purse and coat in the closet. "I guess now I'm going to have to find something else to read this weekend." She looked around the room and over at the bookcases that should have been filled with books but just had a few dusty old ones that no one ever looked at. I felt nervous all over again, scared Miss Thompson thought because of the words Simeon helped me write that I was smart enough to sit and chat with her about her favorite book. I didn't know how long it would take me to read a book this big. And suppose I didn't even like it? Could I really tell her that? I wished again I was like my momma, who would have put her hand on her hip and told Miss Thompson to keep her book, and thank you very much, I got enough books of my own to read.

I tried to imagine being like Miss Thompson, with my whole weekend reading books. By myself. And being a woman whose idea of romance was reading about two poor farmers from China. Momma was alone too, but on Saturday nights, she filled our house with music and dancing, and I wasn't sure which seemed worse, a house filled with people drinking and talking every Saturday night or a house with none at all.

"Thanks, Miss Thompson," I said. The book was too big to fit in my book bag, so I held it heavy with two hands in front of me.

If Miss Thompson thought I was smart enough to read this book, I was gonna read it two times and make sure I knew about every word by heart before I gave it back to her. And I would tell her I loved it too, and talk to her after class about Chinese farmers and all of the romantic parts and find parts that I could call my favorites.

She called out when I reached the classroom door. "Oh, and please tell Simeon I said hello," she said, smiling big.

"Oh, I sure will," I said back. *Lord,* I wondered to myself. *Is* she sweet on Simeon?

LAMB

"**LAMB** baby, I'm gonna need your help today."

On the days when Mrs. Rowland had a lot of fittings in her small shop, she had Momma work at home on the alteration orders. Wasn't nothing I hate more than helping Momma with her sewing. I'm not bad at sewing, but I'm not good at it either. Sometimes I'd watch my momma at night, by herself next to the lamp in the front room, a pile of clothes folded neat by her side that she needed to mend or hem or take up or in, and she looked just as calm as could be. Momma's been working for Mrs. Rowland for as long as I can remember and even though Rowland's Sewing and Alterations is on the Negro side of town, downtown on East Hamilton Street, white folks from all over the city come to her. It's not that Momma minds the work, she just minds Mrs. Rowland.

"Kind of colored who don't know she colored," Momma says when she gets mad at Mrs. Rowland for piling up too much work or Mrs. Rowland yells at her when she doesn't finish an order on time. Momma never said what she meant by Mrs. Rowland not knowing she was colored, but if you walk past Mrs. Rowland on the street real quick you'd hardly know she was Negro. Her skin is lighter than mine, and her hair is straight and she piles it up high on her head. She wears lipstick so red, you could see her from a mile off. I'm sure she knows she's a Negro, because her husband and son, who is grown with his own family, is the same medium brown as Momma and they live just one block away from Mrs. Rowland and her husband in those houses over where some of the Negro doctors live in the nicer section of town. Wouldn't no woman pretending to be white live there with a Negro husband. I suppose some would call her pretty, but to me she looked like she didn't eat nearly enough. I wondered if Momma meant she looked like the white women in magazines, with those little skinny waists and not nearly any kind of behind. But she pays Momma by the piece and better Momma says than those other white folks' shops she worked for when she first got to Jackson. Momma told us she might as well have "stuck to sharecropping," with what they were trying to pay her. Until she found Mrs. Rowland. So even though Momma thinks Mrs. Rowland doesn't know who she is and gives her too much work, she pays her more than anyone else in Jackson, so she keeps right on working for her going on ten years now.

Seemed that what Momma loves best about sewing is that she could make anything prettier with just a needle and some thread. Give Momma an old worn-out dress, and she can turn it into something that looks better than new. I wished sometimes there was something I could do that could fix Momma and Simeon that easy.

"Mrs. Rowland needs all these finished by tomorrow, and I got behind trying to finish last week's order. You can start on the hemming, that's the easiest."

"Momma, you know I'm bad at hemming."

"Stop saying you bad at things just to get out of doing 'em," she said, threading a needle.

"So this means I'm not going to school today?" I asked her.

Momma breathed out her nose and closed her eyes, meaning she was trying not to get mad, but I could see she already was.

"What you want me to do, Lamb?" She looked at me. "Tell Mrs.

Rowland I can't finish? Not have money to buy food this week? Let her find some other colored seamstress to fill my spot tomorrow who can finish orders when she needs 'em?"

"What other seamstress is she going to find that's better than you?" I smiled a little bit at Momma.

"In Jackson, you throw a rock, you hit a seamstress, Lamb, you know that," Momma said in her tired voice.

I reached for the sewing basket. "It's just sometimes..." Momma looked at me with her head tilted to the side, meaning nothing I had to say was more important than what she just told me. But I kept on, "...sometimes it's hard to catch up with my schoolwork. When I miss, that is."

"You?" Momma was already looking down, back at her sewing. "Have Simeon go over your work with you."

I know my momma never had much schooling. That's maybe why she thinks anybody who has any at all knows a lot more than she does. But my momma never counts herself as dumb, just not "book smart."

"There's a whole lot of learning happens outside a book, Lamb," she told me more than once. Not that I asked. I think she was just reminding me not to look down my nose at her for something she never got.

But my momma don't know there's a long way between not having schooling and being so smart that everything comes easy like it does to Simeon. Doesn't seem to matter what it was; I was the meat in the middle of a sandwich, smashed flat in between two hunks of bread that are my momma and Simeon. I picked up the first pair of pants in the pile and waited for Simeon to come out of his room. The pants were a men's pair, a fine dark wool with white pinstripes. Momma had already chalked the bottom, which meant that the customer had come into the store and been measured by Mrs. Rowland, and then Mrs. Rowland gave the order to my momma to tailor. A lot of Mrs. Rowland's white customers were fancy white folks in town and women who seemed to spend most of their time eating too much or too little. I once saw my momma letting out a dress she took in a month earlier. She laughed then, shaking her head. "Damn shame," she said.

"Get a move on, Lamb," Momma said now, and I reached across her for the pins.

Momma put her hand out to stop me. "Go wash under your arms, Lamb. I can't sit next to that stink all day." I stood up. "And eat something too. I don't want you complaining in an hour you hungry."

I walked past Simeon fast with my head down as he came out of his room.

"Too early in the morning to see a face that ugly," Simeon said, covering his eyes.

I smacked his arm.

"What is wrong with you?" he asked.

Don't ask, I said to him with my eyes, tilting my head back at our momma.

He made a sewing motion with his hands. I nodded my head yes. He shook his head no.

Before I could stop him, he went to the front room. To Momma.

"Lamb is missing school today?" he asked her.

"Morning, Simeon," Momma said with a needle in her mouth. "I need help with an order. You want to stay and help me instead?"

"She tell you she has a test today?"

"I tell you we need to eat?" she said.

I walked back in behind him. "Simeon, it's okay. I'll just explain to Miss—" I started.

"Please take your behind to school, before you are sitting here next to your sister," Momma said to him. "Acting like he's somebody's goddamn daddy…" She mumbled the last part under her breath as me and Simeon went on in the kitchen.

Simeon shrugged at me, and I got a knife and bread out of the bread box. We sat at the table. He leaned close to me. "I tried, but you've got to be the one telling her you ain't doing this no more. She paying you to be some kind of seamstress assistant?"

"What else am I supposed to do, Simeon? She needs my help. She's trying to—"

"You ever notice how she can't seem to finish something on the day you have a test? Or when you have a lot of schoolwork? Use your head, Lamb."

I was quiet. I didn't know if what Simeon was saying was true. I know I didn't want it to be. My momma was proud of me in a way she wasn't of Simeon.

Simeon ate his breakfast and packed his schoolbag.

"See y'all ladies later!" he shouted into the front room. I walked him to the door. "I'll get your schoolwork. Go over it with you tonight," he said.

I nodded. "But you need to start speaking up, Lamb. Either you're a student or a seamstress. Up to you to decide." He smiled at me. I could feel tears coming to my eyes.

"C'mon now. Look on the bright side. You are getting all that good practice for your husband. You'll know how to darn his drawers and be the best ole wife this side of the Mississippi."

"I don't want to be no one's wife, Simeon!" I yelled at him, pushing him out the door, laughing now.

Simeon laughed too, and ran down the stairs and off to school.

After I ate and washed up, I went back to the front room and picked up the pinstripe pants. Momma had the radio playing and she was humming along to Count Basie, tapping her foot to the music. If there wasn't school, and I wasn't missing a test, and I liked sewing, it could almost be a nice day.

LAMB

"**YOU** ever think about leaving Jackson, Momma?" I asked her. I was on my third pair of pants now and getting used to the rhythm of sewing next to Momma. She was at her sewing machine now, her back to me.

"Leave Jackson? Jackson's my home now. More my home than Shubuta ever was."

"Why's that?" I ask her.

Momma took a minute to answer. She sometimes has to decide if she wants to go back to remembering out loud the part of her life she wants to keep quiet.

"It never felt like a place I belonged. A place gotta feel like it loves you back. You know what I mean?"

I nodded, but I still wasn't quite sure how a place could feel anything. "I'm not sure how I feel about staying in Jackson. I mean, not my whole life anyhow. I want to go off to college, like Simeon. I'm just not sure where yet."

"Can't be following your brother to hell and back. You gotta do what's right for you."

"I know, Momma. But I think college is right for me. A lot of my teachers say so too."

"Your teachers…mmm mmm mmm…what they know about what's right for you? Only you know that."

"Yup...I guess so...." I kept sewing.

"So what, you thinking about being a doctor like Simeon too?" Momma asked.

"Nah." I laughed. "I don't think that's what I want to do."

"Well, imma tell you like I told your brother. Y'all may have plans, but I ain't got money for dreams. I got money for food and clothes and keeping a roof over our head. I don't—"

"My teacher told me that some of these schools have money they give you if you are a good-enough student..."

"Now you know I don't take nobody's charity." Momma's voice was getting louder. "I can do for mine—"

"Momma, it ain't charity. It's called a *scholarship*. Miss Delacorte, my history teacher, said they give them out all the time. Just need to show you need it and you can do the work."

"And the school's just gonna hand over money to you? Lamb, you need to get your head out the clouds, girl."

Simeon told me he was going to tell Momma about getting into Wilberforce and his scholarship money on his own time. But I could see now he wasn't in any rush to tell her.

"Momma, it's true."

"You mean it's true because your teacher said it's true?"

Momma turned to stare at me, and I wasn't sure if she hated that my teachers were telling me things she could never know about or that she hated that I might believe what they told me over her. Either way, it was the closest I ever saw her face to looking pitiful. Like how she must have looked as a little girl when she was scared.

I tried to make my face plain, and not look like I was feeling bad that she didn't know about scholarships or how colleges work.

"Something you wanna say to me, Lamb, go on and say it. You know I don't like no one holding their tongue for my sake."

"I'm always gonna be your daughter, Momma, no matter where I go."

Momma waved her hand at me. "Don't go getting all sweet-tongued with me, Lamb. Say what you want to say."

I was quiet a minute, trying to get my words right. "You want me to do well in school, right?

"Now, I just needed your help for today, don't go making it about—"

"I know, Momma, I'm just saying. I mean—you wouldn't want me to do bad in school, right?"

"Why would I want that?" she asked me.

I looked at her. My momma would be able to tell if I was telling her a lie.

"So—" I was scared to go on. "So I could stay here with you. And not go to college?"

Now she was quiet. I could always tell if my momma was about to get mad, if she was already mad or not mad anymore. She wasn't any of those. Her shoulders were a little rounded over. And I waited some more. Waited for her to say I was wrong. Simeon was wrong.

"Would that be so bad? To stay?" she said finally.

"Momma...I want to go to college. I don't know where yet. But I want to go."

"They got colleges here too, don't they?" she said.

"Yes, there are colleges everywhere."

"So you don't have to go as far as Simeon is going. All the way up north. So far your momma can't see you."

"I don't have to go that far, no, but—"

"So there you go, you can go to college right here." Momma went back to sewing. Like she had my life all settled for me. Her and Simeon both knew more about what I'm going to be doing than I did. I knew what my momma wanted. Knew what Simeon wanted. Now I just needed to figure out what Lamb wanted.

LAMB

I was out of breath by the time I caught up with the rest of the girls walking to choir practice.

Earvent grabbed my arm when she saw me. "Where you been, Lamb?" she said loud as always. I was hoping no one would notice I wasn't there. They all turned and looked at me. Earvent slowed down. "I waited at the corner. I thought something happened to you."

"What's gonna happen to me?" I laughed.

"Well, you never know. My momma told me last month some ole peckerwood snatched a girl right off the street and—"

"Oh, your momma's scared of her own shadow," NeeCee yelled from in front of us, and everybody laughed. Earvent's momma lets her go out on her own just one time a week and that is on Saturdays to choir practice. She goes to the small Bible school near her house where there are about a handful of students just like Earvent, who as my momma says aren't just *God-fearing* but *life-fearing*, waiting for the devil around every corner.

I hooked my arm into Earvent's. "Nah, I was tired. I went to bed late is all and overslept."

"As long as you're all right, Lamb," she said. Earvent has always been stuck to me like glue since we met in Sunday school when we were little. We were the only two still boohooing long after everyone else had stopped. She was as scared as I was, maybe more. While the other girls ran and chased each other and played games, me and Earvent stayed near the teacher, too afraid to move. One day when the teacher had to tend to some rowdy boys and we were left alone, Earvent slipped her hand into mine and held on tight. She ain't let go since. When my momma had me join the choir, Earvent joined too so she could be with me for Saturday practice and once a month when the youth choir sang. The other girls called us the quiet ones, but some of the girls talked more to me than Earvent, who was too godly for even the preacher's daughter.

"Ask Lamb," NeeCee said, up ahead of me.

Juanita turned and when she did, the whole group stopped. Juanita had on a new shade of lipstick today to match her red dress. Momma always said red lipstick made a woman look cheap, but she must not have ever seen Juanita Hardy. This shade looked like someone made the color just for her. She didn't look nowhere near cheap. She looked like a movie star.

"Lamb, what's that boy's name in Simeon's grade, the one who got in trouble last year for smoking?" she asked me. Only time Juanita really has anything to say to me direct is when she thinks I might know something she's interested in. And that isn't much so Juanita doesn't say much to me. Having Simeon as an older brother means every once in a while, Juanita asks someone to ask me a question about some boy in Simeon's class.

"That was Ritchie, I think," I told her. "Why?" But Juanita had already turned around and was talking to Lucy and Alma.

NeeCee smiled back at me. "He went and got some girl in the family way," she whispered. NeeCee Collins was in most of my classes at school and if it wasn't for Earvent, we'd probably be better friends. But you'd think Earvent went and killed somebody the way NeeCee hated her. Spend too much time talking to NeeCee, and Earvent was hurt. Spend too much time talking to Earvent, and NeeCee stopped speaking to me, so when I'm in school I talk to NeeCee, and at choir practice I stay with Earvent. Just like at home, I feel like the meat in a sandwich, with everybody taking a bite out of me till there isn't nothing left.

I walked on watching Alma, NeeCee, and Lucy up under Juanita all the way till we got to the church, at the same time trying to hear what they were saying up front about Ritchie, but Earvent was too loud whispering in my ear.

"The family way?" Earvent was shaking her head. "That girl is going straight to hell," she said, fanning herself like she was overcome with heat.

"What about Ritchie?" I asked her.

"What you mean?" she asked, still fanning.

"Is Ritchie going to hell too for getting her in the family way?"

She smiled at me, her patient smile. Like she had to explain the ways of the Lord. "Now you know men will always be tempted," she said, "but it's up to us to be ladies and uphold God's covenant."

"God's covenant is only for women?" I asked. Sometimes I ask Earvent questions about the Bible because I want to know, and sometimes I ask because I can't really believe she believes what comes out of her own mouth.

Earvent's lips got tight. And she smiled that smile again. "I know some things don't make sense to you, because—" She stopped and put her head down.

"Because what?" I asked. The other girls had gone into the church and it was just me and Earvent outside now.

"Well, I don't want to say…"

I could tell this was one of those times I could just shut my mouth and go on into choir practice with my friend or I could keep asking and maybe get an answer that was going to make me wish I stopped asking. But seeing her tight lips and patient smile made up my mind for me.

"Say what?"

Earvent breathed deep and looked at her feet. "My momma says—your momma isn't living the life of a Christian, so maybe you don't always know how to—"

"How is my momma not living the life of a Christian?" I asked, wondering if I was madder about Earvent's mother counting all the ways my momma wasn't a Christian or that she was talking about her at all.

"Let's go in, Lamb," Earvent said fast. "You know Miss Twyman hates when we're late." She tried walking past me but I stepped in her way.

"What does your momma know about my momma?" I said again, louder. I couldn't believe I was getting this mad at Earvent. She'd preached to me before, but I could see in her something she was wanting to say but couldn't. About my momma.

Miss Twyman came to the door.

"Girls, rehearsal is beginning. Now."

I stood a second more, looking at Earvent. Her eyes filling with water. She'd never seen me mad at her before. I turned to follow Miss Twyman inside.

"Lamb—" Earvent said, reaching for my hand.

But I snatched my hand away and followed behind Miss Twyman inside the church.

LAMB

BEEN taking care of my momma and Simeon my whole life. Tending to them, making sure neither one was hurting each other too bad. But most times, it was me who was the one who got hurt most. And tired as I got taking care of them, it was Simeon and Momma that helped me to see that just maybe taking care of folks was what I was best at.

Miss Odetta from church worked the night shift at Jefferson Memorial Hospital, the Negro hospital in town. And sometimes on Sunday morning she came straight to church from her shift with her white nurse's dress and cap on and those ugly white shoes to match. If you looked close, you could see her nurse's dress and shoes had spots of blood on them. I think some folks thought it was nasty, coming to service looking like she worked over at the slaughterhouse, but to me, it seemed like she was a soldier out on the battlefield.

Momma once told me that my daddy fought in the Great War against the Germans and for a long time I made pictures in my head, seeing him fighting off hundreds all by himself. A hero. And that's just how I see Miss Odetta too. Only she is helping patients who are weak and in pain fight off sickness to get better again. Helping them to heal. They sure don't give medals for that kind of bravery.

Miss Odetta is round like me and looks like she could care for the whole church by herself if they were struck down with fever. Folks at Farish Street Baptist say she is a little high cotton, knows too much for her own good on account of all of her nursing training at a hospital over in Yazoo City. *Her and all her book-learning,* Momma said once. I guess to Momma, she isn't at all like the midwives who help deliver babies just by knowing the way a woman's body works. *You can't learn that in a book,* I could almost hear Momma spitting out the words. Maybe not, but I'm betting Miss Odetta could deliver babies and more too. Aside from her book learning, Miss Odetta is kindhearted. When I was little, she taught my Sunday school class, and she read Bible stories to us from a big book that had pictures she let us take a long time looking at as she turned the pages, and she let us yell out loud, and she was always quick to smile and hold out a hand to any one of us when we cried and had to go back to our parents or to service. I know she never had children of her own, but anyone could see she would have been a good momma.

Even though I never told my momma when I talked to her about going to college, I was thinking more and more about being a nurse like Miss Odetta. Caring for people and being called smart and tough and kindhearted too. I wasn't sure how Momma would feel about me studying nursing. She'd probably ask why I didn't just go on ahead and be a midwife instead of wasting all that time doing something that came natural to women. But I wanted to do more than catch babies. I wanted to help men and women. Grown folks and children.

But it would take time to help Momma understand all that. I saw the way she sometimes looked at Miss Odetta. Saw the way she rolled her eyes when she came to church in her uniform. My momma feels everybody is trying to make her look like they're better somehow than she is, but most times I think people barely notice my momma. She isn't out volunteering and serving food during coffee hour at church.

She almost never showed up at school or talked to the other women at church or at school. Just kept to herself or her own Saturday night friends. And I didn't see not one of her Saturday night friends in church on Sunday mornings.

Sometimes I wonder why Miss Odetta became a nurse. If she was always good at taking care of people or got good at it later. A lot of times in his sermons, Reverend Greer talks about being of service. About giving and not wanting nothing back. About sacrifice. A lamb of God. Seems like Momma knew what she was doing after all by giving me my name.

SIMEON

THERE were a lot of places I could have worked, but only one I wanted to. When I went downtown with Momma and Lamb and walked past the King Edward Hotel on the corner of Capitol and Mill Streets, I always slowed down to see if I could get a look at the goings-on inside there. Only in the picture shows had I seen a hotel that fancy, and here was one sitting right in the middle of Jackson.

"Don't know what you looking in there for," Momma said to me. "Only colored they let in the doors got to be cleaning, cooking, or serving." Momma never even turned her head to look at the hotel. "The Greystone is good enough for me, though I don't know why I'd ever have a mind to be paying to sleep in a hotel when I got a home of my own."

The Greystone Hotel was over on Grayson Street, and it was nice enough, clean and all, but wasn't no one going to call it fancy like the King Edward. But I didn't say nothing to Momma. It wasn't that I was wanting to serve white folks like Momma said. That was the last thing I wanted. Fact is, I was seeing myself staying in one of those hotels one day. *As a guest.* I want to know what it would feel like walking across those floors so shiny they always looked like someone had just mopped them. And how the white people walking across those wet-looking floors always look like they belong there. Strutting around, smiling big while everyone around them makes sure they keep those smiles on their faces. I wanted to work at the King Edward Hotel, not to serve them and not just to make money to save for college to become a doctor like my principal, Dr. Atkins. But to *learn*.

I was young, but Momma didn't mind me working once I turned fifteen. She said being busy was what a young man was supposed to be. "You can't find trouble when you're busy.

"But you gotta keep up with your schoolwork too. Ain't no sense in you starting working to quit your schooling," she told me.

So I waited like she told me and not one week after I turned fifteen, I walked over to that hotel and when I turned the corner, I didn't strut in the front doors asking for a job. I did like Uncle Chime told me to do.

"Watch first and then make your move." He wasn't talking about getting a job at the King Edward, he was talking about life. And it was on a Saturday night when he'd had too much of Myrtle's punch and liked to come out onto the porch and give me advice, "man to man," he'd say. On one of the Saturday nights, I remembered Uncle Chime saying, "Best thing a man can do is not to go running into something without knowing what he's running into. You get more from looking than doing. So you listen to your uncle Chime and watch first."

So I watched the man at the door first. He looked to be about Uncle Chime's age, and he did a lot of smiling when the white guests walked through, but as soon as they stepped through the doors, he'd stop smiling, put his hands behind his back. He had a look on his face that looked like he was about a million miles away. I noticed he talked to all the Negro porters, so I figured he was someone everybody liked, or at least everybody talked to, maybe even respected. That was good to know. I waited till it was quiet, and I walked up to him. He didn't put his smile on for me.

"Good afternoon," I said to him.

"What you want, boy?" he asked, looking past me. "You see I'm working."

"That's what I'm here for. Looking for work," I told him.

He looked at me, hard. I saw a little smile around the corner of his mouth.

"How old you is? You best come on back in a couple of years."

"I'm seventeen. Old enough," I told him, standing tall as I could. Even at fifteen years old, I was already half a head taller than he was. "Name's Simeon," I told him. "Simeon Clark." I held out my hand.

He looked down at my hand like he wasn't sure if he should take it. Real slow, he reached out and shook it.

"You been working here long?" I asked him. Stopping him before he could ask me more questions. "Looks like it'd be a fine place to work."

"Looks ain't everything, Simeon Clark," he said to me, letting go of my hand. "You ever worked in a hotel before?"

I smiled big as I could, a little like I'd seen him do with the white guests. "There's not much I can't do," I told him.

"Where you live?" he asked, looking around over my shoulder, like I was going to tell him I lived across the street.

"Over on Barrett Avenue," I told him. But as soon as I said the street, I worried he'd know someone on our street and he'd ask about me. And the first thing he'd be asking was how old I was. "Took me all of ten minutes to walk here. I walk so fast, I'm never late for anything."

"I tell you one thing—you ain't no seventeen years old, I'd bet my life on that, but you quick. A fast thinker. And that's all you need to work here. But you got to know when to talk and when to shut your mouth. When to be seen and when to hide. You can do that, I'll see what I can do about getting you a job," he said.

I nodded.

"You ain't got nothing to say?" he asked me.

"I'm practicing," I told him, smiling. For the first time, he smiled back.

50

LAMB

AFTER Daddy left for good, Uncle Chime started coming round more and more. Seemed Uncle Chime filled every inch of space Daddy left behind soon as he walked in the door.

I was guessing that when my daddy lived here, he didn't take kindly to Uncle Chime visiting with my momma so regular and spending his days sitting on the porch talking loud and talking late. Simeon told me a lot of folks didn't like Uncle Chime hanging round too much.

Even Momma said, "Wherever Chime go, trouble follows."

I think Momma thought it was good that Uncle Chime was coming round so we wouldn't miss not having a man in house, but I heard her telling Uncle Chime she was worried too that Simeon, skinny as he was, with his glasses and all, was gonna get beat on by other boys.

"That mouth of Simeon's ain't gonna talk him out of a fight, Chime. More likely to get him in one than out of one, you ask me," Momma said. I could hear her taking a long sip from her Coca-Cola as they sat together.

Uncle Chime laughed at that. "So what? You can't be a boy without getting a beating. Fact is, it's part of being a boy," he told Momma. "But you keep on babying him the way you doing, you going to make it worse for him, not better. You just worried he missing having a daddy, and I ain't so sure he is."

He is about the only one I know who can talk to Momma plain and not worry how mad she'll get.

"You think he ain't missing his daddy?" Momma asked him.

"Well, I know *you* ain't missing his daddy." Uncle Chime laughed. "Maybe he ain't, neither. Maybe he is. What was his daddy doing when he was here? 'Side from fussing and fighting with his momma half the damn time. Now he's gone, he ain't had two words for Simeon. Maybe Simeon just have a chance to grow into something looks like a man."

I heard seat cushions on the old couch they sat on groan and creak. I knew Simeon was listening too on the other side of the wall. But Uncle Chime talked so loud, half the street could hear him when he got going good. "Marion, you got to let chil'ren be chil'ren."

"Says the man who ain't got none," she laughed.

"How you know what I got?"

"None you claiming anyhow," Momma said. "Speaking of, whatever happened to that woman I saw you with last month? Skinny little thing, look about Lamb's age?"

Uncle Chime's laugh echoed into the night. "She just takes good care of herself. Pond's Cold Cream makes her look young." They both laughed at that one.

"You best be careful. They locking up our kind for a lot less these days," Momma said.

"You know better than I do they barely locking up no one. Way I see it, you count yourself lucky if you make it to a jail cell. Luckier still if you see a courtroom. More likely it's the rope or the chain gang."

"Like I said, watch yourself out here with these young girls. Find yourself a woman you can settle down with and—"

"You need to worry about who you got warming your bed at night before you go preaching to me about how to find a woman."

Momma took another sip.

"Don't you worry about me. I'm doing just fine," Momma told him.

MARION ROSS

CHESTER claimed he was coming to pay a visit to my brother Turner. Me and Turner's eight years apart but you'd think we come out my momma together the way we favor each other. Back when the war started and all those boys started heading off to fight, Turner had to stay behind. He was born with one leg shorter than the other but aside from a little limp, you'd hardly notice. He spent his whole life working like two men to prove he was as good as one and the United States government still claimed he wasn't good enough for their army. After the war ended and the men started coming back, I could tell it hurt him the same as when they left. If they'd let women fight, I sure would have been the first to sign up.

Me and Chester ain't never paid each other no mind. Big as he was, I ain't never heard him so much as fussing with anyone, so I didn't know what in the world Chester Clark would be doing in the middle of a war fighting Germans and God knows who else. Truth was, wasn't nobody in Shubuta, Mississippi, scared of Chester. He was always laughing and such. Couldn't nobody say a bad word about him. Can't say I trust people who never get mad. Seems like they got to be hiding something. So when he came round to see Turner, I didn't pay him no mind. But I noticed, he sure seemed to be paying me some. Every time

I looked up, I could feel his eyes on me. Not the hungry eyes I'd see from men when I went into town, a different kind. Smiled at me every chance he got.

"Well, someone is sure sweet on you," Turner said to me one night at supper. My momma stopped eating.

"On Marion?" She laughed. "Ain't no one sweet on Marion for long."

At the end of the table my daddy coughed into his plate and my momma stopped talking. I saw my youngest brother, Chime, sit up straight, look at me, trying to see if what my momma said stung, while everybody else kept right on eating. I tried not to look back at Chime. No need stoking the fire in him anymore, mad as he was at the world already. I remember the feeling of not minding that someone was sweet on me. Especially if it meant it was gonna prove my momma wrong. The next time I saw Chester smiling, I smiled right back.

It wasn't so much that he was *the one*, those words my girl cousins used when they would talk about the boys they had their eyes on, saying this fella or that fella was the one they were fixing to set up house with. I knew right away that wasn't what Chester was going to be for me. I could tell right off he wasn't a man needed to be propped up all the time. Wanting me to fill his head with how much of a man he was. Even if he wanted it, wasn't in me to do it. And he wasn't going to need a woman too godly, walking round with a Bible in her hand. And I could tell Chester wasn't the type who was going to hurt me, least not with his hands. All his wasn'ts made him who he was. More than that, from the first time I saw him I could see my children in his face. I could see their smile in his. Their sweet faces in his big, round cheeks and fat bottom lip, so pink it looked like he was wearing lipstick from the five-and-dime. Clear as day, I could see the babies Chester would make in me. Made me laugh the man had two first names—Chester and Clark. First one sounded like he looked, big and thick.

"You gonna be able to cook enough food to keep that big boy fed?" my brothers laughed, teasing me now every time Chester came round. They needed to be thinking about their old mealymouthed women, tired and worn-looking already after their first babies.

One thing for sure, if it was up to my momma she would have had me married off and out the door years earlier. Said I needed to learn to shut my mouth, that's why the men around town didn't come by.

"Time you got out on your own. You ain't gettin' any younger, Marion. Or prettier. You do right by Chester, he do right by you." She and everybody else sounding like Chester was doing me a favor by courting me. I was young, and he was getting on older. I was thin and he was big as a house.

"What you mean, *do right by Chester*?"

"I hope I ain't got to tell you everything, Marion. Treat him right is all I'm saying. Shut that mouth of yours and look after him right. Chester's a *good* man."

My momma ain't never told me much about how to be a woman. Half the time, I felt like I was one of the boys, a man. Was only when I went into town with her and I could see the men's eyes resting on every part of me that I felt like a woman. My momma would slap me good she see me even look back at anyone staring. "Don't act like trash," she'd whisper. At first I couldn't even understand their looks. Like I was a piece of candy they wanted.

"Keep your eye on that one," some of the womenfolk told my momma after my monthlies came, pointing at my chest, my legs. Like I did something to make my body grow faster than I knew what to do with.

In school, I couldn't be bothered with boys who I used to play with in the schoolyard, all of a sudden not knowing what to say to me. Now I had to sit with the girls at lunch listening to their silly talk. Wasn't but one girl I liked. Laura was a tiny little thing, 'bout as light as a bird.

I remember thinking if I was that pretty, I'd have to look at myself in the mirror all day long. But she was just 'fraid of her own shadow. The other girls picked on her every day till she cried.

"You got to stand up for yourself," I told her one day after she ran off again crying. "You got to fight back, show you ain't scared." She nodded, but I could tell she didn't have any fight in her. Next time the girls started with her, I smacked one of 'em square in the mouth.

"You got a problem with her, you got a problem with me," I told them. After that, the two of us ate alone, talking, laughing near every day I came to school. I could barely stop staring at her, she was that pretty. She had that pretty bright skin and eyes that always looked like she was wide-awake. Half the time she was talking, I nearly had to lean over to hear her, but her voice sounded to me like she was singing. Once I reached out and rubbed her cheek.

She moved my hand away. "What you doin'?" she asked, looking at me funny.

"Had a mosquito on your face," I said, looking away so she couldn't see the hurt in my eyes. I didn't touch her no more after that. I kept looking, though, when I sat behind her in class, and sometimes when she'd wave goodbye on her way home, I'd stand watching till I couldn't see her no more.

But wasn't long before the boys started noticing her too. All that attention gives a girl some confidence. And that's where and how she got it. Bit by bit, she moved away from me and toward the same girls who made her feel like nothing. One thing about girls is you got to be willing to either say less than you want or more of what they want if you're gonna fit. Neither one was gonna work for me, and I just kept away from all of them after that. My tongue got a mind of its own. When my momma told me I was needed more in the fields than in school, I didn't have no complaints.

Chester, he didn't seem to mind my straight talk, and no matter what I told him, behind those girly pink lips, he was always hiding away a smile.

Soon as I could tell he was sweet on me, I told him right off, "I ain't fixing to spend my life farming. You want a wife picking and plowing, you go on and find someone else. I want to move to a city. See if I can get work sewing."

Chester nodded, hiding his smile. "You think I wanna farm, Marion? I watched my pappy get up e'ry morning workin' his plot. He and my momma both. When he died, we should have buried him out there in those fields, right next to his mules. Those fields the thing that killed him. Don't get me wrong, I ain't 'fraid of hard work. But you ain't gonna see me farmin'." He let loose a laugh from the bottom of his belly. "Ain't no wife of mine ever got to worry about farmin'."

Think that was the closest I felt to loving Chester then.

MARION

MOST suitors I had didn't last long. I didn't have patience for young boys all sniffing round for the same thing. But then there was Chester. Looking like he was ready to draw my bathwater and drink it too. Never once did he tell me to "quiet down," or "act like a lady," like those other boys who seemed more scared of me than sweet on me. Chester knew who I was from the get-go, and he liked me just fine. Probably on account of he was older. And traveled some in the army.

We had about as much of a wedding as our folks could do. Married at the church. Daddy gave me away. I picked my own flowers for my bouquet. I wore my favorite dress to get married and wore it again after the wedding when we left Shubuta. The one I made with the little blue flowers and a lace collar. Momma told me I was vain, but I liked it even more then. Chester looked like I took his breath away when he saw me at the church.

Everybody brought food and we covered up some tables with sheets and ate in back of the church. I had every woman from Shubuta telling me how lucky I was. Said me and Chester were going to have a houseful of pretty babies. The men told Chester about plots of land they heard were available for farming. I told him to keep quiet about our plans. I knew how folks liked to go stomping on ideas they didn't know nothing about. He thought everybody would want to know where we were settling. Said it wasn't neighborly to just up and leave like we was sneaking off, shamefaced like we had to get married because I was with child. I knew he wouldn't agree, but he was so happy to be married, he went along.

Momma wasn't sad to see me go. She had Daddy all to herself now. Daddy stood watching us pull off in Chester's beat-up truck that used to be his daddy's. Everything I owned was in a trunk that Chester tied tight with rope. I carried my sewing machine on my lap, afraid all that bumping would break it. I watched my daddy watching us pull off with his lips tight and his hand stuffed down in the pockets of his overalls, like he wasn't gonna let them out to wave a proper goodbye. Chester sang to the radio the whole ride. And I wish I could say he had a singing voice, but he didn't. But I didn't mind that it didn't take much to make him happy. He'd rub my arm or look over at me like he won a prize at the county fair every now and then and go on back to singing. I was so happy to get off that farm, going to someplace, anyplace new, I didn't care about leaving behind my brothers. My daddy. I damn sure didn't care about leaving behind Momma. I'd miss Chime, though. Told him to come see us in Jackson soon as he could because the only reason I'd be coming back to Shubuta was to put Daddy in a grave.

"Not Momma?" he asked. I left that there. I hugged him tight as I could before we left, the only one I did.

When we got to Jackson, we settled first at a boardinghouse outside of town. Chester's cousin said they were waiting for a spot to open up at the lumberyard, but as soon as they did it was Chester's. But he didn't have no trouble finding work. White folks see men like Chester, big, strong, smiling in the way he did, they hired him 'fore he even opened his mouth. He worked a bit at the mattress factory, then at a slaughterhouse. Even worked on a road crew. There wasn't no work he wouldn't or couldn't do. Guess after farming, any kind of work comes easy. Finally the job at the lumberyard opened up.

I fit into Jackson like I'd been living in a city my whole natural-born life. When we first got to Jackson, Chester drove right down Farish Street pointing to the restaurants and stores. "All this here is owned by colored folk," he said, smiling.

I thought he was making fun till I saw wasn't a white person nowhere to be seen. Chester traveled halfway round the world, even to Jackson a time or two, and I had never stepped one foot out of Shubuta. I don't know what I had in my head Jackson was going to be, but it sure wasn't this. Chester loved watching my face that first day, watching Jackson. Watching how the people in Jackson felt alive the way they didn't in Shubuta. Back home, people was barely living it felt like. Just getting by. Work and white folks just about killed them.

Then we found a small house just at the edge of town. Just big enough to turn around in and with Chester working the long hours he did, the money he saved from his service pay and selling his daddy's farm, when we left Shubuta, making sure there was enough to give his momma and sister to go stay with his momma's people, he had enough to buy it. Chester picked me up like a rag doll and carried me in the front door when he got the keys. I held him tight round his big neck. Three bedrooms, each one smaller than the next, all lined up in a row on one side, the front room, kitchen, and inside toilet on the other side. The house felt like a mansion to me. Out the kitchen door was a small back porch with more yard than we had a use for. More than enough to have a garden if I wanted.

"Look like we got ourselves a little piece of Shubuta," Chester said, pointing to the pecan tree setting off in the corner, just like the one in the front of my house back home. I didn't want nothing reminding me of Shubuta, but I let Chester walk me under the shade of the tree and hold me tight with my head against his chest. When he let go, I went back inside. I watched him from the kitchen, under the tree, hands on his hips, filled up and taking in every inch of what he and his daddy's hard work had bought. When he came back inside, we looked in every room again. In the room that would be our bedroom I kissed him hard and long. "Thank you," I told him, and meant it. First time in my life I could call something my own.

Chester was what most would call a good husband. Came home every week with his paycheck. Wasn't expecting nothing outside of what a wife was supposed to give. Probably wasn't up to his liking, but I did the best I could to give it. I was expecting in no time with Simeon, and if I thought Chester was happy before, he was happier now.

I never took to driving, though, like Chester thought I would. 'Specially when he come round in that secondhand Buick he traded his truck in for. But in Jackson I didn't need no car when my two feet would do me just fine. Happy to finally be in a place I could walk just about anywhere I set my mind to. Walk just fifteen minutes and I was downtown to my job and everything else I needed. Another fifteen and I was back home again.

Maybe men and women are different that way. Men need a piece of machinery under them to make them feel like something, make them feel like men. I just needed me.

CHIME

I used to believe there wasn't nothing could make my daddy cry. Not my momma. Not losing his own brother and sister in '18 after the flu took 'em. Not the year it rained near all season and we lost our whole crop. But he cried like I never knew a man could cry when Mr. Charlie paid him a visit. I learned a long time ago, white man got a problem with a colored man, they don't never come alone. They gotta bring five, ten, twenty of their friends along for company. And they don't do no talking in the light of day. Wanna talk when you half asleep in your nightclothes, with your woman and chil'ren half scared out of their minds. That's the way they like to talk it out.

And that's the way they came talking to my daddy. After he lost his crop, he and my momma must have done some powerful praying. They was so deep in the hole for supplies to Mr. Phillips down at the store, we near starved after we slaughtered every hog and chicken we had. Had to hold on to the mule, but there were days I know we all were looking at him thinking he'd be fine stewing in a pot. But we needed God and that mule in equal measure to get us through the next season. Come next season the sun shined down bright, and the crop came back that year and the next. So good Daddy went in town asking about buying another little piece of land to add onto the one we had. He came home feeling like a big man that day, talking to my momma about what they could have if the crop went right. How a man just got to keep his head down and trust in the Lord. My momma didn't say much, but I know she knew something my daddy didn't. Mr. Charlie ain't gonna let you get more than he wants you to have. The next night they paid my daddy a visit, and that was the first time I saw him cry.

"Too much land for a colored man to be owning," they told him. He might want to "be reconsidering" buying up more property, one of them said. Listened to him beg, like a child asking for candy. Like he ain't the one out there every day breaking his back earning every rock he got to dig out and weevil he got to pluck. Told him he was "smart" and a "good colored" but he ought not be forgetting he wasn't no white man and he needed to stop all his "talking biggity." Maybe he needed some help remembering? After they left and my daddy sat at the table, head in his hands, my momma walked right past him to bed. That's when I smelled the smoke.

I ran to the window and saw part of the fields, lighting up the night. Blazing fire up one row and down the next.

I yelled, "Daddy! Fire!"

Momma told me to "hush up" and "get on to bed." My brothers and my sister Marion stayed right where they slept. I grabbed the bucket next to the stove and was heading for the pump when Momma stopped me. "I said get on to bed, *now.*"

"Daddy?" I said one last time, hoping he'd grab another bucket and together we'd go put out the fire without Momma, Marion, and every one of my brothers, Turner, Samuel, Clay, and BoJack. 'Stead of standing up, my daddy stayed sitting and let Mr. Charlie do to him what nothing else could. And all I could do was watch the water roll down his face.

CHIME

IF all it takes to wipe out years of hard work is the cover of night, some white men in hoods, and a torch, doesn't make no kind of sense to spend all my days sweating under the sun working a field when there's easier ways to make money. I so much as told my daddy that.

"The Lord giveth and the Lord taketh away," my daddy said, looking up at the sky at the edge of our land. My brothers were behind him walking, readying to clear land the morning after they came and burned the fields.

"Wasn't the Lord that taketh away," I said behind him. Even with his hood, we all knew the voice talking to our daddy. "That was Mr. Crenshaw, his brother, and they friends."

My brothers all walked along quiet, scared for me maybe or itching to see my daddy bring me down, I couldn't tell. My daddy turned to me. Breathed into my face. "Now, I done tole you once, and I don't expect I'm gonna need to tell you again." My brothers stood behind him watching me. I was starting to feel myself coming up on being a man. Almost fourteen years old. Not as tall as my daddy or my brothers, even my sister, probably never would be, but that wasn't stopping me from speaking my mind neither. My momma and daddy I knew could see that in me. Heard my momma tell my daddy once, "He's wild, that one. You better rein him in 'fore someone else do."

My daddy didn't want to hear nothing from Momma about how to raise his boys and told her so, but he knew it as well as my momma did. Never let me get two steps out of line.

"Last thing I need out of you is your 'pinion on thangs. You here to work, not tell me what you think, you understand?" my daddy said low. "You is young. Too young to know you can't put food on the table when you six feet in the ground. Me losing my head to every white man I get a mind to, means you, your brothers, your momma, sister, they don't eat." He was breathing heavy now. "So, I don't want you saying another word outside today, outside this family, 'bout Mr. Crenshaw, you hear me?"

I stood there looking at my daddy, feeling his breath and mad on me. Remembering the tears running down his cheeks the night before. Where was the mad then? He was quiet when Mister Charlie was talking to him. Thinking about that made me just about smile. I guess I did too, 'cause seeing that smile was when he hit me good square in my mouth. He knocked me to the ground. When I stood back up facing him, he was smiling at me.

"Best you keep your mouth shut now," he said, starting again toward the field.

Thought I said it low, but I guess not low enough, "Hittin' me like you shoulda hit Crenshaw…" I could feel BoJack slow beside me. Clay started singing, hoping Daddy hadn't heard, but he did. I could see it in his shoulders. The way they hung forward now. He never turned round. Didn't hit me again. Just kept right on walking. We all did. Straight out to those burned-up fields. Listening to the sounds of Clay singing, the birds chirping, and feeling the heat of that goddamn sun beating down hard as ever.

SIMEON

THE man who got me the job at the King Edward Hotel was Otis Brisco, and he was the head porter. Turns out I was right about him being respected because he told me he'd talk to the manager, Mr. Finley, and see what he could do about getting me a job, and when I came back the next day, I had one. Momma's eyes got wide when I told her that night at dinner I got a job at the King Edward.

"You mean the King Edward Hotel downtown?" Lamb asked, just staring.

"You know another one?" I asked her, smiling, leaning back in my chair. I was watching Momma out the corner of my eye. Waiting. "The tips I get there are gonna help me save faster than if I work anyplace else."

Momma nodded. "I'm gonna expect some of that money goes to me," she said.

"Why…" I started.

"You gonna be a man, working at a big hotel, making money for college, you gotta be a man and pay your share at home too," she said.

I didn't say anything, just started adding in my head how much less I was gonna have each week to save. "Okay, Momma." I remember thinking that if she thinks she is gonna slow me down from making money to head north, she is surely mistaken.

I started working that weekend as a bellhop, carrying luggage from the front desk up and back to the rooms. I didn't much care for those too-tight double-breasted uniforms and the caps and ties they made us wear along with them. The lace-up shoes made my feet hurt so bad I spent the first weeks limping home, but I liked seeing inside the hotel and the rooms that were prettier than I even imagined. I told Lamb and Momma everything I saw down to the colors of the bedspreads and the feeling of the rugs so thick you'd think you were walking on a mattress. I wondered how rich you needed to be to let you spend this kind of money on a bedroom. But when you walked around the lobby on what I learned were the marble floors under those chandeliers, I could see how just maybe it would feel like you weren't staying at any old bedroom at your house, even if you had a housekeeper and a big, fancy home somewhere in the country. Staying at the King Edward made you feel special. That's what our boss, Mr. Finley, told us at our bellhop meetings. "Remember, our job at the King Edward is to make our guests feel like royalty." *Unless you're a Negro,* I always thought after one of his speeches.

Otis treated me like family, checking in on me now and again, but being careful not to pay me too much attention so no one would think he was playing favorites. I was never sure if he was checking in because he was the one who went on and asked about getting me the job or because he knew I was too young to be working there in the first place and he wanted to be sure I didn't mess up and make him look bad, but I sure appreciated the way he told me what was what. The other men were good to me too, but I was so much younger, they didn't pay me much mind. One of them asked me once if I was any relation to Otis.

"You about the youngest bellhop I ever seen," he said to me. They were trying to earn tips so for the most part, everybody was looking out for themselves.

In the little room in the basement of the King Edward where we put on our uniforms on and took our coffee breaks, the men would sit at the long table on hard benches and talk about women and their families, how the white guests worked their nerves. They'd pass around newspapers they brought in, the ones Momma didn't want me reading at home, like the *Chicago Defender*. I could tell they were only half reading the paper because sometimes a whole argument would break out over just a headline with someone shouting how so-and-so told them something and didn't they hear that story about such-and-such. Things that if they read the whole article, they'd see their arguments didn't even have nothing to do with the story. That's when I'd tell them what the facts were I read in the paper. After that, they started teasing me and calling me "college boy." But not mean teasing, but proud teasing.

"Ask college boy about that fool over in Germany," someone would say in the middle of a fight about Hitler. They let me take all the newspapers with me home to read.

Otis was different that way. He was friendly with the other porters, but still kept to himself. Once they believed me and Otis weren't family, I found out from the other men that he lived alone. Never married, didn't have no children, and outside of the King Edward, no one knew much else about him.

When I watched him that first day, I thought he was Uncle Chime's age, but after working with him for over a year, I could tell he was much older. He bent over a little when he walked, probably from all his years carrying heavy bags, and I knew now when he had that look, when he looked like he was far away, he wasn't so much daydreaming as daydozing, swaying to one side, with his eyes looking glassy and out of focus. The other men saw it too and did their best to cover for him, stepping in front of Otis when he was swaying to meet guests when they pulled up in front with their new cars or snatching up a suitcase when Otis was slow to take it. I did it more than anyone else.

He told me, "You go on and pay attention to your own job. Ain't no one paying you to work my job and yours too," and he patted me on the back.

Those were the times I was sure I was his favorite. Uncle Chime always felt just like what he was, an uncle to me, but Otis, well, Otis felt a little bit like I imagined a daddy would feel. Teaching me, talking to me nice. Sometimes he even called me son. I never told him I didn't have a daddy at home, and he never told me he didn't have a son, but it seemed we were both what each other needed.

One Sunday, when everyone was checking out and the hotel was busy with people coming and going, I had just about sweated through my uniform trying to keep up with the bell ringing and bringing folks' luggage to the front desk or out front. Otis was standing there, stooped more than usual. I looked around for Mr. Finley, hoping he wasn't hanging around, whispering to us to "put some spring in your step," and all the other things he said when he thought the guests couldn't hear.

A young couple got off the elevator with Freddy holding their two heavy bags like they'd stayed at the hotel for a month. I remember hearing from another bellhop that they were on their honeymoon. He said the husband was a "big shot in the making." Which I knew meant to stay out of his way. The one thing I learned working there over the past year was that the nicest people at the hotel were the ones who didn't just have money, but were *used* to having money. They didn't need you to make them feel like something special when they already knew they were.

When the man got off the elevator, I could tell from over by the front desk he was already mad. His wife looked like she'd been crying and was walking fast trying to keep up to him, and he looked like he wasn't even thinking about her, just rushing to get out of the hotel. *First fight.*

Freddy had their bags and they walked past me and toward the door. I heard the bell ring at the front desk, telling me it was time to go upstairs and get another guest's luggage. I looked at the front entrance where the man was heading and Otis was standing, head to the side. I didn't have to see Otis's face to know he was doing his daydozing again, but I knew he didn't want to be doing that anywhere near this mad white man.

"Freddy," I said, but they all kept on walking. I walked closer to Freddy, pretending I didn't hear the bell dinging, and said his name again. Freddy stopped and looked at me.

"Let me get those, they look heavy. You take the bell." Tired as Freddy looked, he sure wasn't complaining. He nodded at me and I rushed along and out the door to the front with the man, his wife, and Otis. Otis had to see to it that the guests' cars were brought around front and help them load their luggage inside. And I could already see the man waving his hand in front of Otis's face. His wife touched his back, I guess to get him to calm down, and when he spun around, she stepped back, put her arm by her side. Otis was looking confused. And the man yelling in his face probably wasn't helping.

I stepped up. "Can I help you with anything, sir?" I asked.

"I told this boy here to have my car brought around and he's still standing there. He stupid or something?"

"No sir," I said to him. "I'll take care of that for you right away." I could feel Otis behind me not moving.

"I want this nigger to do it," he said to me, his spit flying in my face.

I smiled slow. "Yes, sir, I'll see to—"

"Son—son…" I heard behind me. I turned and Otis looked like he was about to fall over. I reached for him.

But before I could grab him the white man reached his meaty hands around me and grabbed the lapels of Otis's uniform. "Did you hear me, boy?"

"Sir, I—" I tried saying, looking at Otis's glassy eyes, but the man wasn't listening.

He snatched Otis, I think to get him moving, but all Otis did was fall into me. His forehead hit mine and I heard the crack of our heads hitting, my glasses breaking, and watched Otis fall to the ground.

"Oh my!" the man's wife half screamed.

Mr. Finley came rushing outside with Barclay, another porter, and they helped Otis up. He looked like he didn't even know where he was. We all looked at the man.

"Who is going to see to my things?" the man asked Mr. Finley, not even looking at Otis now.

"I'm so sorry about this inconvenience," Mr. Finley said to the man. "We'll get everything squared away immediately."

Inconvenience? Otis was an *inconvenience?*

I bent down and picked up my broken glasses. Barclay brought Otis inside and Mr. Finley told me to make sure the man's car was brought around quickly so that he and his lovely bride could get on their way. "In-a-hurry," he whispered, mad, in my ear.

By the time I got back inside the hotel, I went looking for Otis, but he was gone.

"Fired," Freddy told me. "All these years, and Mr. Finley told him he was no longer working up to *King Edward standards*." He shook his head and went to answer the bell at the desk.

Without my glasses, I felt like Otis must have, with everything out of focus and not seeing one thing clear. Glasses or not, I knew I had to get as much money saved as I could and get out of the King Edward Hotel and Mississippi and anyplace that thought white folks were royalty and Negroes wasn't nothing but their subjects.

LAMB

I always hate walking with Momma and Simeon. Their long legs walk twice as fast as my short ones and I got to just about run to keep up. Time we get anywhere, I'm about out of breath.

"Why do I have to go, if it's Simeon who broke his glasses?" I ask Momma again.

"I already told you, Lamb. Every time I see you with a needle, you are squinting like you can't half see," Momma said, up ahead of me.

"Maybe that just means I shouldn't be sewing," I tell her.

Momma didn't look back at me. "If the doctor has time today, we'll see if he can look at your eyes. Make sure you don't need glasses too. Not that I can afford it." She cut her eyes over at Simeon.

"You think I broke my own glasses, Momma? I told you the man—"

"I know what you *told* me," Momma said.

The walk to downtown Jackson wasn't far, little over a mile. We walked down Capitol Street and turned at the corner. Up on the next block was Tremper Optometry. He was the only optometrist downtown who saw Negro patients and that was only on Tuesdays. Momma used to have to get a ride from Uncle Chime to a doctor in Yazoo City to get Simeon's glasses until Dr. Tremper came to town a few years ago and started treating Negro patients. Simeon said he never knew why

Dr. Tremper was even treating Negro patients when he looked like he couldn't stand to be in the same room with them.

"What do he care? The only color that man cares about is green," Momma said, laughing, when Simeon said that. "Colored money is the same color as white people's money. That's why."

We were the first ones in the waiting room, and me and Simeon sat down while Momma went to the front desk. Every time we went, there was a new receptionist. I could see Momma's head nodding up and down at the white lady, trying her best to smile when I could tell she was mad, worried, or both.

"I feel like Blind Willie," Simeon said, looking around the room.

I held out my hand in front of his face with two fingers held up. "How many fingers do you see?" I asked him.

Simeon held up his fist in front of my face. "How many don't you see?" he asked, laughing. "I ain't that bad. Things are just fuzzy is all."

Momma turned and waved us over to her. "C'mon, y'all," she said.

The receptionist said to my momma, "You just remember to see me on the way out about your bill, you hear?"

"Yes ma'am," my momma said, her lips tight. "I will."

"The doctor will see you now," the receptionist said to Momma. "Go on to the back." She was looking down at her desk as she spoke.

"Hello, Dr. Tremper," Momma said when we all stepped into the office. He was sitting at his desk, his back to us. There was only one seat and the examining chair. Momma took the seat, I stood in the corner. Simeon stood next to Momma. "You remember my boy, Simeon? He broke his eyeglasses. Down at this job. He's a bellhop at the King Edward Hotel?" Momma sounded like she was asking Dr. Tremper if he knew where Simeon worked. She laughed nervous. "And he's gonna need a new pair."

In here, in the doctor's office, Momma didn't sound like Momma.

She sounded like someone pretending to be our momma, with her softer voice and polite ways. I wasn't sure the doctor heard her because he kept at his desk, still writing on a pad of paper. We all stood quiet, waiting. His chair spun around, and he looked at Momma and then at me and Simeon. He stayed in his chair, pad of paper in his hand. "Sit down over there," he said to Simeon, nodding his head to the examination chair.

The room was dark with the curtain drawn over the window. There was just the slight smell of medicine in the air as the doctor stood and walked past us and toward the examining chair. I knew that smell. *Whiskey.* The smell of my momma's Saturday nights. I looked at my momma to see if she smelled it too, but she was looking straight ahead at the doctor.

Dr. Tremper looked over his glasses, reaching for a tool from a tray. I noticed his hand shaking. "You got to take care of your glasses, Simon. Your momma don't have the money to buy you a new pair every time you get careless." He kind of half smiled at Momma and she half smiled back. Neither of them looked at Simeon.

"Yessir, I know that, sir," Simeon said in that way he spoke to adults that always made them like him. "And it's *Simeon,* not Simon, sir."

In the small room, his voice sounded like he was shouting. Me and Momma jumped a little at the sound of his voice. "Like in the Bible. With an 'E.' …"

Momma moved closer to Simeon's chair, reached low, and hit his arm that was hanging down soft, so the doctor couldn't see, but I did, and then Momma stepped closer to the doctor. "Simon's just fine, Dr. Tremper—"

The doctor's hand stopped on top of the tool and stayed there. He stared straight past Momma and looked at Simeon for the first time, till Simeon thought to drop his head and stare at his lap.

"You spelling your name for me, boy?"

Simeon took a minute before he answered. Too long. "No sir, I was just—"

"Your boy know he talking to a white man, Auntie?" He stepped closer to Simeon. Breathed down on his head. Now the whiskey smell was strong in the room. I knew we all could smell it. "You look like you might be a smart boy," he said soft to the top of Simeon's head. "Maybe too smart, that it?"

"No sir," I heard Simeon mumble.

"Well, you better act like it."

Momma laughed. "Oh, he understands, Dr. Tremper, don't you, Sim. Don't you, son?"

"Simon," Dr. Tremper said. "Right, boy?"

"Yessir," Simeon answered, whispering now.

"S-I-M-O-N," the doctor spelled.

He turned back to his pad and scribbled something on it fast. Then turned back to his tools. He grabbed Simeon's face, hard, and started the exam. Looked into one eye with his tool, then the other. Took out another tool and did the same. He had Simeon look at a chart on the wall and call out the letters. I didn't know if it was because he was scared, but I ain't never known Simeon to fail a test. But he could barely name one of the letters right on that chart. I kept looking from the doctor to Simeon and back again.

Finally, the doctor sat back at his desk and kept writing on his pad of paper while we waited quiet. Finally he said to his pad, "That'll be all. Come back in two weeks and pick up your glasses. My girl will tell you how much to bring."

"Thank you, Doctor," my momma said. "We appreciate your time." She hit Simeon again low.

"Thank you, sir," he said, so low I could barely hear him.

The doctor looked up and watched us walk out, not saying a word.

LAMB

"**Simeon,** wait," Momma said as Simeon just about ran up the sidewalk ahead of us as soon as we stepped out of the doctor's office.

"I said wait, boy!" When Momma shouted, her voice was deep as any man's. People on the street sidestepped us.

Simeon stopped where he stood but didn't turn to look at Momma, just stared straight ahead. When we caught up, Momma was out of breath.

"You don't walk away from me like that, you hear me, Simeon?" Momma grabbed his arm.

"So *now* it's Simeon?" he asked, turning to look at her.

"I will slap the taste all the way out your mouth, you talk to me like that again. I didn't raise you to be no fool, Simeon. Who do you think you are? You want to live long enough to get to that school up north, then you better learn how to live here in the South. You understand me?"

"Yessah ma'am."

Momma slapped Simeon so loud, seemed like the whole street got quiet.

Simeon looked at her. Without his glasses, his eyes looked so small, and you could see his long, pretty lashes. He nodded his head up and down, up and down, like he was agreeing with what Momma just did.

I was wishing we could go home. Go back to the day before Simeon broke his glasses, back to before the doctor called him Simon. But there wasn't no turning back now.

"Yeah, you keep nodding that silly head of yours. You lucky it's me that's knocking sense into it, instead of…"

"Oh, I know, Momma," Simeon said, his head still nodding up and down. "'Stead of someone who doesn't think I should know how to spell my own name. I know, Momma. I'm so grateful to you." Simeon crossed the street. A car beeped and turned sharp to miss hitting him, and I wondered for a second if Simeon could even see without his glasses. Me and Momma watched him cross Capitol Street and walk through the park. Momma opened her purse, looking for I don't know what.

"Let's go, Lamb. Need to pick up something for supper," Momma said. Her hand was holding on to her handkerchief. But she never used it.

LAMB

I waited, seemed like all night, for Simeon to come home. Through supper and after the dinner dishes were washed and dried. Momma didn't set a plate for him, like she knew he wouldn't be there. Finally, I asked, "Momma, you think we should ask Uncle Chime to go look for Simeon?"

"He'll come home when he's ready," she said. "Boys get to thinking they grown and it's best to just leave them be."

"Momma—" I could see her body go tight. "You don't think Simeon's hurt, do you?"

She relaxed some. "Nah, he'll be home soon enough. Probably out with his friends or something. I'll give him some more time."

Made me laugh inside, Momma thinking Simeon had lots of friends he was out with when he only had but one he was close with.

"What did you think I was gonna ask you?" I asked Momma.

"What are you talking about now, Lamb?"

"That's not what you thought I was gonna ask."

Her body got tight again and she looked at me.

"You thought I was gonna ask about today in the doctor's office."

"You know…" Momma sat down hard in front of me at the table. "You and Simeon spend a lot of time making plans. You gonna get away from here. Get your education up north. Never have to deal with triflin' white folks again. You think you ain't gonna meet Dr. Trempers wherever you go? You think the Dr. Trempers only live here in Mississippi? You think that, the two of you both are too dumb to go to any school up north."

"Simeon says it's different up north," I said. "That it ain't like this, where we always have to be afraid to…"

"Afraid to what? They don't string people up in the North, that it?" Momma laughed. "Maybe not from a tree. But they sure do in a courtroom. Or a jail cell. Please…" Momma shook her head. "Y'all ain't escaping nothing by leaving here. Just getting a different set of problems." Momma stood to pour herself a cup of coffee.

"Simeon read in the *Chicago Defender* that—"

"In the *Defender*? You know how you sound, Lamb? What do the *Defender* know about life here in Mississippi? And I told y'all about bringing that paper in this house. This is exactly why Simeon was up in that office today about to have me lose my job, or worse, about to lose his life over what the goddamn *Chicago Defender* said." Momma's voice was as deep as a freight train. "I am trying to keep y'all—" Momma stopped. Shook her head.

"Trying to what, Momma?"

"I got sewing to do, Lamb, and you need to get on to bed."

Time I washed up and headed to bed, Simeon still wasn't back, so I laid awake listening and waiting.

LAMB

SIMEON was sitting at breakfast like nothing ever happened. Quiet. And Momma too, radio on, sipping coffee. I looked at both of them, waiting for someone to say something. When neither did I went and got dressed and me and Simeon left for school.

"Where'd you go last night?" I asked before we were barely out the door.

"Needed to clear my head."

"From Momma?"

"From everything."

He was quiet still. Wasn't like Simeon to be this quiet. He near talked me to death every morning going to school.

"From Dr. Tremper?"

"Everything, Lamb. So tired of this place, I don't even think I can make it till college starts in September to leave."

"What are you talking about? You have to wait. You don't know no one in Ohio to stay with."

"But I could maybe get a job there, find a room or something till school starts...I don't know...just thinking is all."

"You tell Momma what you're thinking?"

"One day you gonna learn, Lamb, there's people you can talk to, and there's people you can *talk* to. Momma ain't one of those people."

"Yes she is."

"Oh, pardon me." He smiled, first one all morning. "Not one of those people *I* can talk to. I forgot you two are bosom buddies."

"Why do you do that, Simeon? She's our momma. I'm supposed to hate her 'cause you do?"

"You ever heard me say I hate our momma, Lamb?" Simeon stopped and stared at me. And again I couldn't stop staring at how pretty his eyes were. "I hate ignorance. I hate when people are small-minded. But I never said I hate our momma."

"But you think she's those things."

"You know it's more complicated than that. Stop acting like a child," Simeon said in a way that wasn't mean.

"I'm tired of the two of you. Putting me in the middle."

"You put yourself there, ask me."

Sometimes I knew just how Momma felt. I could never out-talk Simeon. You say one thing, he say five, better, smarter than anything you could ever say. Makes you mad and proud at the same time.

We were heading up the road toward school. "Can you see okay?"

He smiled again. "I'll be fine. Glasses'll be in in a couple of weeks. Till then, if you just let me hold on to your arm, I'll be all right." He hunched over a little and hooked his arm around mine like he was a blind man.

I pushed him off. "Always playing," I said.

LAMB

THE front door opened. "Y'all up yet?"

"I guess if we weren't we would be by now," I said when Uncle Chime came into the kitchen.

"Hey there, Chop. Where is everybody?" he asked, his boots clomping as he walked.

"Momma left already. Simeon's sleeping still."

"Then what you doing up?" Uncle Chime pulled out a chair.

"I got a test today I need to finish studying for."

"You gonna hurt your brain you keep up all that studying. You ever study how to have fun?" He closed my book.

"Uncle Chime, it's too early to play."

"Is it too early to talk to my baby girl?" He sat down hard next to me and threw one leg over his knee. Mud was caked all over his boots.

"You going to work today?" I asked.

"S'pose to be. Waiting for a man to call on me."

"How's he gonna find you here?"

"So you can ask me questions, but I can't ask you none?"

I laughed and opened my book back up.

Uncle Chime got up and poured himself a cup of coffee. He took a sip. "You know your momma's coffee tastes like piss?" he says.

"Never had it," I said, looking over at my schoolbook.

"What's that, her coffee or piss?"

"Uncle Chime!"

He laughed. "Just messing with ya, Chop."

"Why can't you ever call me by my given name?" I asked him, not looking up.

"You don't like Chop? You sweet and tender like a little lamb chop." Uncle Chime had a laugh so loud, it felt like the house was shaking.

"Uncle Chime—you gonna wake up Simeon."

"When your momma told me she had a baby girl and named her Lamb," he started, doing Uncle Chime's version of whispering, which was most people's version of talking regular, "I said to your her, 'I know you done lost your mind, Marion, naming that girl Lamb! What you gonna name the next ones? Rooster? Cow?'" He told this story about a dozen times. "'Colored girl have a hard-enough time in this world without you naming her after some animal.' But nah, she didn't want to listen to me or no one else, neither. 'She's my little lamb,' she said. And here you is, Lamb Chop."

"Well, I love my name," I said.

"What other choice you got?" Uncle Chime said, shouting again for the whole street to hear. Simeon really could sleep through just about anything.

"Says the man named Chime..." I laughed.

"Close my eyes and I am listening to Marion Ross herself." He laughed. "You are your momma's girl, that's for sure." He grabbed my head in his hand. "'Sides, you know that's my nigger name."

"*Nick*name," I corrected him.

"Nickname to you, nigger name to me."

He finally let go of my head. "Yessir, your momma was never happier than when she got her Lamb," he said, smiling at me and still sipping on the coffee. "Guess only girl in a house full of boys, she been waiting her whole life for the chance to have a girl, dress her up real pretty. She didn't have the chance to be a girl with us."

"Grandma didn't dress Momma pretty?" I asked him.

"My momma didn't have time for all that with a houseful of mens to feed and land to work!" Uncle Chime was shouting again. "Fact is, she was harder on your momma than she was on us."

"Why's that?" I ask him.

"Well, you'd have to ask my momma that," he said.

"But Grandma died."

Uncle Chime smiled at me, showing off the big gap in between his two front teeth. It almost matched the big part that went right down the middle of his head. He shrugged his shoulders.

"Momma don't talk much about Grandma," I said to him.

Now Uncle Chime was quiet. After a minute he said, "Like I said, she was hard on her. Probably harder than she needed to be."

I whispered, "Like Momma is with Simeon?"

Uncle Chime looked away, cleared his throat. "If you think your momma's hard on Simeon, Chop, then you ain't never seen hard," he said.

Uncle Chime closed my book again. "Tell your momma I came by," he told me, standing up. The screen door slammed behind him.

CHIME

IT wasn't my daddy or my brothers who taught me how to be a man, but my sister. Was Marion who showed me what it meant to stand up, to fight back, just by watching her and my momma every day. From the time she got up to the time she laid down, my momma was on her. None of us but my momma knew why. Most women I know would've cried a river having to hear their own flesh and blood talk to them the way my momma talked to Marion. Told her to her face, she wasn't no better than a fool. Pretty as Marion was, my momma told her that no one wasn't ever going to look twice at her sorry behind. Said it to her plain, just like that. But my momma could see that even the fields didn't take any of the shine off of Marion the way they did other girls. The sun, the work, the tired made every day feel like one hundred more.

Marion never minded work. Never said one word about it. She had eight years on me, and there were times when I couldn't keep up, Marion would come over and help me do my line too when she finished hers. The more my momma tried to beat her down, the taller Marion stood, and that there was what made my momma the maddest. The way she couldn't get her to bend.

Marion would work like two men, and my momma wanted to know why she didn't work like four. Finally, walking out to the field one day, I said to my daddy, "Why's Momma got to be so hard on Marion? What'd she do?"

Daddy stopped and looked at me hard. "Maybe you want to be working in the kitchen today 'stead of out here with us." He pointed to my brothers. "You'd do best to stay out of womenfolk's business," he told me.

"That womenfolk's business or family business?" I asked him again.

My daddy's hand backslapped me 'fore I could barely finish the sentence. I took a step back, but not 'fore I looked at him hard. Let him know his hand wasn't gonna stop me from saying what needed to be said.

"It's the kind of business I say it is," my daddy said through his teeth.

My brother BoJack pulled me along. "Leave it alone, Chime. Marion can take care of herself," he told me.

I wiped the blood from my lip and walked along behind my daddy wondering what kind of man lets his girl have to take care of herself. Lets someone tell his girl every day she ain't worth nothing the way our momma did to Marion. What kind of man don't protect his own? I knew that wasn't the kind of man I was fixing to be.

She was my sister and all, but even I could see how Marion made men start staring and not want to stop. I don't know if my momma was ever that pretty in her day, but Marion was as tall as any of my brothers, not small and stubby like my momma. Her eyelashes were so long and thick it looked like it'd hurt for her to blink. She wasn't fussy about the way she looked. Snatched her hair back in two braids, but even that made her neck look long and you could see how smooth her skin was. She didn't smile much, but when she did, you'd feel like you won a prize seeing her big ole dimples and pretty teeth.

When we'd go into town, time we got home, my momma would be

fit to be tied. "Out there acting like trash." She'd tell our daddy Marion was flitting herself around when Marion didn't do nothing of the kind. I remember the way she looked at our momma. Staring at her as she told our daddy that lie. Then they would both look at him. *Waiting.*

"Say something to her," my momma would tell him. And there would be Marion. Staring at him, quiet, like she was daring him to say something.

"You don't want folks looking at her, then don't take her into town!" he'd shout at my momma.

You had to watch real close to see it, but every time, I could see that little bit on one side of Marion's mouth turn up, telling me, Momma, and everyone else that she won. *Again.*

Seemed like for as long as I could remember my momma walked in Marion's shadow when they were together. We all did. I'd even catch my daddy at night sometimes when she was working on her sewing, just smiling at her from across the room. Course my momma said her head was always up in the air about her looks, but it wasn't. Last thing on Marion's mind was being fancy. Fact was, me and the boys, BoJack, Clay, Samuel, and Turner, all wished she fixed herself up more than she did, 'stead of going out in our hand-me-downs.

Wasn't no one gonna break Marion Ross in two, not even her own momma. That was how my sister taught me to be a man. Don't let no one make you bend.

LAMB

"**WHAT** he say he want?" Momma asked when I was setting the table.

"He didn't say. He said he was waiting on someone to pick him up for work," I told Momma.

Momma just shook her head.

"Only two reasons Chime get up that early in the morning and work ain't one of 'em," she said to herself. "Money or trouble. Where's your brother?"

"He said he was gonna have to work late," I told her.

"Again? You'd think he supporting a family with all that working late he's doing."

"He just worries about having enough money." Momma looked at me. "You know, for when he goes away."

Every time I mentioned Simeon leaving, Momma got the same look on her face. And it wasn't the happy look like I thought it should be.

"Momma—"

She didn't look at me.

"Did you and Grandma used to talk a lot? When you were a girl." Momma was quiet. Kept stirring the pot on the stove.

"You talking to Chime this morning?" she asked me. I could hear her voice change.

"No, I was just wondering."

"So you all of a sudden just up and wondering if me and my momma used to talk a lot when I was a girl?" Now she looked at me.

"Forget it," I said.

"Watch your mouth, Lamb," she said to me. Momma could turn from nice to mean quick, reach out and bite you, like a snake. "You don't tell me to 'forget it.' Do I look like one of your friends?"

"Sorry, Momma."

She turned back to the stove. She waited a few minutes, then said, "Me and my momma didn't talk a lot, no. She was too busy whupping my behind to talk. Any more questions?"

I stood and looked at her. Tall and skinny with her high round behind that I wished I had. She rested one hand on her hip. From behind she looked soft and shapely. Almost as young as the girls in my school. But soon as you looked in my momma's face you could see the hardness around her eyes and mouth you didn't see in her body.

"You lucky you didn't see that part of your grandmomma 'fore she died. But while she was alive, she couldn't find one kind thing to say to me. Treated me like I was some charity case she had to care for. If it wasn't for..."

I could see her whole body get stiff and straight when she talked. "Sometimes, though...when she was teaching me a stitch, or we was sewing together...sometimes she'd talk to me...like a mother. But only when we was sewing." Her voice faded like she was sitting next to my grandma again a long time ago.

I went up behind her and hugged her round the waist. She loved when I did that. "I'm sorry, Momma." Her body relaxed a little bit.

"Let's sit down and eat. You and Chime got me talking about all this ancient history," Momma said, sitting down at the table hard.

LAMB

WHEN it came time for Simeon to go back to the doctor to get his glasses, Momma told me to stay home. Any other day I would have been happy to stay home with time to not be helping Momma catch up with sewing or doing schoolwork and just be alone in the house reading. But I was scared Simeon was going to get smart again with the doctor or Momma or both so I went.

Simeon knew too. "You my protector?" he whispered in my ear when Momma was locking the door behind us.

"No, I wanted to come." I smiled at him sweet.

"What is that in your hand, Lamb?" Momma asked, staring down at my book.

"Oh, I forgot, I'll put it—"

"Nah, we ain't got time for all of that. You can't be dragging a book all over town. Books are for school, Lamb. Or when you doing your schoolwork. You lose it, don't expect me to pay for a new one."

"Books are for school?" Simeon asked Momma.

Already I was wishing I just stayed home. "You do know that people read books for pleasure, right? The library is filled with books for just that—"

"You do know you are not too grown to get popped upside your head again in the street, right?" Momma told him.

Simeon breathed slow out the side of his mouth.

"This isn't a schoolbook, Momma. Miss Thompson, my English teacher, loaned this to me. It's her favorite, and she thought I'd like it. I'm trying to hurry up and read it and give it back to her before school ends."

"Well, just be sure you do," Momma said.

Simeon rolled his eyes behind Momma's back and I tried hard not to laugh.

I noticed Momma put on her nicer dress this time, like she was trying hard to look respectable for the doctor. Maybe hoping he'd forget about the last time. Maybe hoping he wouldn't call her Auntie. I didn't know what dressing nicer meant to white folks. Did it mean we were nicer?

I'd never seen the waiting room so filled on Negro Day. Every seat was taken with only one left, and Simeon threw out his arm and bent his knee, waving Momma toward the seat like Momma was royalty and he was her subject insisting she take it.

She gave him a look that said, "Keep playing with me…" and he smiled wide at her. They both knew she wouldn't hit him in a waiting room. I stood with my back against the wall, glad I brought my book.

Miss Thompson was right about some parts of it being romantic, but I couldn't help feeling so bad for the woman O-lan and the way she worked, longer and harder than even her husband, and never once complained. It looked to me like her whole life, from the day she was born, was going to be a hard one, filled with work. Each time I opened the book I was hoping things would get better for her and also hoping that her husband's mean old father would just go ahead and die already. But there was something too about that book that made me want to open it up each day, reading not about farming and China like

I thought, but about how two strangers came together and dreamed of something better. Sometimes after class, she'd ask on my way out the door, "How's my book coming, Lamb?" and I would just smile and say, "Good, Miss Thompson, thank you." But now I could tell her how this was the part I liked the most so far. *The dreaming.* Almost like me and Simeon.

Simeon found a spot on the floor and began talking to a boy next to him wearing glasses. Before I knew it the two of them were stretched out on the floor taking turns pushing the boy's toy car back and forth. That was the thing about Simeon, one minute he was as serious as an old man, the next he was like a little kid again.

The white girl behind the front desk looked like she wasn't much older than me, with hair the brightest color of orange I had ever seen. It looked worse because of her yellow sweater. She called out the names so soft you could barely hear them if you weren't listening good, and she had to say them over and over again until someone would finally hear her and get up to go into the doctor's office. I knew then she was the reason the waiting room was so crowded. After Simeon's new friend and his family were called, I found a seat near Momma and settled in a hard chair with my book. Momma's head had fallen to one side, and I could see she was asleep.

"Si-mon ?" I heard the girl at the front desk whisper. "Simon?" she said again, not much louder. I nudged Simeon with my foot.

"Simeon, they're calling you."

He looked straight at me. "She called *Simon*," he said.

I felt the hair on the back of my neck go up. *Not again.*

I stood up and tapped Momma. "Momma, come on. We're here," I said to the girl at the front desk. Simeon still didn't move.

Momma wiped the side of her mouth, smoothed down her dress. I saw her pull up her nylons. She walked to the desk.

93

"You called Simeon Clark?" Momma asked.

"Um, says here Simon. Is it Simeon? Sometimes I can't read the writing in these charts," the girl said, squinting down at the folder in front of her.

My momma shook her head but all of a sudden Simeon was right beside her. "Thank you," he said. "It is Simeon, just like in the Bible."

Momma turned slow and looked at him long.

"Of course," the girl said, looking at him smiling. She took out a pen and scratched out one name and wrote a new one above it. "S-I-M-E-O-N. Okay, there we are, all fixed. Go right on in," she said.

She's not going to last long working here, I thought.

"You're reading my favorite book," she said to me as I walked behind Momma.

"Excuse me, ma'am?" I said, eyes low.

"*The Good Earth.* That's my favorite book. You like it?" she asked me.

Momma looked at me. I didn't know where to look now.

"Yes," I said, nodding my head. I rubbed my hand over the cover, looking down at the book.

I felt like I was onstage with everybody staring at me, waiting for me to act out a part in a play I didn't know the words for. I kept rubbing the cover.

"What part are you on?" the redheaded girl asked, smiling big. "In the book?" she asked, head nodding and pointing to my hand. My momma looked at me and cleared her throat. I could feel Simeon at my side moving from one leg to the next.

Everybody, I could tell, was waiting.

LAMB

"**THEY** coming or what?" I heard from behind me, and we all turned to see Dr. Tremper walking toward us, his face red. Mad maybe he had to wait for a Negro patient.

He looked at Momma, then me. Let his eyes rest on Simeon long. Even though I knew Simeon could barely see the doctor's eyes, he could see him staring. He looked down at his shoes.

"There a problem here?" Dr. Tremper asked, his eyes moving fast from Simeon to the redheaded girl.

The girl reached out and touched Dr. Tremper's arm and giggled.

"No, Daddy, sorry. It's my fault, honest," she said, smiling big at him now. I wondered if she could stop smiling.

"Now how could it be your fault," Dr. Tremper asked her, his voice changing to soft and purry as a cat. He looked again at us like we did something to make her keep us waiting. I realized, this new voice must be the one Dr. Tremper used when he saw his white patients.

"Well…" She tilted her head at the doctor. "You know how I get to talking.…"

Please don't mention the book was all I keep thinking to myself. I moved my hand with the book behind my back, hiding it.

"We are here to see to folks about their glasses, darling, so let's not try to keep them too long. In and out, right, sweetheart?" He smiled big right back at her, and I could see now how they favored each other. I didn't believe Dr. Tremper even knew how to smile, but here he was with just about all his teeth showing, one in the front brown from tobacco. "Now let's get these people seen quick as we can."

"Yes, Daddy," she said, looking ashamed.

"It's okay, honey," he said, putting his hand on top of hers. "It's your first day. You just keep on doing a good job." Problem was, she *wasn't* doing a good job, least not as far as Dr. Tremper would have liked, making sure patients got in to see him orderly, like the last woman at the front desk. But she was nicer than the other woman. Looking each person in the eye, saying *please* and *thank you,* like she was raised right. Like it didn't make no difference to her at all whether you were white or Negro, just so long as you were a patient in her daddy's office.

In Dr. Tremper's office, I stood again off to the side in the corner while Momma took the seat. On his desk were a lot of small boxes of eyeglasses and a stack of charts. I saw now a picture of him and an older red-haired woman, the girl when she was young, and an older boy in a picture frame in the corner. *Her momma and brother.* For just one second I thought about me, Momma, Simeon, and my daddy, wondering if before my daddy left, they took any pictures of the four of us together and maybe before Momma stopped talking about him and us, they put that picture in a picture frame and hung it in our house. If people came to the house, saying how much I looked like my daddy and how much Simeon looked just like his momma. Maybe there were pictures like that, and Momma took them all down and had them in a shoe box somewhere in her room she hid the minute my daddy shut the door behind him.

Momma spoke up. "Your girl, your daughter out there—she's real pretty, Dr. Tremper."

Dr. Tremper was quiet.

"And she's doing a fine job too," Momma added in.

He looked over at my momma. I was thinking he'd at least say, "Thank you, Auntie," but all he could manage was to nod his head. He turned back to his desk.

Dr. Tremper reached for one of the boxes with the name SIMON CLARK on it, took out the new pair of eyeglasses, and polished them with a big soft cloth.

"Sit down," he said to Simeon, not turning around. Simeon sat in the chair holding tight to both the arms looking like he was scared he was gonna fall out. Dr. Tremper spun around finally and put the glasses on Simeon's face.

"Read that chart," he said to Simeon, pointing to the one on the wall he had to read before. This time Simeon passed the test. I smiled over at him, but he didn't smile back.

"You folks gotta learn to take care of your things," Dr. Tremper said to Simeon. "That's how they last, right Auntie?"

"Yessir Dr. Tremper," Momma said, not looking at Simeon. She smoothed down her dress. The whiskey smell was gone today but the room still smelled like cigarettes and something old. Old and dead.

"Thank you, Dr. Tremper," my momma said quiet. She tapped Simeon's leg as he got up. I saw him brush her hand away fast. He walked toward the door. I could see the scared in Momma's eyes.

"Thank you, sir," I said, loud, hoping my "thank you" would help Dr. Tremper not notice that Simeon hadn't said anything.

"You did a fine job, Dr. Tremper," Momma said, backing out as Simeon opened the door and walked into the hallway.

Dr. Tremper nodded his head at Momma and tried to look past her toward Simeon but I stood in the doorway. Momma bumped into me backing up and we both turned quickly and made our way back to the front desk. Simeon was sitting out in the waiting room, and Momma looked over at him. I wished I could walk home another way or at least by myself. Listening to the two of them fussing all the way home about Dr. Tremper and thank-yous and knowing your place was just about the last thing I wanted to do. Momma walked over to Simeon and leaned down to whisper loud in his ear. I turned away and the redheaded girl looked up.

"Hey, what's your name?" she asked.

Momma was still whispering to Simeon and he was leaning his head away from her. I was scared their whispering was going to turn into a fight. "Lamb," I said, louder than I meant to.

"Lamb?" She laughed. "Like a sheep? Like the hymn, 'Lamb of God'? That's one of my favorites. We sing it every Sunday in service."

It's my favorite too, I said to myself, letting myself smile just a little at her.

"I don't think I've ever heard of anyone with that name before. You're lucky to have a name so different," she said.

That's why I love my name too, because it's different. I kept on talking to her, just in my head.

"I'm Marny."

I still didn't say nothing out loud but nodded at her. Just like her daddy did to my momma in his office.

"Okay then," she said. "I hope you like the rest of the book." She called out the name of the next person waiting.

As Simeon stood to leave I walked to the door and waited. I looked at the book cover thinking, *Now that's two people loving this story.* I'd still need to wait and see what I thought but it sure would be nice to find out why she liked it. I wondered if this red-haired girl thought it was romantic like Miss Thompson or if she felt bad for O-lan, same way I did. One thing I knew for sure, I was never going to find out what she thought because I didn't know which of our parents would be madder about us talking over that book together, her daddy or my momma.

LAMB

WE were barely outside when Momma started in. "Didn't I tell you not to bring that book?" I didn't say nothing.

"You could tell that girl is slow-witted or something, thinking you are her little friend. What is her daddy doing having that girl at the front desk?" Momma just shook her head.

Even Simeon was quiet.

"You ain't got nothing to say?" Momma asked, stopping to look at me.

"How was I supposed to know she'd ask me about my book?"

"And this is why I told you that books are for school, and you needed to leave it at home, where it belongs."

"Because you were worried that a silly white girl would be reading the exact same book and might just ask her about it?" Simeon said to Momma.

I breathed in deep, getting myself ready for what I knew was coming.

"Oh, and I know you and your stupid self ain't talking about someone being silly. You already moved north in your head but your body still alive and well in Mississippi."

Simeon shook his head and looked at me. I kept walking, almost as fast now as Simeon and my momma, just wanting to get home.

"That girl don't know she can't be your friend?" Momma asked more to herself than me.

"I don't know, Momma," I said, already out of breath, trying to keep up.

"Well, Dr. Tremper ain't had time to check you for glasses, Lamb, but I'm gonna hope that girl ain't there the next time we have to go. I don't know who's a bigger fool, her or your brother."

"Wasn't Lamb the fool for bringing the book?" Simeon asked. I swear sometimes I think he wanted Momma to beat him in the street.

"You ain't gonna have me out here shaming my name, Simeon Clark. But when we get home, I'm gonna tell you who's a fool...." Momma said, walking so fast with her long thin legs, it was like she was near running.

I looked at Simeon, my eyes begging him. *Let it go.* He smiled back at me. *Good Lord,* I thought to myself, *he actually likes this.*

LAMB

I didn't know if Momma and Simeon even knew I went to bed early, but after listening to them fighting all through dinner and washing up the dinner dishes, I picked up my book and went to my room. I could still hear them out there carrying on. I couldn't stop thinking about the red-haired girl, Marny, and her asking me about the book. I never much liked talking to girls who were quiet as me. Too much work to just get to know each other if together we had to try to find the right words. But whenever I met someone like Earvent and NeeCee, who did all the talking, it was easier. Or like this girl Marny. If she was Negro, that is.

If she was Negro, I might have said the things I thought in my head. Or told her what part I was on in the book. Or rolled my eyes with her when Momma and Simeon started up. If she was Negro I might have told her how "Lamb of God" was my favorite hymn too, maybe told her how I was in the choir, asked her what church she went to. If she was Negro, she would have asked me if I knew so-and-so, or if I had people over on Deer Park or what school I went to. But she ain't Negro. And I ain't no white girl, so that's that.

I went back to my book and kept reading. Was she slow-witted like Momma said? Or just friendly? Did her daddy know she was at the front desk spelling out folks' names the right way and asking about what books his Negro patients were reading? At Simeon's job, he has to talk to white folks all the time. Says one way whites and Negroes is alike is that both want to be treated like they are important and treated with respect. The difference between them is the way they do you if they don't get it. Momma says whites and Negroes are about as different as night and day. "Something in 'em makes them evil," Momma told us about white folks. "That's just how they're born."

This Marny didn't seem evil. But it did seem funny to me that I was thinking at all about a white girl with a daddy as close as I could imagine to what Momma was describing. Maybe my momma was only half right.

LAMB

THE next time I saw the red-haired girl it wasn't at her daddy's office. I was walking home along the trestle bridge not far from home. Taking my time because I knew Momma had to finish Mrs. Rowland's order and knew if I was home, Momma would find a way to make me help. "Just catch this hem for me right here," she'd say, and next thing, I'd be sitting under her all night with her passing me pants and shirts to mend. She didn't need me for the tailoring and nice stitchwork she did on her own.

I almost never walked along the trestle bridge if I could help it. Sometimes it scared me looking down into the grass below, piled with trash, and I imagined all manner of bugs and nasty animals feeding off it. Looked like it was just waiting to swallow up somebody who slipped and fell from the bridge. So when I walk across, I look straight ahead. Minding my feet to walk slow and careful over every tie. I saw her from a ways off, her bright red hair tied under a red scarf, wearing another yellow sweater, this one a twinset with a string of pearls around her neck. She looked like the movie stars do in the picture shows, wearing dark sunglasses in one of those cars with no top.

Simeon told me you could talk to a white person all day long and the next day too and they'd still walk right past you like you were a ghost. "They never remember our faces," he told me one day when he was reading the paper. "But let them testify in court and they are always *absolutely* sure it was *that* Negro right there." Simeon said, pretending to be a white man on the witness stand pointing to a Negro man. He stood up tall and puffed out his chest. "How would they know," he said, sitting back down and shaking his head, "when they can't tell one of us from the next?" Truth be told, only reason I knew it was her was because of her red hair and yellow sweater. I nearly fell off the bridge when we got close enough to pass, walking as close to the edge as I could, but she slowed down, looked right in my face, and said, "Lamb?"

I looked at her. "It's me, Marny," she said, like she was an old friend I didn't recognize. "From the doctor's office, remember?...You were reading *The Good Earth*."

"Yes, I remember," I told her, hoping I could get on my way.

"Well?" She stepped closer, her head tilted.

"Ma'am?" I remember my momma saying she must be slow-witted, and with her head tilted to the side, smiling like we were friends, she sure looked like it.

"Did you like the book? I was hoping you would." She smiled.

"I still haven't finished it. Almost, though." I looked over her shoulder when I spoke to her, not feeling right looking her in the eye. "But it's good so far."

I was scared standing close to the edge of the bridge but I was scared too with her standing closer to me than she ought to be. I took a baby step forward, and she didn't move. I kept staring over her shoulder.

"I knew it," she said, so excited her purse slapped up against her hip. She turned around to see what I was looking at. "Like I said, it's my favorite."

We stood quiet. She opened her large purse and started tearing

104

through. "The thing is…" Her head was down, and she started digging around for what I didn't know what. All I could think was, suppose she wasn't just slow-witted but crazy in the head and pushed me over the edge of the bridge, down below with all the trash and critters? I moved to the side and she didn't notice.

"I'm a bit of a bibliophile." She looked up now, smiling still. "I can't get enough of books. It worries my daddy, of course. He thinks they are corrupting my mind." She shook her hands over her head when she said the word "corrupting," and laughed out loud. "You know what I say to that?" I wondered how long you could have a conversation with your own self. "It corrupts your mind when you *don't* read!"

That really made her laugh. "Of course, I never say that out loud to Daddy. He'd have me in the sanatorium for sure." She tilted her head again. "He's hoping that keeping me busy in his office will keep me from reading. And then you walk in with my favorite book! I guess that didn't work, huh?" She poked me with her elbow, and her touch made me lean back.

"Whoa there." Marny reached her hand out to grab mine and I grabbed back. "Careful," she said, yanking me toward her.

We were so close now, I could smell the perfume she was wearing, florally. Gardenias maybe.

"You okay?" Marny asked. I nodded, not realizing at first how heavy I was breathing. I was still holding her hand, but didn't let go yet.

"That's a long way to fall." She smiled. Finally I let go of her. I wiped my sweaty hand on the side of my skirt.

"Well, I got to get on home," I told her. She finally stopped smiling.

"Have you ever read any of Pearl S. Buck's other books?" she asked. For a second I tried to remember who she might be talking about. And slowly I caught what she was saying—*Pearl S. Buck. The woman who wrote* The Good Earth. Now *I* felt slow-witted.

"No," I told her. "She wrote other books?"

"Oh my goodness yes," she said, reaching again into her purse and pulling out a book. This one had a cover that was beat up and one edge on the corner missing. I read *Sons* on the cover.

"This is the book she wrote after *The Good Earth*, called *Sons*. It's the sequel."

Without even thinking I reached for it.

"It's not as good in my opinion, but it is nice to read what happens next," Marny said.

"So this is about what happens to their sons?" I asked, looking at the back of the book.

"Can you believe it?" Marny's face started getting red. "I nearly died when I heard there was more."

"Did Pearl S. Buck write any more books?" I asked, still looking at the book. "Any more... sequels?"

A big smile spread across Marny's face. She didn't answer but nodded her head up and down, up and down over and over again. "I just ordered it. But don't tell my daddy," she said to me. I prayed, for her sake, she knew there was no way in the world me or anyone else in my family would ever be talking with her daddy about anything beyond eyeglasses. I was betting that if Miss Thompson knew about this series she wouldn't be reading the same book raggedy every Saturday night.

"I'm sorry," Marny said. "I'm making you uncomfortable."

"No ma'am. It's just—" I looked behind me.

"I know, you have to get home. I'm sorry for keeping you," she said. I thought again about how different she was from her daddy. How she must have got all the manners in her family and left none for him.

"Where do you live?" she asked me.

"Ma'am?"

"Ma'am?" She laughed so hard she snorted. "I'm not your ma'am. Why, I bet we're in the same grade. It's Marny."

I started wondering now if maybe she wasn't born in Jackson. She had to know it didn't make no difference what grade I was in, I couldn't go around calling her Marny.

I did my best to smile.

"So, where do you live?" she asked again.

I didn't have dealings with many white folks, but I knew enough to know that when white people asked where you lived, couldn't nothing good come of it.

"Over near Farish." Trying to sound like I was telling something I wasn't.

"Well, I'd like you to take this book," she said, pushing the beat-up book toward me.

Now I tilted my head.

"Ma'am?"

"And stop calling me that." She snorted again. "You can only call me Marny. Well...truth be told, it's Marion, but I think Marny suits me better, don't you?"

Which name suited her better was just about the last thing on my mind.

"My momma's name is Marion," I said before I could stop myself.

"Another thing we have in common." She laughed again.

"Here, take this book," she said again, pushing it toward my hand. "You'd be doing me a favor. It's hot as Hades out here, and I don't feel like carrying it."

First off it wasn't hot. As she was talking, a cool breeze blew in, lifting her scarf in the back. And second, last thing I wanted was a gift from a white girl who thought she could be friends with Negroes.

"I am not taking no for an answer." She pouted like that was gonna make me change my mind. I could tell she was the type of girl who pouted every time she didn't get her way. Probably worked most times too. But a white girl pouting at me expecting me to feel sorry for her was about the same as Eve thinking she could sweet-talk the serpent in the Garden of Eden.

I could see two people walking onto the foot of the trestle behind her. Couldn't tell if they were white or Negro. Either way, it wouldn't do me no good to be standing here chatting with a white girl.

I snatched the book harder than I wanted to. She stopped pouting.

"I'm just borrowing, right? Not keeping it?" I heard enough of Simeon's newspaper stories to know that too many times, borrowing from white folks one day meant a Negro was stealing from them the next. You had to say everything plain. "How am I gonna get it back to you?" I asked, speaking low but fast.

She put a finger to her chin and tilted her head like she was thinking as hard as she could. The people were walking slow, taking their sweet time, but I knew I had to move fast. But Marny kept thinking. Just when I was about to give the book back to her she held out her arm and pointed behind me.

"See over there." I turned and saw a big old broken-down barn. I nodded. "Meet me there next week, same time, after you read it," she said.

I could see the two women were older white ladies, holding each other's arms to keep steady. *I got to go.*

I nodded. "Thanks, ma'am—Marny," I said, walking backwards first till I turned and started walking fast toward home and well ahead of the two older white women coming near. I could hear them stopping to talk to Marny. I put the book in my bag wondering how trying to avoid one thing got me mixed up in something worse.

LAMB

SUPPER was cooking when I walked in, but I didn't see Momma.

"Momma," I called out, and in came Uncle Chime through the back door.

"She gone on down to her job. Had to drop off her order. Said to wash up and go on and eat. She'll be back soon."

"What are you doing here, Uncle Chime?" I asked, getting plates out to set the table.

"Is that how you greet your favorite uncle?" he asked, grabbing my head under his arm.

I laughed. "You're gonna mess up my hair," I said, smoothing it down.

Uncle Chime sat down hard at the kitchen table. "Ooh Lord, they 'bout worked me to death today. See if your momma got a beer in the icebox," he said.

"Where did you work today?" I asked him. Uncle Chime never has one steady job. He just works day jobs when they need men to work hard labor for one or two days at a time. Momma says that's about as long as Uncle Chime can last on a job without getting fired.

"Had me haulin' scrap metal. Felt like I was back on the farm." I handed Uncle Chime a beer, pressing the cold bottle first against my cheek.

"You hauled metal on Grandpa's farm?" I asked him, sitting down. If Uncle Chime started talking and drinking, something good was bound to slip out.

"Girl, Marion ain't teaching y'all nothin' in this house?" He took one long swallow. "Parchman Farm. Penitentiary?" He shook his head and mumbled, "Grandpa's farm…mmm…mmm…" He laughed to himself.

"How was I supposed to know?"

"Anyhow, let's see what's cooking in those pots. Maybe a hardworking man can get something in this house 'side from some questions."

I fixed plates for me and Uncle Chime and as soon as I said grace, Momma came in the front door.

"You still here?" she asked Uncle Chime.

"I can see where your daughter gets her hospitality from," Uncle Chime said, his mouth full.

Momma didn't even look at him. "And where were you?" she said to me. "You should have been home long before I left."

"I had to stay after school," I said, "to talk to my teacher."

Momma stared in my eyes. Momma once told me one of the things she most loved about me was that I never could lie to her or anybody else. "It ain't in you. For some folks lying is about as natural as breathing, but not you. You can't do it. I look you in the eye, you look away or cry. I'd know if you were lying." But here I was lying now, staring right back at my momma. She turned to the stove.

"Damn, Chime, you eat up all my food?" she said into the pot.

Uncle Chime burped. "Too much salt in them greens," he said, laughing, and got up to leave. "And you need more beer.

"See you later, Chop." He leaned over and kissed my forehead. His lips were greasy but warm and soft. "Marion, teach this girl something, would you?" he said.

Momma looked at me, and I rolled my eyes like Uncle Chime was crazy in the head.

Momma sat down across from me with her plate. She had lines between her eyebrows and for the first time I noticed how the veins in her hands looked big and bulgy.

"Simeon ain't home yet?" Momma asked.

"Nope, not yet," I told her.

"Well, set his plate aside, and wash up these dishes 'fore you go to bed," she said.

"You tired, Momma?" I asked her.

"When ain't I?" she asked, eating a spoonful of pinto beans. Her hair was pulled back tight into two braids on either side that she rolled in a bun in back. Her momma, my grandma Ophelia, used to wear her hair the same way, only her hair was gray and my momma's was jet-black. Only my momma could look like a young girl and an old woman at the same time. I felt bad now about lying, especially about a white girl. But if I told my momma I was late because I was talking to Dr. Tremper's daughter, there was no telling what she'd do. There was no way round telling her that Marny wouldn't stop talking or I almost fell off the bridge or I wanted just a look at that second book in the sequel. I sure couldn't tell her that there was something about that Marny girl that kept me standing there listening to all her silly talk when I knew I should have come right home. And until I could figure out what kept me standing on that bridge, I wasn't ready to start telling my momma the truth.

LAMB

I rushed to get through *The Good Earth* and tried to finish reading *Sons*, but I couldn't get through both of them in time to meet Marny. When the day came for the two of us to meet at the old barn near the trestle bridge, Momma could tell right off something was wrong.

"What you all nervous about?" she asked me at breakfast. "You got a test today?"

"Yeah," I told her, "a math test."

"Well, don't go and get yourself all worked up like you do. You need to learn to relax."

"Mmmhmm," I said, biting into my biscuit.

"Relax about what?" Simeon said, walking into the kitchen and sitting in the chair next to mine.

"Lamb gonna make herself sick over these tests when all she needs to do is relax. Math ain't nothing but numbers," Momma said.

"Well, math is more than—" Simeon stopped himself. "You don't have a math test today," he said to me.

I looked at him and then at Momma.

"I didn't tell you about it," I said.

Simeon laughed. "Girl, are you—"

"I'm not stupid, Simeon," I almost shouted. "I can pass a test without you."

I heard Momma laugh to herself. "Guess she tole you."

"No one saying you can't. It's just usually we review together is all. Good for you," Simeon said, looking like I hurt him.

"I just want to try to do it by myself this time," I told him softer. "To see if I can."

He nodded at his plate.

I wondered now that I made all this fuss, how I was going to find a way to get around showing Simeon a test I didn't have and not asking for help on the next one I needed to take. This Marny girl was already more trouble than she was worth.

The whole day I barely heard what the teachers were talking about, thinking I shouldn't even meet this girl. Thinking there was no way she was gonna remember to meet me anyhow. What did she need with this book if she had enough money to just order a new copy? Suppose someone saw us out there talking to each other and it got back to my momma? Or worse, her daddy? And that was when I decided wasn't no way I was gonna meet that white girl.

My last class of the day was Miss Thompson's class and seeing that I finally finished *The Good Earth*, I waited until everyone left after class and walked to her desk.

"I finished, Miss Thompson," I told her, putting the book at the corner of her neat desk. "You were right, it was a very good book."

Miss Thompson raised her eyebrows. "Now you know that just won't do." She smiled at me and sat down. She nodded her head toward a chair for me to sit. "Why, anyone can *say* they *liked* a book, but few can tell you *why*."

Lord, I thought Miss Thompson would never let me leave once we started talking about the Lung family and the ways their lives changed through good luck, hard work, and a little bit of both. "And isn't that the way it is for all of us?" she said to me. "But O-lan never gave up, did she? Even through the hardest times." Miss Thompson's eyes looked watery.

"No ma'am," I said to her. I wasn't sure I wanted to see Miss Thompson crying over made-up people in a book, even if they felt real.

"Have you ever read the sequel?" I said, reaching in my bag to pull out the copy of *Sons*.

That did it. Miss Thompson's eyes dried up. She reached for the book. "Now where did you get this?" she asked, turning the book over to read the back of the jacket, just like I had when Marny showed it to me on the bridge.

"A—friend. A friend loaned it to me," I told her.

"Well, I haven't gotten to this yet," she said slowly, still reading. "But I'd sure like to."

"And there's another one too," I said too loud. "My friend told me. Called *A House Divided*?"

"Your friend is quite a fan of Pearl Buck, I'd say." She smiled.

"Yes, she is," I said.

"Is she a student here?" she asked me, standing now.

"No," I said fast. Hoping she wouldn't ask more.

"I see." She smiled. "Well, do let me know how you like the other books. It seems that now I will have to catch up to you," and she laughed.

"I sure will, Miss Thompson," I told her. I stood up to leave.

"And you are so lucky to have a friend who is feeding your interest in books," Miss Thompson said. "Very lucky indeed."

I nodded my head. "Yes, I am," I told her.

As I left Miss Thompson's classroom. I made up my mind one more time. I was going to meet Marny. And all I was going to do was thank her and give her back her book. I might have told Miss Thompson she was my friend, but this white girl wasn't ever going to be any friend of mine.

LAMB

I was out of breath by the time I reached the barn. My back was sweaty, and I was breathing like I just ran a race. And of course, she was nowhere in sight.

I knew it. You can't trust white folks for nothing in the world, I thought, leaning against the barn to catch my breath.

"Why are you so late?" I heard behind me. I turned, and Marny was walking from around the other side of the barn, this time wearing a baby-blue dress with a shiny matching belt. I realized every time I saw her I was noticing what she was wearing. One thing about having a momma who sewed was that even though Momma never had money to buy me store-bought dresses, she could always make what I had look better or sew me up something nice with the fabric left over from her orders. But Marny's clothes weren't homemade. Her clothing was bought from stores. *Fancy* stores.

"Sorry. I had to stay late with my teacher," I told her, still out of breath.

"Were you in trouble?" she asked, smiling.

"No. No, I wasn't in trouble," I told her, feeling mad she'd think I'd be in trouble with a teacher. "I had to give her back her copy of *The Good Earth.*"

"Well, today is your book return day then, isn't it?"

"I guess so," I said. I reached in my bag for her book.

"What school do you go to?" she asked.

"Lanier High School, over on Lynch."

"Oh, that's the colored school, right?" she asked.

I ain't never once thought of Lanier as the colored school, but I guess that's how white folks thought of it.

"Which school you go to?" I asked her.

"Well, Central High School, of course."

"I don't know anybody who goes there."

"I don't suppose you would," she laughed. "They don't exactly allow—" Marny stopped herself from finishing.

I looked at her. Not bothering to look over her shoulder, but right in her eyes. They were green, I could see now. "Well, here's your book," I said, handing it to her.

She breathed hard. "I want you to have it," she said. "As a gift."

"I don't want it," I said, trying not to sound as mad as I was feeling. "But thank you."

She tilted her head to the side like I remembered her doing the last time. Like doing it would make me smile along with her. Make everything all right. Like maybe I wouldn't notice that she was some rich white girl who wore fancy dresses with a mean daddy who called my momma *Auntie* and my brother *Simon* and *boy* and went to a school that didn't allow Negroes. I smiled back with the same face we all had to have when we talked to white people. When we were saying one thing but thinking another.

"Just sit with me for a minute," she said. "Please?"

Lord she looked pitiful. Not pitiful like she made me feel bad for her, but pitiful like she made me want to run on home even though I was still tired from running here.

She found a space in the grass, out of sight from the bridge and the sun, and we sat down. Together. Not close enough to touch, but close enough that I could smell that florally perfume again.

She reached in her purse and took out a fan. "Aren't you hot?" she asked, and started fanning herself.

"Mmmhmm," I said softly.

"Well, where's your fan?" she said, fanning herself like there was no tomorrow.

I laughed. "I don't have no fan." She was quiet.

"If you're so hot, why do you always wear long sleeves?" I asked her.

"The sun." She pointed up to the sky. "I burn just as red as a beet. Here," she said, moving closer to me, "come and get some of this fan," and she started fanning the two of us. Seemed rude to move away, so I sat still while she fanned warm air on both of us. Wasn't bad sitting quiet in the grass being fanned.

With the sun beating down on us and me swatting away the flies and ants crawling up my legs, we sat like that quiet at first. But then me and this white girl, Marny, we started talking.

LAMB

I didn't do nothing but listen when Marny first started talking to me about her family. Her older brother George, her daddy—and then her momma, passed now going on two years. Marny took out a handkerchief when she talked about her. Patting at her eyes, then her cheeks. I looked away, over toward the bridge.

"Sickness just ate her up," she kept on. "At the end, I'm not sure she even knew who we all were. George and Daddy couldn't bear to see her like that, but I'd go in and sit with her and read to her like I know she would have liked." Water was pouring down Marny's cheeks, and I didn't have no words for her. "We both loved books."

"I think I saw a picture of your momma in your daddy's office. She was real pretty," I said, trying to find something to make her stop crying. She did and finished drying her face.

"Thank you," she said. "Does your momma like reading too?"

I shook my head no. I could tell the more questions she asked, the less I was going to want to talk.

"Poor Daddy," she said. "He took it hardest. He hasn't been the same since. I thought maybe spending more time with him working in the office might, you know, make him happier." She looked down.

I thought about the smell of whiskey in his office and how that man never looked happy. I was thinking it was Negroes making him sad-faced, but maybe that was just a part of what was making him drink.

I couldn't even make my face look sad when she was talking about her poor daddy, thinking of the way he made us feel standing in his office.

"You best be grateful every day for your momma and daddy," she said to me.

They give you a scrap of anything and tell you to be grateful, I could hear Momma telling me. And I knew it wasn't the same thing Marny was saying now, but somehow a white girl telling me what I needed to be grateful for made me understand just what Momma was saying.

"Mmmhmmm," I said quiet.

"I'm sorry," Marny said, putting her handkerchief back in her purse. "I didn't mean to go on like this."

"No, it's fine," I told her. But it wasn't fine. Being with her made everything harder. One minute we were sitting quiet in the grass, and the next she was boohooing about her dying momma and she kept talking to me like I wasn't Negro and she wasn't white and none of it felt right. She dried her face. Smiled half a smile at me.

"You have any other brothers or sisters?" she asked me.

"No. There's just me and Simeon."

"Well, of course." She smiled big again.

Now I tilted my head at her. *Of course?*

"Momma, daddy, we both have one brother? We have so much in common. What's your daddy's name?"

"Listen, Marny," I said, standing up. "I got to get going. I just wanted to return your book."

"Wait—what? Did I say something wrong, Lamb?"

"No, no. You're real nice and all, Marny. Real nice to loan me your book, but I gotta—"

"It's because I'm white, right?"

I looked at her. "You know we ain't supposed to..."

"You care about what people say we're *not* supposed to do?"

I never once thought about that question before, but I guess I did. I cared about what my momma thought. What Simeon thought too. Earvent, NeeCee, Juanita, my teachers. I spent so much time caring about what other people thought, I barely paid attention to what I thought. Marny didn't give me time to answer.

"Well, I don't care one bit what people say," Marny said. "Soon as my momma knew she wasn't gonna get better, she told me one night, 'You gotta live your life for you, baby girl. Not your daddy, not for any of these ole biddies round here, always whispering and judging folks, but for you.' She told me she spent her whole damn—my momma was God-fearing, but she still cursed now and again—she lived her whole life for other people and now...now here she was...at the end of it..." Marny took out her handkerchief again.

I leaned toward her and she waved me away. "Just go on then," she said. She smoothed her hair down, tossed her head so it moved out of her eyes. She bent down to pick up her purse and the book and started walking back toward the bridge.

"I'm trying not to care," I said to her back. She stopped. "But I do still."

"Well, that's a start, Lamb." Marny turned and started walking back toward me.

LAMB

I thought I wouldn't have nothing to tell Marny about my family. I figure I'd just let her keep talking about losing her momma and how sad her daddy was. She didn't say much about her brother. "Georgie" she called him, to me sounded almost like a girl's name, and I was betting if Marny didn't have much to say about someone it was because she didn't think much about them, even if it was her own brother. But when she kept asking me questions about my family like she really wanted to know, I told her a little bit about Momma, a lot about Simeon, and nothing about my daddy.

"Where does he work?" Marny asked me.

"Simeon works over at the King Edward Hotel."

"Not Simeon, silly," she laughed. "Your daddy."

I shrugged. My knees were pulled up under my chin and I was yanking out the dandelions in the grass as we talked. Now I looked at my shoes.

"Oh, I'm sorry, Lamb," Marny said. She reached out and touched my arm. I jumped a little then, hoping she didn't notice.

"Sorry?"

"Did he pass on?" she asked. "I should have known when you weren't saying anything. And me and my big mouth. I'm sorry, I just—"

"My daddy didn't pass on," I told her.

She was quiet. Waiting for me to say something.

"I don't remember him much. My momma and daddy...they don't live together anymore."

She breathed in quick. "Well, do you still see him?"

I shook my head.

"That's a shame," she said.

"I'm not sure it is," I told her. I couldn't believe I was even talking to Marny about my daddy, something I'd never done with anyone aside from Simeon. "It's like he was never even there, so I don't think about him much."

"Hmmm...Well, I can't imagine that. Maybe you just think you don't think about him. He's your daddy, you have to—"

"Not everybody lives with their daddy." I could feel myself getting sweaty.

"Well, of course I know that, Lamb," she said, her face red. "But you never wonder about him? Maybe he's thinking about you?"

I didn't want to start thinking about whether or not my daddy was thinking about me. If I thought about that too much it would make me start thinking things about my momma too, and why they weren't together and why my daddy never came to the house. Sometimes the answers ain't worth the questions.

"Well now, I really do need to get on home," I told Marny, standing up again.

"Me too," Marny said, brushing off her pretty dress. "Gloria Jean will have dinner on the table soon. And she gets so mad when we're not on time." I didn't need to ask to know Gloria Jean was her colored help.

"Which way do you live?" she asked, holding her hand over her eyes to block out the sun.

"Just over there." I pointed.

"Oh," she said, nodding. "I live over there," and she pointed in the other direction. "Lamb—" she said, real soft. "Can we meet again? Next week?"

I took a deep breath. *I can't do this again.* "Okay," I said. "Next week."

LAMB

TRY asking my momma anything about my daddy and right away her eyes start rolling, and before you can ask much more she says, "I ain't in the mood, Lamb." I once even tried asking Uncle Chime, but I guess Momma told him to keep his mouth shut too. But the Saturday night after Marny got me talking about my daddy, I followed Uncle Chime onto the front porch. He was holding a half-empty bottle and feeling no pain and Momma was in the kitchen laughing with Myrtle and a couple of others who were in no hurry to go home, so I went out and sat on the front porch with Uncle Chime. The broken-down couch creaked when I sat next to him.

"You coming out to visit your uncle Chime? I ain't got no money." He laughed. His words were all slow and lazy.

"I don't want any money." I laughed too. "Just fresh air."

We sat quiet. It looked like there might be some other Saturday night parties too because house lights were on late up and down the street with laughing coming out of open windows and doors. Uncle Chime was tilting over to one side and I knew he might be falling asleep soon, so I started right in. "How tall was my daddy, Uncle Chime?"

"How tall is a tree?" he laughed, slapping his knee. "I don't know, Chop, never took out a yardstick to measure him."

I smiled to make him think he was funny. "But he's taller than Momma, right?"

In the dark, his eyes looked thin as slits. He tilted his head. "Chester is taller than e'rybody, not just your momma."

I nodded. Held my breath. "You seen him lately?"

He took a sip of his drink. "Lately? Not lately. But I see him when I'm passing the lumberyard over on Ellis. He ain't stopping by my way for a cup of coffee or nothing. But I say hello if I cross his path. You got me out here talking about Chester and now you done killed my high." He stood up and swayed a little bit.

The lumberyard over on Ellis? "You okay, Uncle Chime?" I stood up and he leaned against me. We walked inside with his arm around me. Good old Uncle Chime and his whiskey gave more than I asked for.

All these years I'd wondered where my daddy was and thinking he must have been far, far away because why else wouldn't he have come to see his children unless he was someplace he couldn't get to us? And now to find out he wasn't but a mile from home. I wasn't sure who I was madder at, my daddy or Momma for letting me believe a lie.

LAMB

I wasn't sure how long I sat across the street watching. But it gave me time to imagine what it would have been like to have him living with us every day. To see Momma with a husband, a man by her side, taking some of the weight she carried.

I never expected to see him, just wanted to see first the place where my daddy worked, but I waited so long I heard a whistle blow and men came pouring out of Davis Lumber. Then I crossed the street. Standing at the gate, I watched the man I knew right away was my daddy. Not because I'd seen pictures but because of the daddy I remembered and because looking at him was like looking at me. There he was, about as tall as Uncle Chime said, laughing, talking to two other men, his laugh louder even than Uncle Chime's. When the two men turned to leave he looked over and saw me standing there, squinted a bit. From where I was standing, I couldn't tell if he was frowning. He took a few big steps and there he was in front of me, on the other side of the gate.

We were both quiet.

Finally he said, "Come on around to the side," pointing to an opening.

I walked down, slower than I needed to. I walked inside the gate. There was a bench at the end of the lumberyard, and he walked toward it, and I followed behind taking in every inch of him, from the curl of his hair under his cap all the way down to the cuff in his pants before they hit his work boots. He waved his hand for me to sit down on the bench. He grunted when he sat at the other end, further away from me than I sat from Marny, like I was white.

"I only got fifteen. Boss man watching us like a hawk," he said, unwrapping a sandwich. I could smell the baloney, and he took a big, fast bite.

"I just found out you worked here," I said. "Uncle Chime told me he sees you now and again."

"Chime," he said, shaking his head, his mouth full. "Working here ever since you were born." He was looking straight ahead.

"You mind me coming?" I asked him.

"Your momma know you're here?" he asked.

I pretended not to notice he didn't answer my question about minding if I came. "No," I told him.

"Why not?" He didn't look at me yet.

I shrugged. "I just needed…"

Now he turned and looked. Uncle Chime was right. He looked as tall as a tree. Bigger even. His skin looked darkened from the sun, but I could tell we were the same shade.

He leaned toward me. "You sure grown-up," he said, shaking his head. "Prettier even than the last time I saw you, and you were some pretty then."

I didn't expect to, but I turned away, my face hot.

"When was that? The last time you saw me?"

"You was about four. Nah. Maybe you was five."

"And you never came back? To see me? And Simeon?" I didn't dare ask about Momma.

He finished off his sandwich in one bite, looking away again. He shook his head. "Me and your momma talked about that. Thought it best I stay away." He wiped his hands on his pants.

"You mean *you* thought it best you stay away?" I said. I couldn't believe I sounded this bold. Almost like Momma.

"You came over here to ask or tell? 'Cause if you want to know, I'll tell you. No matter what your momma said." He looked back over his shoulder.

"Time for you to go?" I asked.

"Nah, I got a few more minutes."

He lowered his voice. It sounded soft now, gentle. Like he was about to tell me some bad news. "You old enough now to know the truth. And the truth is your momma didn't want no husband. She wanted to get out from under her momma and daddy." He smiled to himself. "I know that now. I just helped her do it. I was dumb enough to believe she was feeling something for me."

I loved the shape of his lips, so full. Everything about his face was soft like mine. His cheeks, his round nose. I was staring at his eyebrows when he caught my eye. Smiled at me. I never saw Momma smile much, and I wondered if he made her laugh when they met. Could I ask him that?

"Your momma wanted something to call her own. She wanted you and Simeon. And she wanted to get on up out of Shubuta. The only thing she didn't want was a husband, that's for sure."

"Did she tell you all that?" I asked.

"Folks ain't got to tell you something you already know. Remember that. Your daddy ain't tell you nothing else, you remember that." He nodded at me.

Daddy. I wondered if it sounded as wrong to him as it did to me.

"Soon as you were born, your momma could barely look at me."

"I thought you just got tired of being with us."

"Wasn't never tired of being with y'all. Was tired of fighting to keep a wife that didn't want to be a wife, that's all." He wiped his mouth with the back of his hand.

I kept waiting for the whistle to blow. I wanted him to keep talking and wanted him to stop too.

"A man got to be a man, Lamb. That's all imma say about that." Now he wiped the sweat off his forehead with his other hand. "But we both knew we had to let go."

He waved at two men passing by. One slowed and looked at us hard.

"Expect Tyson have some questions for me when I get back in," he said, shaking his head. He leaned down to tie his shoestrings. Watching him, I didn't see none of Simeon in him. His body, the way he moved, talked. Simeon was all Momma, and I was all our daddy.

"He doesn't know you have children?" I nodded to the man he called Tyson.

"My business is my business," my daddy said, like having a family was some kind of secret you were supposed to keep.

I stood up to leave.

My daddy nodded again at me. "Usually take my break 'bout this time," he said to me.

"Okay," I said.

"Don't mind the company."

"Okay," I said again.

"Your momma ain't got to know," he said.

"I wasn't planning to tell her."

"You gonna bring your brother back next time?" he asked.

"Not sure I'm coming back," I said.

He stopped smiling. He nodded his head.

"Simeon's got his own mind," I said.

"That he do," he said. "That he do."

Finally the whistle blew, and he stood up now. "You looking good, Lamb. Your momma was right. Your name suits you fine. She done right by you," he told me.

Like I didn't already know it.

CHESTER CLARK

My momma and pappy were never prouder than the day I left for the war. I always stood 'bout a head taller than my pappy, but he looked up at me that day at the train station like I never seen him look before. Didn't take much to get Momma boohooing, but seeing Pappy look at me the way he did made me feel like I knew I had to come back to them, in my uniform, *alive*. I knew every single one of the soldiers I served with over in Europe musta said the same when they left behind their families, but I carried my pappy's face with me everywhere I went those four years.

I was stationed in France, and if we colored soldiers signed up thinking we were going to fight for our country, didn't no one tell the United States military. They treated us worse than the Germans. Put us outside in tents like somebody's dog while the white soldiers slept in warm barracks. Got us up with the sun, digging as many trenches as graves. Ain't no way I was ever gonna live out my life digging, planting, and picking with a shovel in my hand. I'd just as soon dig a trench for myself and lay down in it. Night after night, I could hear soldiers next to me, so cold and tired and hungry they were crying for their mommas. Colored troops in the Ninety-Second Division saw some action on the lines, but the truth is we knew every white division and commander was wanting us to fail. They didn't want to see colored with weapons fighting for something they didn't think we should have. I left my pappy at that train station feeling proud to be doing my part protecting my country. Signing up to fight, you started to believe that maybe you were helping the world change just a little bit when you went and put on a uniform. It took coming back to Shubuta to remind me that in some places, the clock ain't never gonna move forward.

I knew Marion growing up. Always saw her as one of the boys. She could work longer, run faster, and fight harder than most of her brothers. Me and Turner was friends coming up. Stopped by to see him when I came back into town and Lord, I thought Marion was his wife. I said to him, "I see you got yourself a pretty young thing," when I saw her standing on the porch.

"Fool, that's just Marion," he laughed. Instead of arms and legs, she was all curves now. And woowee she was pretty. I traveled halfway round the world, and I don't think I seen someone prettier. But Marion wasn't giving me a second look. My momma and sister were the type of womenfolk always kept to themselves. Let me and my pappy do the talking for them. Marion wasn't that type of woman. You could hear her yelling from down the road and knew what she was thinking 'fore she even opened her mouth. Folks always said Marion was a little rough around the edges. She took some getting used to, but I figured I was the right one to smooth her out. Every day I called myself coming by to see Turner until one day he'd gone into town to pick up feed. Instead of leaving, I stayed talking to Marion, right on through supper. Her momma looked happy to see me. I bet she was thinking wouldn't no man be brave enough to take a second look at Marion.

Marion was about as interested in farming as I was and that was how I knew we could make a go of things.

"I'm fixing to get up on out of here soon," I told her. "Gotta cousin over in Jackson holding a job for me over at the lumberyard where he works."

"You taking me with you?" she said, smiling that pretty smile of hers. God dawg if that girl didn't have a smile that could just about break a man's heart in two.

"I'll take you wherever you want to go," I told her. Wished I had something smoother, but sitting with Marion made me lose my words sometimes. She asked, and I'd answer yes before even thinking it through.

Deciding to go to Jackson happened before Marion but right after the bridge. Shubuta, Mississippi, ain't but a couple square miles but word travels fast as a locomotive. Someone sick, someone in need, home on leave, you can bet everybody's gonna know. So when we got word about two boys gone missing, last thing I thought was that it could be kin.

Talk started traveling fast. First word came through that nine coloreds were hanging from that ole bridge over the Chickasawhay River. Turns out it wasn't nine colored at all but four. And that was four too many. Seems just when you thought things might be getting better, someone told white folks and they turned around made it worse. Two of those hung were my cousins, younger than me, good boys, trying to make their own way. When the news came by the house, Momma started right in crying, praying, and carrying on so my pappy had to hold her up. I went into my room, sat on the edge of my bed. So tired I felt like I could've slept for a week, but I was holding on to a mad that wouldn't let me close my eyes.

Major and Andrew were working out at that devil Mr. Johnston's place. Johnston wasn't known to ever do right by anybody working his land. Work two weeks, he barely want to pay you for one. Tore me up something bad I wasn't here to tell them about ole Mr. Johnston. Alongside Major and Andrew they hung two sisters by the name of Alma and Maggie, both girls big with Mr. Johnston's babies. Well, Mr. Johnston turned up dead. Now, everybody knew Mr. Johnston been chased, beat, and threatened more than once over wanting a woman that wasn't his. And now these white folks gone and hung two sisters right alongside family for something it's likely one of their own did. I heard one of the girls, maybe the oldest, Maggie, was working to pay off a sewing machine she likely paid off years earlier. Ain't none of them barely grown and here they go hanging from a bridge.

Ain't no one round here wished death on no one, but let's just say, no one was shedding a tear either for old Mr. Johnston. When I heard, took all I had not to run out the house with my pappy's rifle, put all that army training to use. But that was just what white folks were waiting on. Got the ropes tied and ready. Waiting.

Every one of us men made our way over to my uncle's. Thought my pappy wasn't going to hold up. He looked like he was 'bout to burst from holding back all he had inside. But now he knew he needed to be strong for his brother. His nephews swinging from that bridge hurt the same as the thought of me not returning from the war. Gone is gone. Both dying for something ain't your own making.

Since the hanging, the sheriff and mortician been telling my uncle he needed to get on into town and claim his boys' bodies. But when white folks tell colored it's in their best interest to do anything, you had to think twice 'bout doing it. My pappy told me to round up some of the men. Figured grieving is no time to go making decisions. Best to let more heads talk it through, so we met up at my uncle's, trying to decide what to do. Could be they had something waiting on my uncle too. We just needed word from someone with ears so there wasn't five bodies hanging instead of four. First time I was glad my aunt passed on years back. Seeing what they done to her two boys would have killed her for sure.

My pappy sat in the truck shut-mouthed on the ride over. As if losing Major and Andrew wasn't hard enough, ever since last week, when the sheriff paid us a visit, my pappy ain't been himself.

CHESTER

IN all the years we been in Shubuta, we never had cause to have the sheriff at our house, but there he was standing on our porch. Momma came to the door when he knocked and near had a fit. She called out to us in the field. And we came quick. Pappy went on out, but I stayed back, behind the screen, waiting.

"Sheriff?" my pappy said to the sheriff, still out of breath from hurrying to the door.

Didn't even have the decency to say "How do you do," or take off his hat, the way any man would have done standing on another man's porch. Instead, he said to my pappy, "Heard your boy's back in town."

"Yessir," he said. "Just served over in the war and he's back home now, helping me farm, just like he used to. He's a good boy." Heard my pappy asking and telling at the same time.

"Y'all must be mighty proud. Isn't that right?"

My pappy nodded his head. I opened the screen door, walked out slow onto the porch, and stood behind my pappy. My pappy turned and looked up at me, his eyes telling me to go on back inside, but I stayed right where I was.

"How you do there, Sheriff, sir," I said to him. He looked at me and went on talking to Pappy like he had wax in his ears.

"Well, I know you don't cause no trouble, Uncle. No trouble at all. But you see, your boy there—" He nodded his head at me. "I'm coming out here as a favor to y'all."

"A favor, Sheriff?" my pappy asked.

"Does your boy know he's breaking the law? Now I don't want to have to go an' arrest a...veteran"—look like he about choked on that word—"but in these parts, law says I can arrest any colored wearing their uniform more than three days."

"Three days?" I said, forgetting myself for a minute.

He looked at me then. Looked like he wanted to spit.

And then he leaned over the side of the porch and did.

"You heard me right, boy. I see you walking through town in that uniform again, you and me gonna spend a little time down at the jail."

Pappy looked back at me slow. Waiting.

"I served this country. Sir," I told him.

"And now you are living here in Shubuta, Mississippi. I don't expect I'll need to make another visit, right, Uncle?" he said, smiling at my pappy.

"No sir," Pappy said in a whisper. He stood watching the sheriff's car disappear down the road. We both did. "You best go on and put that uniform away, son," he said to me. Went on inside.

My pappy died not three months later, out in the fields while he was plowing. Everyone said his heart just gave out. But I knew that after four years of waiting for me to get home alive, and having his heart filled to bursting with pride, the sheriff's visit just made his heart give up. After Pappy was gone, I knew then it was time for me to get on my way. I just never expected it'd be with a pretty wife by my side.

LAMB

I couldn't decide whether to tell Simeon about seeing Daddy or not, so I did what I always did when I couldn't decide whether to tell him something. I told him.

"You did what?" he almost shouted at me.

"I saw our daddy?"

"At the lumberyard?" he asked.

"Yes, at the . . . You knew he worked at the lumberyard?"

"I got ears, don't I?" he said.

"Well, I got ears too, and I sure never knew he worked at the lumberyard till Uncle Chime went running his mouth." I waited. "You didn't think I should know?"

"And look what happened as soon as you found out. You went visitin'." Simeon shook his head.

"I had to see for myself."

"See what? Why his sorry ass never came back?"

"There's more to it than that."

"You spent what, five minutes with Mr. Clark and everything is all right with you? Let's go in and tell Momma." Simeon made like he was getting ready to walk out the room toward the kitchen.

"He asked about you," I said, stopping him.

"What's he asking about me for?"

"He wasn't really asking about you, he just said I can bring you next time."

"There's gonna be a next time?"

"I don't know."

"I can't wait to see Momma's face now."

I looked at Simeon like he lost his mind. Simeon held up both hands.

"You the one who's so honest and all. Always wanting to tell the truth and shame the devil..." He smiled.

"Thing is," I told Simeon, "he wasn't at all like I remember."

"Is it what you remember or what Momma told you to remember?" Simeon asked.

"Maybe a little bit of both? He was... It was like... he wanted to be our daddy."

Simeon nodded.

"Could that be true?"

"Maybe for you."

I hated that every time we talked about something from the past, I remembered it one way, Simeon another. His memory was like a nightmare to my daydream.

"He said Momma never wanted to be married. She just wanted to get out from under Granddaddy and Grandma. And have babies."

Simeon nodded quiet.

I kept on. "I can't even picture them married."

"Jesus himself would have packed his bags married to our momma." Simeon laughed.

When I didn't laugh back, he tried to hide his smile behind his hand.

I rolled my eyes and said out loud what I already knew.

"You gonna bake him a cake too?"

"I just wanna know—"

"Know what? There's nothing our daddy can tell you that's gonna change anything about the life you are living today, tomorrow, or yesterday. Leave good enough alone. We got enough on our plate as it is."

"You got enough on *your* plate," I corrected him.

"My plate is your plate."

I shook my head. "My life is my life, Simeon."

LAMB

OF all the things I was sure I'd never talk to Marny about, my daddy was at the top of the list. But there I was talking a mile a minute about going to see my daddy at the lumberyard.

"I think you were right about him wanting to see us too."

"You see there, I knew it," she said, bright specks of orange in her teeth. She had brought a whole box of candied orange slices along. "My daddy orders them from a candy store over in Vicksburg. He used to get them for my momma. Oh she had a sweet tooth. I don't love them like my momma did. Course I can't tell my daddy that, so I eat some and share them with Gloria Jean. She takes them home to her family, and they just love them."

Well, I loved them just as much as Gloria Jean because as I was talking about my daddy and answering all her questions, I looked down and nearly the whole box of slices was gone.

"I'm sorry," I said.

"For what?" She laughed. "You just saved me about five pounds."

"The last thing I need is five pounds," I told her, putting the last of the candy in my mouth.

"You have a lovely figure," she told me. "Me, I'm wide where I should be narrow and narrow where I should be wide."

141

We both laughed at that. Truth is we were about the same size. Full-figured girls, some folks would call us. My legs were thicker than hers and she had a lot more bosom than me, but we were about the same.

"My momma used to say to me, 'Now Marion, you keep eating the way you do, and you are never gonna find a nice Jackson boy to marry you.' And I used to think to myself, 'Well, I better keep on eating because I sure don't want one of these boys!'"

I let myself laugh out loud.

"Do you have a boyfriend, Lamb?" she asked me.

"No," I said. "I don't think any of these Jackson boys want me."

"Well, I find that hard to believe. Why's that?"

I shrugged. "I'm just not their type, I guess…I'm not exactly…" I didn't finish the sentence.

"Popular?" she said.

I nodded.

"Well, me neither," she said, her face serious.

"You?" I asked.

"Yes me. Strange, fat Marny, too smart for her own good, whose head is always in a book, with the momma who died and the daddy who…" She stopped.

"The daddy who what?" I asked.

"Nothing, it ain't Christian talk."

The daddy who what? Who drinks whiskey while he treats his patients? Was that it?

"You seem like you would be popular," I told her. Even though I had no idea all of a sudden what would make a white girl popular. Marny wasn't so much pretty. But she had personality, and she talked a blue streak. She had money and nice dresses and confidence like Juanita. Wouldn't that make someone popular? I didn't have any of those things, so it made sense I wasn't popular. But it had to be different for white girls.

"Well, those things don't matter now anyhow," she said leaning back, closing her eyes.

"Why not?" I asked her.

"Because, silly." She opened her eyes wide. "Because we're friends now. We have each other."

Now I leaned back and closed my eyes. How could we be friends when we had to hide? When there was so much we could never talk about? When I couldn't even tell her where I lived or tell my momma about her?

Marny sighed next to me. I couldn't meet her again, but I didn't know how to tell her.

"Would you like to come over to my house tomorrow?" she asked. "Meet Gloria Jean?"

"Mar-ny," I said slowly. "You know I can't do that."

"Well, why not?" she said with her pouty face. "Gloria Jean would love to meet you."

"Do you think I can just walk over to your neighborhood and knock on your front door and say, 'Howdy, my name is Lamb, and I'm here to pay a visit to Marny'?"

She looked like she thought about that for a long while. "Well, how about if I come to visit you?"

I laughed out loud. She looked hurt.

"Gloria Jean took me once. To her house. I couldn't tell Daddy, of course, or Momma. But she let me go with her, when there was an emergency and she had to go home."

"Mmmhmmm," I said. It was all I could say.

"No one at her house seemed to mind. Everyone was nice."

No one *could* say anything. I wondered now about Marny, remembering what Momma first said about her being slow-witted. Did she really think Gloria Jean's people would be nasty to the daughter of the white folks she worked for? Say what was really on their mind?

"Well, my momma would say something to me. We can just meet here." I did it again. I wasn't going to meet her anymore and now to stop her from talking more about meeting at my house I was setting up another meeting.

"Oh all right," she said with her pouty lips. "Oh, I almost forgot." She grabbed her bag and dug deep inside. "This is for you."

She handed me a gift wrapped with a bow.

"Marny, you didn't have to give me a present," I said, but I was so happy to get a present wrapped so pretty I barely wanted to rip the paper off.

"I wanted to. Go ahead—open it."

I untied the bow real slow, taking my time. "Hurry, silly!" Marny yelled.

I took off the paper but before I did I could tell by the feel of it that it was a book. *A House Divided*. "You bought me a book?"

"It's the last book in the trilogy. I have a copy too, and this way we can read it together so you don't even have to return it to me." Marny looked like she was about to burst.

LAMB

THE front door banged open, and I heard Simeon's fast steps coming into the kitchen. "You see this?" Simeon asked, pointing to the bottom of the front page of the *Jackson Daily News*. Me and Momma were sitting at the kitchen table. Momma liked to have a cup of coffee while she did the last of her finish work in the parlor and I got ready to go to bed. These last few weeks Simeon was working late so it was time me and Momma were both getting used to being alone together. Not always talking, but we enjoyed the feeling of the soft early summer air at night blowing in through the windows. Simeon slammed the newspaper down on the table so hard my glass of water fell on its side.

"What is wrong with you?" I asked, grabbing a dish towel from the sink and wiping up the water.

"They got another one!" he yelled.

"Who, Simeon?" I asked. "Who got another one?"

"Another one of us!"

"I know you better keep down that shouting in my house at this hour," Momma said, reaching over to take the dish towel from my hand.

"Don't none of y'all care?" Simeon snatched the newspaper back and sat down across from me, his arms folded.

Momma looked at me.

"How is you raising a fuss this time of night gonna change any of that?" Momma said. "You need a newspaper to tell you things ain't fair to colored? Boy, you make me laugh sometimes." Momma finished drying the table and refilled my glass. She went back to the stove to start making her coffee.

Simeon opened up the newspaper again. He pushed his glasses back up on his nose like he does whenever his nose gets sweaty, and started reading out loud.

I looked up and pretended to be listening but all I heard was "Negro fiend…assault…white woman…set upon by avengers." I sat quiet while Simeon turned the page.

"Let me stop you right there," Momma said, not turning around.

He looked up. He was mad, I could see, but the way his shoulders were hunched forward I could see he was something else too. He was about to cry. I was hoping Momma couldn't tell because more than Simeon acting like he knew everything, Momma hated when Simeon cried. I heard Momma tell him once when he was young, "Pull yourself up like a man," when he ran in the house screaming after he just about cut his hand wide open on a limb when he was climbing the pecan tree out back. He closed his mouth tight while Momma washed his hand with water and then poured something on the cut from a brown jar and he had snot running from his nose, but he ground his back teeth and he stopped screaming. After Momma finished wrapping his hand with a clean white cloth, she leaned close to him and said, "That's a good, strong boy." And Simeon nodded his head up and down, but I could see how bad he was hurting still. And later that night I heard him crying soft in his room to hisself. Probably hoping Momma couldn't hear him. Since then, I hardly ever saw Simeon cry, only when he was mad. Like now.

Momma looked over her shoulder at Simeon and then turned away.

"How many colored you think been strung up this year? This month? This week?" she asked.

"I don't know, but everyone is too..."

She sat down. "And how many you think you saving by reading about 'em here in my kitchen?" she asked.

Simeon stared at Momma. His eyes were dry now.

"You think I don't know what's going on?" she asked him. Her voice so calm and soft she could have been asking Simeon what time he had on his watch.

"I *lived* it, and you *reading* about it," she said to him. "You don't want to live it too, I suggest you shut that mouth of yours and remember who and where you are."

Simeon opened his mouth and then slowly shut it again. "So..." he said slowly, "just be okay with lynch mobs making it their job to kill us? And just be happy it ain't me, is that it? Be a good nigger?"

Momma crossed one leg over the other and tilted her head at Simeon.

"Can't say you ain't smart," she said.

"How 'bout this, Momma? How 'bout I keep on reading about what they are doing to our Negro brothers and sisters here in the great state of Mississippi, so one day, if they come for me, I'll be ready."

Momma laughed. "And how you gonna do that, Simeon? Fight 'em? With a newspaper?" Momma stood up again, turned back to the stove, and waved her hand. "I ain't got time for this. Go on to bed." Momma filled her coffee cup till it was almost spilling. She never added milk or sugar. Said she liked it hot and black. She took a long, loud sip and got up from the table. "Good night," she said, leaving me and Simeon sitting there.

MARION

MOMMA never made much of a fuss about any of our birthdays, but especially not mine. If I asked nice, and if she was in the mood, not too tired, she'd make a cake, but birthdays, mine at least, was same as every other day. Breakfast, work, midday meal, work, and supper. Go to bed tired and get up and do it all again. She might get me some new fabric for a dress. But on my fourteenth birthday I didn't even get that.

Soon as we got in from the fields my daddy and brothers washed up and changed into clean overalls. Mr. Collins came by earlier, and told my daddy there was to be a meeting over at Mr. Clark's farm that night.

"What's going on?" I asked my momma.

"Men's business," she told me. When I looked at her she was wiping her face with a rag.

"Someone die?" I asked again.

My momma usually saved up all her curse words for me, but now she was cursing under her breath at no one but the rag she was holding. BoJack came rushing past me, and I followed him out the front door. I grabbed his arm before he ran for the wagon all loaded up with my brothers.

"What happened? Where y'all going?" I asked him.

"What you mean what happened?" he yelled. "They strung up Major and Andrew Clark, that's what happened!"

His eyes were wet, his fist balled tight. He and Major were friends coming up. Folks used to say they were together so much they started to look like brothers. BoJack wasn't nothing like Chime. It'd take a lot to get him riled up, but I sure hoped my daddy and brothers got him straight 'fore they got to where they were going. Last thing they needed was BoJack talking 'bout what needed to be done or what he wanted to do to Mr. Charlie and get him and a few more hanging too. Didn't make sense leaving women out of a conversation where they rightfully belonged, but this was one time I was glad to stay home.

I didn't know what talking was going to do. By my count, this was the fourth hanging since planting season started. White folks worried 'bout a war going on miles away when colored right here fighting and losing one every day right outside our door. I went back inside, and Momma was sitting at the table, her head in her hand. She didn't look up when I sat down across from her. She mumbled something soft.

"What's that, Momma?" I asked her.

"Saw one with my own eyes, coming up, you know…" she told me, still looking at the table.

I didn't ask what. Didn't have to. "They took off all his clothes. Cut off his privates. Said he raped a white girl. He ain't did no such a thing. His only mistake was working for her daddy. Walked into a barn one day and there she was. Said what he was s'pose to, 'Mornin', miss.' Maybe he didn't say it loud enough. Maybe she was on her monthlies. She went and told her daddy that night over supper, that boy looked at her *funny*. When she was alone in the barn. Next thing her daddy gathered up his friends. Swear they just waiting…" Momma shook her head. She looked at me. "They strung him up good from a tree out near the main road so's we all could see it that mornin' when we were heading to the field. He was burned but we could still see what they done to him. They wanted us to see that. All because he said 'Mornin', miss…'"

I got up, put on the kettle. But Momma said, "I'm going on to bed." Hard as my momma worked, I ain't never seen her go to bed till well into the night. She looked more tired now than I ever seen her.

"You want tea?" I asked her.

Momma shook her head and got up from the table slow. I poured myself a cup of milk. Sat at the table waiting for my brothers and daddy to get back. Only when I heard the wagon coming down the road did I realize I'd always remember two things about that day. It was one of the only times I could remember sitting with my momma and not having her fuss at me. And I'd remember that it was my birthday. My fourteenth birthday.

LAMB

MARNY'S job at her daddy's office meant there was only one day we could meet. After staying up late to let Simeon talk to me about lynch mobs half the night, I sure wasn't in the mood to meet Marny, but seeing it was our meeting day, I went on ahead. She had on yellow again, her favorite color.

She told me once, "I know they say redheads should never wear yellow. My own momma wouldn't be caught dead wearing the color, but I just love it. Makes me feel like I'm spreading sunshine." When she said "sunshine," she opened her arms wide like she was going to give me a hug and I took a step back.

"Sorry, Lamb, sometimes I am a little bit theatrical." She laughed.

"No, it's all right, Marny. I like yellow too," I said.

"Well, why don't you ever wear it?" she asked me.

Sometimes it was so hard explaining to Marny the things I never had to explain to any of my other friends. Things like I didn't always get to pick my outfits because I liked the color. I had to pick what my momma had the money to buy or whatever leftover fabric she had. I tried to picture myself telling my momma I only wanted to wear yellow silk dresses from now on because they made me feel like I was spreading sunshine, and I wasn't sure if she'd laugh out loud or take me straight to the sanatorium.

Today Marny had on sunglasses and her hair tied up in a ponytail with a matching yellow scarf. *Pretty.*

"I thought you'd never get here," she said.

"Sorry, I was up late," I told her. "I was tired this morning."

"Up late? Doing something exciting, I hope?" Marny hit me with her elbow. We both knew I wasn't doing anything exciting, but it felt good to imagine I could be. I smiled a tired smile.

"Nah, just talking with my brother."

"Simeon, right?" she said. Marny tried hard to remember everything I ever told her.

"Yes, Simeon." I couldn't even remember what her brother's name was.

"That must be nice to have a brother you can talk to," she said, looking away.

"You don't talk to . . . you don't talk to your brother?"

"Me and Georgie talk?" She laughed. "As in 'Pass the salt, please?' Or 'What time is Daddy going to be home?' Does that count?"

"How old is he?" I asked.

"Twenty going on a hundred," she said. "Since our momma died, he thinks he's my daddy. Our daddy's daddy even. Telling me what's 'appropriate' and how the Trempers 'have a reputation to protect.' Bunch of horseshit. Pardon my French, Lamb."

I smiled and nodded, and thought something about George reminded me a little bit of Simeon. Not the protecting our family reputation part, but the part about the way Simeon acted like he was my daddy and always knew what was best for me and Momma.

"Sounds like we got a little bit of the same brother," I said. She nodded back at me.

"Well, I only got one daddy and it ain't Georgie Tremper. Anyhow, what were you and Simeon up late talking about?"

I breathed in deep.

There was a whole lot of things I was never going to talk to Marny about—my momma, me and Simeon's plans to go north to study, what Negroes really thought of white folks, the way I felt about her daddy—but in the time we'd spent together over the past month, I told Marny more than I ever thought I would. Even though I kept fighting hard against it, Marny was starting to feel like a friend.

"Well, he read something in the paper," I started, "and it got him pretty upset."

"Oh, that story about those Nazis?" she said. "Aren't they just horrible? My daddy was talking about it over breakfast."

"No, not that story. The other one." I was quiet. Waiting.

"About the lynching," I told her.

"Oh, that horrible man who ravished that woman. Well, my daddy and Georgie said he got just what he deserved."

Marny could have been talking about what she had for breakfast. Like it meant nothing to her.

"He didn't deserve no trial?" I asked. "White folks get to accuse someone of a crime and convict them too?" I could hear my voice getting louder.

Marny's face got red. "Well, I'm just saying, would you want that man walking around your neighborhood putting you and your momma in danger? They were doing you a favor if you ask me."

"Do they hang white men that way?" I asked her. "Without a trial?"

"Well, how many white men—what I'm saying is, what do you care about all of that? He hurt a woman and got what he deserved. George said, it's a way of keeping these men in line, is all."

"Who are *these* men?" I asked her, feeling now every bit like Simeon. Mad enough to cry.

"Men who would hurt women. Lamb, why are you getting so upset with me? I didn't do anything to that man. Let's talk about something else. Anything."

"So now you agree with George?" I asked her.

"Lamb. I'm sorry. I shouldn't have said that. Let's just talk about something else."

"There ain't nothing else to talk about," I told her.

Marny's mouth hung wide open as I stood to leave. Funny, I thought to myself, I was more tired now than when I got there.

MARION

ONLY when I close the door to my room at night and make my way into my bed, alone, is when I let myself breathe out all the air it feels like I been holding in all day. When I'm taking my braids out, combing my hair through, greasing my scalp, I look in the mirror and see someone so tired looking back I hardly know myself. Lamb is always carrying on about how young I look but all I see is the scared in every line on my face. Putting on my nightclothes and feeling my own ribs and dry elbows and cracked fingers, I remember the way I used to fill out my dresses had men staring for miles around. Myrtle says I'm still looking so good she can't keep her eyes off me, but that's just love talking.

After Chester left, Lamb started coming in to lay up under me at night, but she didn't know it was the only time I had to close the door to the scared I was feeling of one day seeing her and Simeon gone from me. Only the hurt of it was what kept me from letting her in. I worried if I held her too close, I wasn't never gonna be able to let her go.

They are the only two things in my life that's ever mattered to me. But I don't say all that. I tell 'em how the world is outside this house, outside of Jackson. That the North is just as bad as it is here. But Simeon was born knowing more than I could ever tell him. And one thing he knows, in the North he got a chance at a life he's never gonna have here. He know it, I know it, and he know I know it. That's what I love most about that boy. He talk all the damn time, but he got all kinds of secrets he ain't never gonna open his mouth to tell. He look in my eyes and know every truth about me. Lamb look at me and only wants to know the lies. I let them both believe what they need. Soon they both gonna be gone, and when they do, things ain't never gonna be the same for them or me again.

I know the hardest thing for Simeon to do is to shut his mouth when he got so much to say. To play dumb when half the time he know more than the teachers. But that's about the only way I know to keep him breathing.

Lamb is just as smart as Simeon, only she don't know it yet. But one day she will.

The Saturday nights and Chime used to help me to forget what was coming. When I filled my house with people, and drink and cards and music, seemed like it filled what Chester left behind, but it ain't never gonna fill what my babies will leave. Back in Shubuta our house never once felt like this one here. Like home. Like a place I fit. But at the end of every night, alone in my bed, here that scared feeling come again.

Even when Myrtle makes her way to my bed and her soft lips are on mine, it don't never go away.

When Simeon's teacher started showing him those newspapers from Chicago, at first I took them out back and burned them. For a colored man to survive in Mississippi you had to be deaf, dumb, and blind. That *Chicago Defender* paper gave my boy more ideas than sense. Trying to get him killed before he could even get north. Later I told him, he could read them, just keep them out of my sight. He's just too bright a bulb to dim.

I never quite understood why people got to pack up all they know, start from scratch, and go north to make something of theirselves. I've seen 'em come dragging their sorry tails back home, shamed to find out the streets up north weren't lined with gold like they thought they were. Mississippi is home for me. Always has been, always will be.

It ain't gonna be like that for Simeon, I know. He's going for schooling. He's a child born for the North, for bigger thinking and a place that lets him run off at the mouth like he needs to. Sometimes I lie in bed at night and picture him, maybe as a teacher at one of them colleges. With a tie and all, shoes shined nice, his little glasses. Speaking more proper than he do now, in front of a classroom full of folks paying to hear him talk about the ideas he has about colored taking their place in the world. What was that he said he wanted to be? *Doctor Simeon Clark.* Sounded like it fit him just about right.

I can just hear folks asking me, "How's your boy, Marion?" and I'd have to wave my hand at them, "Oh, Simeon? He teaching now at a college. He's a professor," I'd tell them, and just watch their faces. That's right, *Marion's boy.* I could just make myself laugh thinking about it. That's one secret Simeon don't know. How his gifts are mine too. Every time one of them teachers would tell me, "Your boy is really going places," it was all I could do not to shout it out loud, hoping my momma, wherever the Lord took her, could hear them and see me. I hope she knew then, it was me that did the choosing of their daddy. Me that had these two babies, so smart, so special, just about all of Jackson can see it. It's me who raised them up right and saw to their schooling. *Marion.* The one you thought was worth nothing. But the only way my boy gonna get north, his sister too, is if here in Mississippi, he stay deaf, dumb, and blind. And Lamb, she gotta stay true to the name I gave her. Quiet. Meek. She got to listen good.

LAMB

THIS time I waited at the fence. Right about the time I knew he'd come out for his break. When I heard someone yell, "Clark," I looked up, searching through the men coming out until I saw him. I saw now he had a limp when he walked that made his arm look longer on his left side than his right. He was in a group of men as he walked past and at first I said it soft, like I was trying it out, but then I yelled it out loud so he could hear.

"Daddy." A few of the men looked over, but he was the last one to look. I saw him say something to the others and they watched him close as he walked toward me. He was smiling, nodding his head as he walked.

"Lamb," he said as he came to the fence.

"You got time?" I asked him.

"Sure do. Just my break. But I got time."

I walked down the fence over to the bench where we sat the first time. He was waiting. Already eating his sandwich. He handed me half. I shook my head. "I'm not hungry."

"Glad to see you back," he said, looking across the street.

"I wasn't sure—well, I wanted to see—wanted to talk to you some more."

"Don't mind talking," he said. "Your brother, he didn't want to come?"

I shook my head no.

"Is that no as in never or no as in maybe one day?" he said, smiling big.

"There's no telling with Simeon," I told him.

"He's hard to read, maybe, like his momma."

I didn't think he was asking a question.

"You and Momma were in love when you got married?" I asked him.

"I thought so," he said. "She was about the prettiest woman I ever seen. Spoke her mind, some said too much, but didn't bother me none. We could talk about just about anything."

"Like what?"

He crumpled up the paper his sandwich was wrapped in. I never seen someone eat so fast. "Well, she was aching to get out of Shubuta. Said she wanted to get off the farm and get a job sewing. And she was tired of living scared. Think we all were, but not many of us were brave enough to do something about it."

"Living scared of what?" I asked him. Asking him questions about Momma made me feel scared I was gonna find out more than I wanted to know. He turned and looked at me.

"Of what?" He laughed. "Of everything. Scared of saying too much, too little, trying to buy an extra plot like your granddaddy and they come and burn your land. Everything."

"They burned my granddaddy's land?" I asked him.

"Girl, you—there got to be a reason your momma ain't telling y'all none of this. And I don't want to get in the way of that," he said.

"Were you scared?" I asked him, wanting him to keep talking. His deep voice sounded so familiar to me.

"Ain't something I let myself think much about, I guess. More mad than scared. I spent those years fighting for what I thought was freedom and turns out the freedom I was fighting for wasn't mine after all." He shook his head. "Nah, not scared, just sick and tired and mad."

Men walked past us now, looking longer than they should. My daddy nodded at them.

"I told them you my daughter," he said, looking at me. "Not that everybody couldn't see it." His eyes stayed on mine. I could see the pride in them.

"Do you think—" I started.

"I gotta go on back," he said.

"Do you think you could ever come by the house? To see me? And Simeon?" I breathed out. Waiting.

He stood up and looked down at me. "You'd have to ask your momma 'bout that," he said. "And your brother too. But if you asking, I'd surely do it."

"Thank you," I said to him. "Daddy," I added, wanting to see his face again when I said it out loud to him.

He looked at me again long in my eyes. If I didn't know better I'd think he looked like he was getting ready to cry.

"Do you live here in Jackson too?" I needed to know. For all I knew he could have been our next-door neighbor and Momma kept that from us too.

"Sure do. Not far from Farish over on Gallatin. Little bit of a house I'm renting right there on the corner. Can't miss it if you try," he said, smiling. "It ain't much, keep meaning to get around to fixing up the front steps, and it ain't nowhere near as nice as the home I bought us." He said *us,* like he wanted to be sure I knew it was him that did the buying. "But it's clean and a place I can cook and lay my head every night."

"That's near where we go to church," I told him. "At Farish Street Baptist."

He laughed. "So you the one waking me up every Sunday morning with all that praising?" He leaned into me when he laughed, and I nearly fell off the bench. He patted my knee.

"I sing there," I told him. "In the choir." Felt shamed soon as I said it. Like I was being boastful.

"Sing?" He looked away from me. "Sing," he said again to himself, softer. He leaned forward with arms resting on his legs. Folded his hands together like he was praying. Quiet.

I wasn't sure if I said something wrong.

"Okay," I said to him. "I know you got to get back." I stood up but he kept sitting.

"My momma—" he started. "Your grandmomma, and my sister Ruthie, your aunt. They sang in the choir. Folks said the two of 'em had voices like angels. Bet you do too," he said, looking up at me.

"I'll come back to see you, Daddy," I said, not wanting to leave.

"You do that, Lamb," he said, standing up. He grabbed my hand quick. Squeezed so hard I closed my eyes. When I opened them he had let go and was walking back into work.

LAMB

THE knocking woke me up. I knew Momma left early for work and even half asleep, I heard her moving around, making coffee and closing the front door soft behind her. Simeon could sleep through just about anything. Usually Uncle Chime found a way to get in even if Momma locked the door, by jiggling the doorknob just so or coming round through the back window only he knew we could never get to lock. Sometimes we'd get home from church service or an event at school and find Uncle Chime sitting at the kitchen table waiting.

"Where you all been?" he'd say, flashing the big gap in his teeth.

Made Momma so mad she'd say through her teeth, "One of these days you gonna find yourself with some buckshot through your eyes, you keep it up."

I had a hard time believing he started listening all of a sudden but why else would he be knocking this early in the morning? I pulled a sweater over my nightgown and went to the door.

"Uncle Chime, it's too early—" I said, unlocking the door and swinging it wide open. But it wasn't Uncle Chime.

"Marny?" I said, not believing she was standing on my front porch.

"Lamb, I'm sorry but—it seemed like it was quiet inside, so I figured your momma was at work—"

"Marny." It was early, but I looked up and down the street, hoping no one was out who could see us.

"You can't be here." I was whispering.

"I know I can't. I rode my bike over from my daddy's office. I told him I was just going to get a soda pop and I'd be right back, so I rode as fast as I could. I got your address from the office. Well, your brother Simeon's chart and I know I wasn't supposed to do that, because my daddy said a patient's chart is confidential, but I knew you wouldn't mind seeing we're friends and all."

I saw now her face was red and sweaty, probably from riding her bike or talking too fast or both. But I didn't care about any of that now. I cared about this white girl on my porch and someone telling my momma. I pulled her inside and shut the door behind her. Soon as I did, Marny started looking around. Up at the ceiling, the walls, past me into the parlor. I imagined she was taking in every inch of the first Negro home she'd ever been in aside from Gloria Jean's.

"Marny." She looked back at me. "What do you want?"

"I came to apologize is all," she said. "For those things I said the other day. It's just that my daddy and George go and get all worked up about things getting out of control around here and people not knowing their places and all that kind of talk sometimes and I guess—"

"You just believe it?" I finished for her. "That we need to know our place?"

"Not that I believe it, Lamb," she said. "But they go to their meetings and all and come home and it's just—"

"Their meetings?"

"Oh, it's just men talking about silly things and blowing off steam, the way men always do. 'Men gotta have a hobby, something to keep them busy.' Least that's what Momma used to tell me," Marny said.

"What are they talking about at these meetings?" I asked her.

163

"You think they're gonna tell me? Silly ole Marny? George thinks I need to be spending my time learning how to bake cakes and play hostess at teas, he sure isn't talking to me about what goes on at his men's meetings." Marny laughed.

"You ever think about what your daddy would say if he knew I was your friend?" I asked her.

"Of course I thought about it, Lamb." Marny looked like I hurt her feelings. "Truth is...I thought about telling him."

"What?...Marny, we can't see each other no more," I told her.

"Now I knew you were going to say that, Lamb. Just because our families don't agree—"

"It's more than not agreeing Marny. It ain't safe for us—"

I heard the floor creak behind me.

I turned around. I thought just about nothing could wake Simeon, but here he was, standing behind me with his hands on his hips. He tilted his head to the side, staring hard at Marny. Then back at me. "You want to introduce me to your friend, Lamb?"

LAMB

I thought Simeon wasn't never going to stop shouting. After a while I had to just stop listening.

"What in the world were you thinking?" he asked me for about the twentieth time.

"I said I didn't invite her over here, Simeon," I told him.

"The point is," he said, shouting louder, "she thought she had the *right* to come over, Lamb. And waltz her white behind up to our front door and *pay a visit*?"

I breathed out slow. "You asking me a question or telling me a story?"

"Don't get smart with me," Simeon said in a voice that sounded like overnight he had become my daddy.

I could tell he was only listening to his own self talking now.

"Oh, Momma is gonna love this." He was walking back and forth across the kitchen floor.

"Well, Momma ain't gonna know nothing about this, right? Remember, 'There's some things you can tell and some you can't'?" I said, reminding him of what he said to me every time he asked me to not tell Momma something he didn't want her to know.

"Oh, you think I'm gonna tell her? Or every person on the street watching you and your friend out on the front porch having tea this morning is going to tell her?" he said. "Or better yet, maybe someone will let it slip to her daddy that his precious baby girl is hanging with some niggers on Barrett Avenue and see how that goes over."

"You trying out for a part in the school play?" I asked Simeon, getting mad now. "Ain't you making more of this than there needs to be? One, I checked and no one saw her come to our house. Two, if anyone saw Marny, they sure wouldn't have the nerve to go and tell her daddy. Three, they don't know what she was doing here. Maybe she came to collect a bill."

Soon as I finished my number one, Simeon was shaking his head back and forth.

"'Hi, Simeon,'" he was saying now in a high voice, trying to sound like Marny. "'I'm Marny, Lamb's friend.'" He laughed out loud. "Lord, lord, lord, if I ain't seen it all."

"Simeon—"

"Oh, I know, why don't we invite Marny"—he spit her name out like it left a bad taste in his mouth—"and her folks for Christmas dinner? Wouldn't that be fine? Why, we could all sit around—"

"Shut your mouth, Simeon!" I yelled.

He finally stopped talking.

"Marny ain't my friend. Well, she was kind of my friend. I know she's white, Simeon, but she ain't all bad. She got her problems too."

"Are you asking me to feel bad for Marny Her Daddy Hates Colored Folks Tremper?" Simeon laughed out loud.

"She can't help who her daddy is," I said.

"You do know the expression, the apple doesn't fall far from the tree, right?" he said.

"Well, you don't have to worry about any of that. Like I said, me and Marny ain't friends. She loaned me a book is all and we talked some. But that's over now."

Simeon looked like he calmed down some. "So we don't need to set an extra plate at dinner tomorrow?" he asked me.

We were both quiet. And then started laughing.

I was so glad me and Simeon were through with talking about Marny for now. I could count on one hand the number of times we fought, and I sure didn't want to be fighting over Marny. So I didn't see any need to tell Simeon that when I walked Marny to the front door, and we whispered our goodbyes, I agreed to meet her again.

LAMB

"YOU sounded good in there, baby," Momma said when I came out for breakfast. I sat at the table, putting the brush and comb down beside me.

"It's a new song Miss Twyman wants us to sing next week. I'm not sure we're gonna be ready."

"Well, I don't know about everybody else, but you're ready. I don't know why she keeps putting that Juanita girl up there singing solo every time when she knows—"

"Momma, please stop. Juanita has a really nice voice," I said.

"Yours is better," Momma said.

"You gonna have to do that yourself this morning, Lamb," she said, looking at the comb and brush. "I got to go with Myrtle to the doctor."

"She sick?" I asked her.

Momma nodded her head. "Women problems," she said. Myrtle was something else Momma never talked much about. I knew she was Momma's friend, probably her only real friend, but that was about as much as I knew. Myrtle never stayed for supper. Never came to church with Momma. We'd never even been inside of Myrtle's house, though I knew she lived over the grocery store downtown where she worked on Farish Street. She was loud and danced with Momma sometimes when

168

she had too much to drink, and when Momma had her Saturday night parties, she always brought over her Bourbon Street punch that was red and sweet, and she said it was something they drank where her people were from in New Orleans in a greens pot, and people dipped cups in it all night long till it was gone. And she made just about the best sweet potato pie I ever tasted. I once asked her how she made it, and when she said to me, "I'll have to come on over one day and show you," Momma heard that and took her hand, pulling her away from me. "I'll get you Myrtle's recipe, baby, and I'll make it with you, right, Myrtle?"

I could see the hurt on Myrtle's face but she shook her head at Momma and walked away. She never talked to me much after that. Myrtle was the only one she let sleep over, in her room. And I heard them in there laughing and carrying on. In the morning, by the time we got up to go to church, Momma's bed was made and Myrtle was always gone.

On one of those nights, when I made my way into Simeon's room, I was lying in his bed with him on the floor, and I asked him, "Can two women kiss?"

In the dark, he was quiet. "I suppose they can."

"Can they be in love?"

"I don't see why not," he said.

"Do you think Momma and Myrtle kiss?"

"Go to sleep, Lamb," he told me. "I'm tired." I could hear him turning over.

And I realized it was the only time Simeon hadn't answered a question I asked him.

"So you can't do my hair real quick?" I asked Momma now.

Momma took a quick sip of her coffee and looked at the clock.

"You old enough to do this yourself, Lamb," she said, snatching up the brush and comb. Both of us knew this was our favorite part of the day, her doing my hair. The way she parted it and worked her way through with a brush and comb. A little bit of grease and she could take my thick mess of hair and make it look shiny and pretty in one bun with a big, thick braid wrapped around it. When I tried to comb it, all I felt was the pulling and the comb popping every single nap. But when Momma did it, I could almost close my eyes and fall asleep with how good it felt. And I think she loved the feel of my hair against her fingers. Sometimes, she'd take a minute and scratch her nails along my scalp or tell me, "The Lord blessed you with a headful of hair." Hers was so much thinner and finer and easier to comb through, but she made me feel like I was the lucky one.

"There you go," Momma said, brushing up the back. She took a last sip of her coffee. "I'm not sure how long I'll be. You and Simeon figure out dinner on your own today, okay? I may need to stay with Myrtle for a little while. No telling when I'll be back."

"That's okay," I said. "Earvent asked me to come over to her house for dinner after choir practice." Me and Earvent hadn't spoken in over a month now. Seeing her at practice with her head bent low was hard at first and then I just stopped thinking about her. Some days she didn't even show up to practice. Not like the other girls missed her. I knew I should be better, but thinking about what her and her Bible-thumping momma might be saying about my momma made me mad every time I thought about her.

Miss Twyman asked me before practice if something had happened. I lied and told her I wasn't sure what was going on with Earvent. I saw her asking Earvent the same thing and watched her head hanging low as she was crying.

NeeCee said behind me, "What's Little Miss crying about today? Her momma told her how babies were made?" A couple of the other girls laughed loud, and Miss Twyman looked up at them, mad. Just when I was thinking about going down to talk to Earvent and putting it all behind me, remembering what it means to be a Christian and to forgive others, I saw Earvent run out the church doors. Miss Twyman shook her head and went back to the piano.

"Let's get started, ladies and gentlemen," she said, snapping her fingers.

LAMB

TODAY after practice NeeCee asked if I wanted to walk with everybody over to the Blue Heaven Lunch Stand to get something to eat and I told her I had to get right home to help my momma. I ain't never lied so much in my life as I had since I met Marny. And as easy as it was to blame my lying on her and the things this white girl was making me do, it wasn't that hard at all. I was starting to like being a different kind of Lamb. The kind of Lamb that had secrets. That wasn't as boring as everyone thought I was. I had a white friend, a daddy I talked to, and for once I didn't wait for anyone to give me permission to do something I wanted to do.

I waited until I couldn't see the girls anymore and then I doubled back past the church and through downtown past People's Funeral Home and Hunt & Whitaker's Loans. I was looking careful up and down the streets because I knew Myrtle lived just a block away over the grocery store, but I walked fast and kept my head down until I turned onto Gallatin Street. I remembered the house he described. And there I was standing on the corner in front of his "little bit of a house" with the broken-down steps thinking *This can't be it*. I looked around to ask someone, but the street only had two men sitting outside on crates further down, and I sure wasn't going to ask them. I stepped up and knocked on the door.

A woman who looked like she was still wearing last night's lipstick answered. Her hair was in those tight waves and she was what some folks might have called pretty in her day, but she looked too mean to call pretty now. She looked at me sideways.

"What you want?" she asked. *This definitely ain't the place.*

"I—I think I have the wrong—I think I have the wrong house," I told her. "I'm looking for Chester. Chester Clark?"

"Well," she said slow, her head leaned all the way to one side, "you got the right place, but who the hell are you?" She didn't move from the doorway.

I tried to look around her. And she moved to block me. "I'm Lamb."

"Kind of name is Lamb?" she laughed.

"Who's that, Velma?" I heard my daddy's voice behind her. She stepped to the side, and my daddy came to the door. She stared at him staring at me, looking just as mean. He had on a dingy white T-shirt and suspenders holding up his pants. He was wiping his mouth with his hands, and I couldn't tell if he just finished eating or was just waking up.

"Lamb?" he said, stepping back.

Velma put her hands on her hips as soon as he said my name.

His face reminded me of how mine must have looked when Marny came to my door.

"I'm sorry—I didn't know." I backed up out onto the sidewalk. I felt so stupid thinking I could just walk into his house. Thinking he didn't have a woman. Of course he did. What did he tell me? *A man got to be a man, Lamb.* So, so stupid. And here I thought he was alone and maybe wanting my company and I... I was walking fast as I could as I made my way back up the street.

"Lamb!" I heard behind me just as I turned the corner. "Lamb!" he said again louder. "I can't walk that fast, girl." And when I turned I could see he had his feet shoved halfway into some boots and he was limping. I stopped walking. He was out of breath when he reached me. He took a minute to catch his breath.

"I'm sorry," I said. "I didn't mean to. I mean, I didn't know your wife, or whoever, was going to be there. I just wanted to—"

"You ain't got to explain nothing!" He sounded like he was shouting at me. "She ain't got a right talking to you like you some vagabond off the street. She was thinking you something you ain't is all." He smiled at me. "If you get my meaning."

"You mean, she thought I was...your girlfriend?"

He nodded, smiling bigger.

We both laughed. "I think she owes you an apology," he said.

"No, I understand," I told him. "But is Velma your...wife?"

"Wife?" He laughed about as loud as Uncle Chime then. "Last time I checked, law says you can't have two wives at the same time," he said. "I'm still married to your momma."

He saw the look on my face. "Some things ain't meant for you to understand, Lamb." I nodded my head at him. "Me and Velma keep each other company is all."

I didn't know what to do, so I stood staring up at him.

"Well, we ain't got to keep talking out here in the street. Come on back and let me see what I can put together for us to eat. Velma went on home, so she'll have to give you that apology another time."

He stopped and bent down to put his feet in his boots and tied up the laces. "Almost broke my neck out here chasing folks in the street." He laughed to himself. It made me smile to think about how much he laughed at one thing or the other. Not at all like Momma. When he stood up again, he pulled up his suspenders and held out his arm for me to hold. I looked up at him. *Tall as a tree,* and I took hold of my daddy.

CHESTER

I ain't had much chance to be a daddy, so after we finished eating and Lamb started talking to me about this girl Marny, this white friend she gone and got herself mixed up with, I wasn't sure what I was supposed to tell her. She wasn't telling Marion nothing. She was afraid to talk to her brother. Seems I was the only one who could tell her something straight. But the truth was I barely knew her. My own girl, I barely knew.

There were times when my girl was talking I had to remind myself I wasn't listening to my very own momma. Same soft-spoken way and with her hair pulled up on top of her head and those big, round cheeks. All's was missing was my momma's pink housecoat, and I'd have thought the Lord himself raised my momma from her grave and sat her across from me at my kitchen table. Hard as Marion was, this girl didn't have a lick of it in her, just like my momma. Just as pretty as Marion, but in her own way, with a sweetness to her face. Can't say I was ever gonna trust much about Marion again, but she done right by naming her. Day she was born, she told me she was gonna name her Lamb, and I thought she must have come on with a fever bringing her into the world. Figured we give her some time and she'd come to her senses. Name her right. But nah, Lamb is what she had in her mind. And once Marion got something in her head, ain't no getting it out.

Lamb had us both worried at first. The girl barely cried, she was so quiet. Then it seemed she couldn't find her words. "Leave her be," Marion would tell me, holding her tight, like she was her baby doll.

I leave for work, Marion was holding her. I come home, Marion was rocking her. "You ain't got to hold her like that all day," I'd tell her. Seemed like she'd never let her go. "And you ain't got to tell me what to do with my babies," Marion said to me. *My babies.* Every time she said it, felt like she took a piece of me. "You know I'm their daddy, right? Was me who made those babies?" Marion would just smile at me then. Showing me all her pretty white teeth. I ain't never been a man to lay my hands on a woman, but only time I ever thought about it was when she smiled like that at me. Like she was trying to make me hurt. Making me ask myself *Is you really their daddy?* Marion barely wanted to be with me in the way a wife should, so I knew she wasn't the type to be out in the streets with other men. If Lamb didn't look so much like me, she would have had me asking questions in the wrong kinda way.

Simeon, though, was all arms and legs, brown and skinny just like Marion and her people. Talked more than he cried. Bothered me at first to have a brother and sister not even look like kin, but Marion told me, she and her brothers all looked like copies of one another, and except for Chime, she'd just as soon pass them on the street than say hello. "Looking alike don't make you kin," she told me. She had me there. Seemed to me Marion was right about that too. Lamb sounded like Simeon stepped in the place where I was, looking out for her like a brother and a daddy, whether she liked it or not.

"Daddy?" Lamb asked me. The way she said "Daddy" made my chest hurt.

I pulled my chair closer to the table. Looked down and saw she didn't finish half of the plate I made for her from last night's supper. I picked it up and brought it to the sink to keep her from seeing all's I was feeling.

"Sounds to me like your brother is just worried about you is all," I told her, my back to her now.

"I don't know if he's worried about me or worried I'm going to ruin his plans," she said.

I sat back down. Looking at Lamb, she looked like she'd be too scared to say two words. But sitting here on one of my rickety old chairs, seemed like she had a whole lot to say. Like she been saving up years of talking for just these weeks to tell me. I was wishing on the one hand I could go back to being her daddy every day so I would have never missed a minute and on the other not minding hearing her having to talk more than she was used to talking.

"I'm sorry," she said finally, looking down. "We can talk about something else if you want." She folded her hands in her lap. My girl was what I know some folks called *refined*. I was trying hard as I could to listen, talk, look at her, not look at her, and wonder how Marion did it. Raised this girl and Simeon too, up better than anybody could have done, daddy or not. But then I thought about Marion. She get her mind set on something and no one gonna tell her it wasn't gonna happen. And the one thing Marion wanted was her children. I never quite knew why. She didn't much seem cut out for mothering. But sitting looking at this girl, so fine and proper, I saw now, Marion was just that.

"You talk as much as you like," I told her. "Wish I had some better answers for you than I got."

"That's the thing," she said. She put her head in her hand. "I don't know what to do. Something's telling me to leave Marny alone, but I like her. But I don't want to be lying all the time either…."

"Her daddy know about you?" I asked, sitting back down in front of her.

She shook her head no, looking sad.

"Look here," I told her. "I know I ain't been much of a daddy to you—and I'm sorry 'bout that." I had to stop and take a breath. "But that don't mean—" I had a hard time looking at her. "Don't mean I stopped caring about y'all...I'd drive past the house sometimes..."

"You drove past our house?" she asked, her mouth wide open.

"Yes I did. Usually at night. When I knew y'all were sleeping. Don't know what I was looking for exactly. Maybe I just liked knowing my children were there in bed in a house I provided for 'em. I saw you once...sitting out front. You and Simeon, on a Saturday night. Two of you were laughing and Simeon got up...Lord that boy is skinny." I stood up then and showed her how Simeon was dancing. To hear her laugh made me want to keep dancing like that all day. I sat back down out of breath. "That's just how you were laughing that night." I cleared my throat. "I never stopped caring about you. But this right here. This don't seem safe," I told her.

"You mean with Marny?" she asked me.

"Yes, with Marny. With your momma and brother not knowing where you are half the time. Nice as she is, sound like her daddy and brother may be mixed up in something you don't want to be nowhere near."

I could see her eyes getting wet and I reached out and touched her hand. "I know," she said. "I know."

We sat at the table quiet. "It's getting late," I told her. "And I don't want you to have to make up any more stories today on account of me." I smiled at her. "Why don't I drive you home?"

We both stood. She waited while I changed into a shirt and we walked to the car. The ride home was quiet. I watched her looking out the window.

"Lamb," I said. She looked over at me. "I say something back there made you upset with me?"

"No." She shook her head.

We pulled up in front of the house, and I was glad to see it didn't look like anyone was home yet. "Thank you, Daddy," she said. I thought she was leaning forward to open the door and get out, but instead she leaned over toward me. Kissed me right on my cheek. She jumped out quick, and I watched her walk up the steps and into the house. Close the door behind her. I just sat watching the house for I don't know how long. Hard as I tried, something was making it hard for me to drive away.

LAMB

I walked as slow as I could to the barn. Knowing it was the last time I'd see Marny made me feel some mix of mad and sad for how things had to be. And I hated that Simeon seemed smart not just about school things and his life and plans but it looked like my life too. Even when I tried to do things my own way, it seemed I still needed him to tell me how to do it better. I walked around behind the barn and Marny ran up behind me and threw her arms around me.

"Marny!" I yelled, sounding madder than I wanted to. "Stop." I pulled her arms from around my neck.

"I wasn't sure if you were going to come," she said with her pouting face.

"And don't make that face neither, Marny. I can't stay," I told her.

"What do you mean you can't stay? You came all the way here, least you can do is sit down for a bit. You can do that, right?" She tilted her head to one side.

I sat down in the grass and she sat down close to me.

"You should have never come by my house," I said finally.

"I know that," she said.

"If my momma had come home…"

"I said I know, Lamb. I was just worried—you know—I didn't know what else to do." Marny's head was down, looking in the grass, and I was wishing I hadn't come after all. Seemed like it would have been easier to not even say goodbye. But who's to say Marny wouldn't have shown up again at my front door? I looked over at her. She had on a yellow-and-white polka-dot skirt with tennis shoes.

"Your skirt is pretty," I told her.

She looked at it, half smiling, and smoothed down the pleats. "My momma told me I had to be careful wearing prints. You know, with my figure and all." She looked up at me. I could see the water in her eyes. "I ain't never had a friend like you, Lamb."

I nodded.

"Maybe I'll be needing eyeglasses one day soon," I said, smiling at her. "And I'll see you back in the office."

"My daddy says soon as school starts back he's going to hire another receptionist," she said, "so I can focus more on my studies. Of course Georgie says it's because daddy thinks I'm too friendly with the color—well, hell, you know, with the colored patients. But if I wasn't, I wouldn't have met you, right?"

I tried to make myself smile.

"What in the heck is—" Marny said, turning around quick.

We could both hear the sound of a car radio blasting from behind the barn, and Marny stood and reached out her hand to pull me up. We looked at each other not saying a word, and we saw a blue pickup truck driving fast and swerving toward us. I jumped to the side, expecting Marny to jump too, but she stood still, staring at the truck.

A car horn beeped and a white man sitting behind the wheel pulled up and stopped short in front of us in the grass. I backed away, looking for where to run, when I noticed Marny walking to the truck.

"Marny?" I said soft.

The window rolled down, and the music turned off.

"What are you doing here, Georgie?" Marny shouted at the truck. *Georgie? Her brother?*

I walked over to the grass where I'd left my purse. "Marny, I'm going to get on home—" I said, turning to leave, but as I started walking the truck moved forward, almost touching my leg.

"Georgie, knock it off!" Marny shouted.

"Where's your friend going?" George said over the truck engine. "The two of you, get in the truck."

"We're not going anywhere with you, George!" Marny shouted louder.

I was looking at Marny's face getting red. "I really gotta go, Marny—"

The truck door opened, and her brother George got out. He was as tall and skinny as Marny was short and round. *Just like me and Simeon.* He was as handsome as I could imagine a white man could be. I guessed from Marny's momma because his looks sure didn't come from their daddy. A piece of his red hair fell in his eyes, and he brushed it away quick. He looked like he was in a hurry.

"I gotta get her home," he said, looking at me. "You get in too, girl. I may as well drive you on home. Y'all shouldn't be out here. Don't you know there are big bad folks just looking for pretty young things to scoop up and carry away?" He smiled big.

"How did you find us here?" Marny asked, walking toward his truck.

"You're not hard to find," he laughed. "You used to run away here, remember?"

Marny rolled her eyes. "Well, we don't need any saving, right, Lamb?"

"Well, you gonna need saving from Daddy, he finds out you were sitting out here with a ni—your new little friend here."

Marny put her hands on her hips. "There's no call for that, Georgie, and you know it."

I stood still.

Marny turned to me. "C'mon, Lamb, get in the truck."

"Nah, that's okay. I'm going to walk." I snatched my purse from the grass.

"Now, didn't you just hear me tell you it's not safe for the two of you to be out here by yourselves? If it ain't safe for two, it sure ain't safe for one. C'mon, girl, you're gonna make me look like I ain't no kind of gentleman," George said, swinging open the passenger door and smiling.

Marny shrugged her shoulders at me and climbed in. She waved her hand at me to get in beside her. I didn't see no way out of it. I climbed up slow into the truck and got in, sitting as close to the edge of the seat as I could, and closed the door behind me.

LAMB

I barely closed the door before George started speeding off.

"What's the hurry anyhow?" Marny asked, falling over on me when he sped back around the barn.

"Daddy said he needs you home now," George told her, looking in the rearview mirror. "Didn't ask him why. Maybe he just missed you." He grinned down at her.

"Oh, shut your mouth, George Tremper," Marny said. "And Lamb lives the other direction, near downtown."

"Well, look at you. Y'all pay each other social calls?" He laughed. Made me feel like I was back home listening to Simeon talk about Marny.

I looked at Marny but she looked straight ahead. Finally she said quiet, "I would like for you to drop Lamb home first. Please?"

George kept driving. "I told Daddy I'd get you home, and that's what I intend to do. Won't take but a minute." He jabbed her with his elbow. "You know how fast I drive." He smiled.

I leaned across Marny. "You can just drop me over here," I said, pointing at the corner up ahead. Even though we were heading away from the direction I lived, I knew we were still close enough where I could walk home. "I'll walk from here." I could just see Momma's face she see me getting out of a pickup truck with a white girl *and* her brother.

George kept right on driving past the corner.

"George, did you hear Lamb?" Marny shouted in his ear. "Pull over there and let her out. She can walk from there." I was so glad Marny was trying to help me out. I could tell, though, it wasn't going to do much good. That the more she asked, the more George was going to say no. I could see why she didn't have much to do with him.

"Daddy told me if I didn't get you home right away, there would be hell to pay. You know how he is when he gets worked up. I'll take you home, then drop your friend." He patted her knee, and she pushed his hand away. With her other hand she reached for mine.

"How about right there?" I pointed at another corner. This neighborhood wasn't familiar at all, and I could tell it had a lot of white folks. I wasn't even sure I wanted to get out here.

"I'm doing you a favor, girl! You'll be home in a minute. Now sit back and shut your mouth," George said to me.

"You shut *your* mouth," Marny said. "You ain't nobody's daddy."

He laughed and turned a corner onto a quiet street with trees up and down both sides. The houses weren't as big as some I'd seen in Jackson, but these were nice enough, each with a little lawn in front and set back a ways from the street. Marny's house was white with a black door with big gold numbers 1 and 6 on the door. If me and Marny were still going to be seeing each other, I could tell her, that was another thing we had in common. Her house number was sixteen, just the same age we were. There was a wide driveway next to her house, and George swung in quick.

"Hurry up and get out so I can get your little friend home," he said. I opened the door to step down to let Marny out, and after I got back into the truck, she looked up at me. *I'll miss you, Lamb,* she mouthed to me so George couldn't see.

I closed the door.

George sped back down the street. "I live over near Farish," I told him.

He smiled big. "My sister already told me, remember?"

We hadn't driven two blocks before he said to me, "You know colored ain't supposed to be riding in the seat next to a white person, right?"

I nodded.

"I wasn't sure you did since you think it's okay for you and my sister to be meeting and socializing and all?" He hadn't once stopped smiling.

"I know it's not right. And me and Marny weren't planning to see each other again," I told him.

"Marion tell you to call her that?" he asked me. "Marny?"

I nodded yes.

"And you know when I ask you a question, the answer is yessir or nosir? Didn't your momma teach you nothing?" He stopped smiling now.

"Yessir," I said. My stomach started getting tight.

"You and my sister are just as thick as thieves, ain't you? So sweet." He said "sweet" the way Simeon said the name Marny. Like it made him sick.

"Mar—Miss Marion is just real good people," I said to him. White folks always made it so there wasn't no right way to talk to them.

"Real good people what?" he said, looking over at me.

"Real good people, sir," I said, turning to look at the road rushing by.

"Am I good people?"

"I don't know you," I told him. I could hear how shaky my voice sounded but I wasn't sure he could tell.

"You don't know me…yet," he said, looking over at me. He looked so much like Marny, I had to look away.

I looked up ahead and noticed he had turned onto a road that was headed out of town.

"I live over on Barrett Avenue," I said. Then added in "sir." Loud so he'd hear me.

"Now why do you keep telling me where you live?" he asked me. "I just feel like taking a little ride. How we going to get to know each other if we don't spend time together? You like my sister, I'm betting you'll like me too."

"No sir, I like you fine. Miss Marion said you are real nice, but I got to get on home." I reached to put my hand on the door handle, and he reached over and hit it away. The truck swerved a little bit. Up close, he even smelled like Marny, not like her florally perfume, but like they lived in the same house, but his smell was mixed with the smell of cigarettes and that smell of men. I could never tell if it was sweat or something else.

I could feel my eyes filling with water. He laughed again. "Relax yourself," he said, resting his hand on my knee. I looked down at it, smooth and pale and freckled. I never knew hair on someone's knuckles could be so long.

"Better now?" he said, tapping my knee hard. "How'd you and my sister meet?" he asked like we were at a church picnic.

"At the doctor's," I said, my voice shaky. I knew he could tell I was getting ready to cry. "Your *daddy's* office. She was working at the desk." I said "daddy" louder than the rest, hoping just thinking of his daddy might make him start thinking straight.

"My daddy's office, huh? You getting glasses?" The more he talked, the more we drove further from my house.

"No, but my brother Simeon was."

"Mmmhmmm." He nodded, his hand rubbing my leg faster. "So the two of you just decided right then and there in my daddy's office"— he said "daddy" loud like I did—"that you were gonna be friends?"

"Well, no, not just like that."

"Don't keep me in suspense," he said, looking ahead at the road. "How did my sister get to be best pals with a colored gal?"

I was quiet still.

"I'm waaaaiiitttinnng."

"She liked a book I was reading," I said quiet as I could, thinking if I didn't say it too loud it wouldn't sound half as bad.

"A *book* you were reading?" He whistled through his teeth. "My sister does love her books. Me, I've never been much of a reader. But I guess you are, huh?"

I nodded.

"I think I've heard it all today," he said to himself. "You both love *books*."

Up ahead I could see dirt rising from the middle of the road. I started thinking maybe I could open the door quick and jump, but if it was someone white, the two of them would catch me easy. I didn't know if they could help me if they weren't.

The dust cloud got bigger as we got closer, and I could see a truck coming toward us through the smoke.

"Put your head down," he said in a whisper. I leaned forward, ducking my head toward the dashboard, but he grabbed the side of my head near the window and pulled it toward him.

His hand was covering my ear as he pulled my head hard and laid my head in his lap. The driver in the truck beeped and he beeped back, put his hand out the window to wave. After the truck passed, I moved to sit up.

"Stay down. We don't know it's safe yet." His dungarees were scratching my cheek and he let his hand up off my ear and reached toward the radio.

"You like music?" he asked. "I do," he said, not waiting for an answer, and turned up the radio loud.

He put his hand on my cheek and moved his hand down to my shoulder, rubbing in time to the music. He started singing along.

"You are my sunshine, my only sunshine…"

"You know this song?" I could feel him looking down at me.

I didn't move. Finally he pulled the car over to the side of the road and stopped. I went to sit up.

"Stay there," he said, his words slow and deep. "Stay right there, Lamb." It was the first time he said my name.

He rubbed my hair, then my cheek. "Lamb," he said. "That sure is a pretty name, Sunshine."

George moved his other hand down and rubbed himself through his dungarees. "You stay right there."

Sunshine. I closed my eyes and thought then of Marny and her favorite color.

SIMEON

EVER since Lamb's been seeing that white girl Marny, she changed. She's always been quiet, sometimes too quiet for her own good, but it was like this white girl was making Lamb become something she wasn't. First she started sneaking off to meet her, and then out of nowhere, this girl showed up at our house like she was company who came calling one fine afternoon.

The truth of it was, I wasn't sure if I was madder that Lamb was becoming friends with a white girl or that she was keeping secrets from me. Lamb ain't never been one to lie. Our own momma always said Lamb just didn't have it in her not to tell the truth. But lately, either she snuck off somewhere with her new friend or met up somewhere with our daddy and she wasn't saying one word to me about it.

Where was our daddy all these years when Lamb needed help with her schoolwork, and she needed to figure a plan for her future? And now he wanted to play like he was some kind of savior from up on high?

I thought about telling our momma just what Lamb was up to. Let her set her right. But it ain't my place, and Lamb's kept her tongue all these years, far as I can tell and never once told Momma the things I asked her not to.

Even tonight when Momma asked me when I'd last seen Lamb, I told her I saw her earlier with some of the girls from choir. Told Momma she told me she'd be home a little late when Lamb said no such a thing. I ain't Lamb. I don't care one lick about telling Momma what I got to do keep her off my back, but I sure as hell ain't gonna keep lying to cover for when Lamb was out with that Marny girl or someone who pretended to be a part-time daddy.

I laid in bed waiting for her till I heard the front door open and close quiet.

I heard her in the parlor talking to Momma. Telling her she wasn't feeling well. Telling Momma she was going to bed early. No, she wasn't hungry. No, she didn't want any tea, she was just going to go lie down. "Good night, Momma."

Lamb had the nerve to walk past my room, quick to hers, and close the door behind her. I waited. Let her get her nightclothes on, and then I got up and went to her room and closed the door behind me. The lights were off, and she was in bed, her head under the bedspread.

"I hope you weren't out with that Marny girl," I said to her soft, in case Momma was listening the way I know she liked to do. "'Cause I sure don't plan on lying for you anymore for that girl."

Lamb was quiet.

"And I know you ain't 'sleep that fast," I said to her. "The least you can do is thank me."

She didn't move.

"Lamb?" I could see covers moving up and down but not from her breathing or sleeping. I could hear now from the catch in her breath that Lamb was crying.

I pulled the covers back. "What's wrong?" I asked, leaning over her in the dark.

She pulled the covers back over her head.

"You're really sick?"

She was holding the covers so I couldn't pull them down.

"Well, if you're sick, I'm not going to feel right leaving you here alone. I'll just sit with you," I said, pulling up a chair next to her bed.

"Simeon, leave me alone," she said from under the covers.

"Well, that don't sound to me like someone who's sick," I told her, and waited some more.

Lamb pulled the covers down so just her eyes were showing. I turned on her bedside lamp. Her eyes were swollen and red. She wiped them with the covers and turned away from me.

"Turn the light off, Simeon," she told me.

She kept up her crying.

"She ain't worth it, Lamb," I said. "I promise you I am not going to say I told you so if that's what you worried about. But I don't want you wasting one more tear over someone who doesn't deserve it. That girl is just like the rest of them, Lamb. They can't help who they are, they say one thing—"

She turned back to me. "This doesn't have anything to do with Marny, Simeon."

"Then what—?"

I could see her looking at me the way she did when she was trying to decide whether or not to tell me something she didn't want to tell me.

"Lamb—" I said, looking in her eyes.

She wiped her face. Pulled the bedcovers down and sat up.

"It was her brother, Simeon," she said. "Her brother, George."

SIMEON

I sat with Lamb long after she told me what happened with George. I sat with her till she stopped crying. Till she finally fell asleep. I pulled the covers over her, turned off her light, and went back to my room. The street was quiet, and I listened to the sounds of Lamb and Momma sleeping, and it seemed almost like if I listened hard enough I could even hear George Tremper too, sleeping real good in his bed on the other side of town. The only one who wouldn't be sleeping tonight was me.

All night long, I played it over and over in my head what Lamb told me. *Is something wrong with every single one of them Trempers?* I wondered. I already knew the answer to that question. That nasty drunkard father. His spoiled daughter and now his son who thinks he can have his way with any Negro girl who crosses his path. Are they just going to go on hurting folks who can't fight back? How long we Negroes gotta keep taking before we start giving? Every time I closed my eyes trying to go to sleep, it was like it was those nights when Lamb would come into my room when she was scared. I'd always feel her breath on me, standing next to my bed. Then she'd lean down and whisper, "Simeon?"

Even if I was sound asleep, I'd have to make room for her in my bed or sleep on the hard floor so she wouldn't be scared. Sometimes hold her hand till she fell asleep. She never told me what scared her, but I noticed it was right after our daddy left for good she started coming in and she'd tell me, "I don't want to sleep all by myself."

Every year she came in less and less. There were nights I'd miss our talks in the dark. The things we could say to each other when the lights weren't on. But tonight, I was wishing what she told me about George Tremper was all a bad dream.

And then he turned up the radio, Lamb told me.

"Turned up the radio?" I asked her. *What kind of man does this to a woman while he's humming a tune?*

"Yes, Simeon," Lamb told me, crying. *He was...he was...singing. Said he loves music.*

I felt like I couldn't breathe. But for Lamb's sake, I kept on nodding, like I was just listening, not mad, just trying to understand her story.

"And that's when he touched you?"

She nodded. I nodded back.

I reached for her hand, but she pulled it back. *You can't tell Momma, Simeon. You can't say anything.*

I kept nodding. *Breathe,* I told myself. *Keep breathing.*

"Momma's the last person I'd be telling. But are you gonna say something to your friend?"

She shook her head no.

"You're just going to let her brother get away with this and not say a word to her?"

"Quiet down, Simeon," Lamb said, looking at the door, waiting I guess to hear if we heard any sounds from Momma. But the house was quiet. "Today I told Marny it was the last ime I could see her," she said.

"Seems I heard that before," I mumbled.

194

"Well, I meant it this time. We both said goodbye. She doesn't—she won't ever know what happened."

I intended to keep my promise to Lamb. I wasn't going to say one word to our momma. But when the sun was just starting to come up, and I finally felt my eyes getting heavy, I knew who I was going to tell.

CHIME

I wasn't exactly no easy man to find, so seeing Simeon waiting on me in front of my boarding house got my heart racing. Knew right off something was troubling him, and I tried to read him to see if it was my sister or his.

"I need your help," he said, walking toward me fast. His hands were in his pockets, his hat pulled low. Looking like the wind could blow him over. Had me thinking again, *Marion don't feed this boy nearly enough.*

"What, not even a hello?" I said to him, smiling.

But Simeon didn't have time for none of my pleasantries today, as they say.

"Need to talk to you, Uncle Chime. Man to man," he said.

"We need a bottle?" I asked him, thinking now, this wasn't nothing but some women problems he ran into. And didn't nothing solve women problems faster than some talk and a bottle.

He shook his head no.

"My landlady don't allow me to have no company, so you keep quiet, hear. Follow me," I said, putting my finger to my lips, and we headed in the front door. He nodded his head. It was early enough Miss Richmond was still in bed, just like I was hoping. And I didn't have to hear her yapping 'bout rent, my late hours, my drinking, or all three 'fore the sun was barely coming up. And Simeon walked quiet like I told him behind, on up to my room on the third floor. My room wasn't nothing to speak of and I could see him looking round thinking the same, taking it in, and I stopped him 'fore that mind of his got going good.

"This is just temporary," I told him. "Till I get some more money coming in."

He shook his head, but I could see in his face how he was feeling about the little bed pushed up in the corner of that dark room and the hot plate and burned-up coffeepot. He sat in the chair at the table, I sat on the edge of my mattress.

"What's on your mind?" I asked him, taking off my boots. I laid back, closed my eyes.

"I need... I need..." Simeon's voice cracked. "I think I need a gun."

I opened my eyes and at the table he was bent over, head in his hand.

I sat up. "Nephew. One thing I know about women. They can just 'bout tear your heart in two. But they can also heal it. Saying that to say, get on back out there and see who you can find to heal the hurting you feeling now. You young and—"

"Uncle Chime." Simeon sounded like he was choking. "Someone hurt Lamb. Bad."

I stood up. "What you talking 'bout, nephew?" I could feel the sweat starting on my back.

He shook his head. Tears were running down his cheeks. I ain't never seen this boy cry. Always thought Marion took the soft out of him, but here he was crying now like a newborn baby. I walked over, put my hand on his back.

"You got to talk to me now."

"A white man…"

I held on to the edge of the table. I could feel something rising in my chest all the way up to my throat. The way he was crying, I could see it clear as day. *A white man. Lamb.* "Marion know?"

He shook his head.

"You know who this white man is? What his name is?" I asked. Feeling the calm come back to me. Started me thinking about all the white men from my past, thinking they were owed something they weren't. Crenshaw and his brother. Frank Murdoch, the man who tried to cheat me out of my wages I had to settle up with in my own way. The ones who liked to hide at night, under hoods. The ones who were safe with badges and guns. The guards at Parchman on horses with whips. Trying to take away every last ounce of manhood you had. Always finding some way to beat down on someone they thought couldn't fight back. Soon as I got out of Parchman, I came straight to Jackson to my sister. See if I could step up, be a different kind of man. One that could see to her and her children after Chester left. I thought maybe it was working. And now… *my Chop?*

Simeon nodded yes.

I walked back over to the edge of my bed. Sat down. "Tell me what you know," I said to him. "Don't leave nothing out."

Simeon watched my face as he was talking. Watched me walk to the coffeepot and warm it up. My back to him. Open a window to get in some air.

He asked, "Uncle Chime, you listening?" I was quiet, nodded my head.

Every single word he said I stored away. Like I was sitting next to him writing notes in one of his classrooms. *George Tremper. Twenty years old. College boy. Pinecrest Circle. Pickup truck. Daddy Dr. Tremper. Sister Marny.* The key to making a plan is to not look like you making a plan. That ain't something Simeon would know. Or should know. But it's something I learned when I was running 'shine back in Shubuta. It's what got me time in Parchman. Took me years, but I learned the same lesson my daddy did. White folks ain't got much of a problem with colored long as they ain't messing with their money. Soon as you do, they gonna find any way to stop you. Setting your fields on fire. Burning a cross. Shipping you to Parchman. Hanging you from a tree. My 'shine business messed with a lot of other white folks' 'shine businesses and 'fore I knew it, I was standing before a judge. My momma and daddy never even showed up for the trial. Not one of my brothers neither. But Marion came out to Parchman once on a visiting day. A fifth Sunday. Wrote me a letter or two. Told me I always had a place with her. And I went, soon as they saw fit to let me go.

To look at us, you'd think me and Simeon 'bout as different as night and day. Simeon always been the smartest one in his class. Not a book he can't read. A test he can't get an A on. I'm willing to bet he smarter than most of his teachers. Me, I never took much of a liking to school. Sitting in a schoolhouse while someone talked at me, telling me what they think I ought to know, never seemed worth my time when a big whole world of learning was waiting outside the schoolhouse doors. But different as we seem, me and Simeon both was alike in one way. We never waited for anyone to make a way for us. Difference is, he did it his way, and I did it mine.

I knew farming a plot was never gonna be my way. Watching my daddy and brothers every day, hunched over a crop, planting, picking, sweating, waiting. Waiting for a crop to come in. Waiting for the white man to decide if they could own a piece of land they earned with their own sweat wasn't what I called living. Especially when down the road was money to be made, not under a hot sun, but in the cool of the night. Just needed me, a few friends, a still, some upfront cash, and we had ourselves a business. A friendly business. Easy money. That's the way me and Simeon are just alike. We were tired of waiting for white folks to decide. We went and decided for ourselves what our lives were gonna look like.

Marion always told me to keep my mouth shut around her boy. "Don't go telling him any of your crazy stories or giving him ideas about those shortcuts of yours. Only thing that's gonna get him is jail, hurt, or worse."

"What's worse than waiting on life?" I asked her.

"Not having a life to live!" she yelled in my face.

I laughed then. "What happened to you? You scaredier now than our daddy."

She stared at me in a way Marion ain't never looked at me. Long and mean. The way she looked when she had one drink too many. Or when someone been cheating at cards. Or lied to her. "One thing you don't do," she said almost so soft I could barely hear her, "you don't tell me what's right for me and my children. If being scared means keeping them alive, then I'm gonna stay scared. Live your life anyway you want, but you gonna keep your mouth shut about things gonna get my boy in trouble. You understand?"

I ain't never planned the way my nephew do. This boy must plan what time he do his business every day, you ask me. He been planning since the day he was born, like he can see just where he gonna be years from now. He and my Chop, good kids, trying to live life right. But me and Marion never had it easy. We had to fight our way through life every day. Now I know some would say I made it harder on myself but there's hard learning and easy learning.

Simeon finished talking and sat waiting.

"That it?" I asked him.

"Is that it?" he shouted.

I put my hand to my lips. Pointed to the floor, reminding him about my landlady. He put his head back down.

"You don't need no gun," I said.

"Yeah I do," he said plain. "He gotta pay."

"And you gotta life ahead of you. You forgettin' your plan? College? North?" I asked him. Every time I thought about this boy and Lamb too doing something me and Marion could never even dream of made my heart just about burst out of my chest. I couldn't have been prouder if I made them myself.

"So we're just gonna let him get away with it?"

"This here needs thinking on," I told him. "And not your thinking, but my thinking. You need to go on home and let me figure this out."

He looked at me. "I need to do this too. For Lamb. This ain't just your fight, Uncle Chime. It's mine too. I was supposed to be…" I could see the tears starting again and I made my way toward him. He held up his hand to stop me. Looked at me with dry eyes now. Dead in my face. "She's mine to protect," he said to me. Not like my nephew. Like a man.

SIMEON

UNCLE Chime wasn't going to give me the kind of help I was hoping he was. And he definitely wasn't going to give the kind of help I needed. I wasn't a child. I didn't need for him to figure out nothing for me when I knew what needed to be done. George Tremper needed to pay for what he did to my sister and it was up to me to see to it. Uncle Chime was right about one thing. I did have a plan for my life, and it didn't include me going to jail for murder. So it probably wasn't a gun I needed. Mad as I was, I knew I wasn't no murderer. But there's plenty of ways to make someone pay without killing them, right? I needed to hit George Tremper where it hurt most.

Walking home from Uncle Chime's, seemed like every car that passed was a blue Dodge pickup truck. I'd slow and look to see if I saw anyone sitting behind the steering wheel with red hair, hoping it was him. I wasn't even sure what I'd do if I saw him. I just wanted to look at his face for now. Just thinking about his sister in my house not a week ago, *Hi, I'm Marny.* And her daddy, *You spelling your name for me, boy?* Made me want to rethink that gun idea and kill every single one of them Trempers.

Another pickup truck came speeding around the corner and down the street, windows rolled down and music blasting some song I ain't never heard and wouldn't care to again.

He asked me if I liked music. And then he turned up the radio so loud and was singing along when he was touching me.

His radio, I thought to myself. What about his car radio? I never owned a car and neither did Momma, but it seemed to me that for most folks, a car was just metal on wheels without music from the radio.

And George Tremper ain't nothing without his truck, his music, and his radio.

I remembered my first day of high school when I found out that every single girl had to take home economics and every boy had to take automotives. "Guess they're getting us ready to be housewives and auto mechanics," I said to Lamb, laughing at the kitchen table while Momma cooked dinner. "At least you already know how to sew, so you're ahead of the game. Me, this is the first class I'm likely to fail."

I remember Momma giving me one of her looks.

"You don't know what kind of job you're gonna have. Not everybody gets to plan their life, Simeon."

"Well, I know I ain't going to be no auto mechanic. Someone come to me to fix their car, they may as well start walking, because I barely know a carburetor from a tailpipe." I winked across the table at Lamb. She didn't look up at me, but I could see her laughing into her book.

Momma snapped her head around from the stove. "You so book smart, you think you can't learn to work with your hands?"

"Well, I didn't say all that. I just don't want to be working under the hood of no white folks' car."

"How 'bout colored folks? Can you learn to work under the hood of colored folks' cars? Or is it just white folks you worried about?"

Lamb looked up at Momma. Her voice had changed the way it did when she's had enough.

I sat quiet. Talking to Momma always made me wonder what kind of momma didn't want something more for hers. Something better.

"Is that what you want? For me to work with my hands?" I asked her.

Now Momma was quiet. Beating at cornmeal batter like she was beating a rug out on the line. Hush puppies were gonna be hard as shoe leather tonight with all that beating.

"I don't want you to get your hopes up, that's what I want."

Lamb stood up.

"Momma—" She knew Momma was about to say something that was going to make it another one of those nights that stretched a few words into a long fight.

"Nah, Lamb, sit down. Momma wants to tell me how I shouldn't have dreams. Oh, and by the way, get your apron ready. Because you are gonna spend your life behind a stove chasing after all the babies you're gonna have as a homemaker. Let's listen."

"Yeah, you better listen, Simeon. You walk round here like you ain't got to answer to nobody but yourself."

"I gotta spend my life listening to white folks, is that it? You ain't tired of that?"

Lamb didn't wait for Momma to answer. Always feeling like she had to fix things between us. Me and Momma, we our own way. I won't say it's broken, but it never has, probably never will, work quite right.

"Everybody's tired of it, Simeon," Lamb said to me, one eye looking over at Momma. "Momma just gets worried."

"Is that it, Momma?" I said directly to her back. "You're worried about me?"

Momma choked out a laugh and turned to me.

"You worried about me, Simeon? About Lamb? Or you just worried about you?"

I looked down at the table and Momma walked out of the room.

"She didn't mean that, Sim."

"We both know she did. Me wanting to do something with my life is about me being selfish." Lamb went back to her book. I sat there, drumming my fingers, looking at the part running down the middle of her head. When me and Momma fought each other, it always felt like Lamb was the one who got hit the worst.

"What you working on?" I asked her. Hoping to change the subject just to get her smiling again.

"I got it, Sim…" She sighed. Lamb is smart, but she always has to work a little harder than I do to figure things out. I help her as much as I can, hoping to get her grades up, but I want, no, need her to help herself too, for when I'm gone and can't help. With just her and Momma, I'm already worried Momma is gonna try to keep her home from school to help her with her sewing. Lamb won't say no.

I leaned over the table. "Let me see what you got…"

"I said I'm fine," she said, as mean as she could. Felt like she slapped me. I sat down.

"I was hungry," she said, looking at me.

I tilted my head.

"Momma was making dinner, and now we can't eat."

"You could miss a meal, Lamb." Said it joking but that wasn't how Lamb took it. I could see her eyes fill. "I'm playing, La—"

She stood up and closed her book.

"Then I'll just take my big self to my room. I know Momma's hard, Simeon, but maybe she's right about one thing. Maybe you are always just thinking about you."

I remembered feeling like she'd slapped me again.

LAMB

ONLY when I heard Momma leave for work, and Simeon's door close telling me he was getting ready to head out too, did I make myself get out of bed. Momma came in this morning again and sat down on the chair in my room and pulled it close to my bed. I felt her smoothing the bedcovers and she let her hand rest on top of mine. I kept breathing slow and steady, hoping she'd hear my heavy breathing and leave again like she had been doing for the past week. But this morning she stayed put and rested her hand on my head. She started whispering quiet to herself, "Lord, please...please heal her, Lord..."

I opened my eyes. "Momma?" My momma stopped her praying. My momma ain't one for prayers unless she was in church and Reverend Greer asked the congregation to bow their heads.

Momma was quiet again and looking down at me. The skin around her eyes was dark and wrinkled and her lips were dry.

"Hey, baby," she said soft. "You feeling any better?"

I nodded.

"I made you some toast," Momma said. "You wanna try to eat something?"

I was about to tell her I still didn't think I could hold down any food but then I looked again at her face. "I think so," I said.

She smiled a little. "Myrtle said she gonna drop off her sweet potato pie tonight. She said ain't no way you gonna say no to that." Momma rubbed my arm.

If Momma was letting Myrtle come by during the week to drop off a pie for me, I knew she was scared. "Thinking maybe I should call Dr. Prescott to come by and see you tomorrow," she said. Momma never had one kind thing to say about Dr. Prescott. Thought he was one of those high yellah doctors who just wanted colored folks' money.

"No, Momma, I'm starting to feel better." I sat up. She looked in my eyes. Trying to see if I was telling her the truth. She thought I was.

Momma patted my arm soft. "All right then. Imma head on to work. Simeon's about to head out too. I'll be back early today. I told Mrs. Rowland you weren't feeling well."

Momma's voice sounded far away, and I wasn't sure how long I could keep sitting up trying to look like I was feeling good. Finally Momma stood up.

"Toast is on the stove," she said before she left. I smiled one last time and closed my eyes and went back to sleep soon as I heard the front door close. I was too tired to eat or talk to Momma or Simeon. I wished I was too tired to think about Marny and George. I could still feel his hands, baby soft, like he never did an honest day's work in his life, reaching down the front of my dress and under my brassiere. Squeezing me so hard I could still see the marks his hands left. And I could hear him laughing when he pushed his hand between my legs.

"Awww, don't go acting all innocent on me now," he said. "I know how you colored girls are."

We colored girls? I barely had time to think before he was on me again. I ain't never been with one boy in my life. Not that I didn't wonder what it would feel like to kiss and do the things I sometimes heard the girls at my school talk about. There were boys I liked. Who I wished would like me back and ask me out on a date. But it seemed like none of them ever even noticed me. And now here was George Tremper breathing heavy, his lips all over my face and my neck, telling me he knew all about me because I was colored? As if colored girls would want him. When he finally got tired of me fighting and crying, he shoved my head against the door, shouting, "Fine then! Niggers, white girls, y'all just the same. A bunch of teases." He sat up and zipped up his pants. The truck took off so fast I hung on to the door handle and closed my eyes as he was driving, listening to him curse me under his breath. He slammed on the brake blocks from my house and I opened my eyes.

"Get out!" he yelled, just about throwing me out his truck like I was garbage he was tossing onto a heap. He flung my purse out the window and everything fell out onto the road. "And you best stay away from my sister, you hear? I see you two together again, imma finish what we started tonight." He flung his hair back again out of his eyes.

Before I could even stand up he was speeding down the street, his radio blasting. I wiped the dirt off my dress as good as I could before I got home and brushed up my hair. My behind was still sore from when I fell out of the truck. And in between my legs...I started crying again. I reached down and touched myself soft. It was still sore where George tried to shove his fingers. *What kind of girl did he think wants that?* I wished I could have hurt him back. My head started pounding and I squeezed my eyes closed tight.

Because Momma was coming home early, I knew I had to get up and look like I was really feeling better. My nightclothes were sticking to me and I could smell myself. I couldn't remember if I'd taken a bath since I'd gotten home that night with George, so I made my way to the bathroom holding on to the wall. Looking into the mirror, I could see why Momma was praying. My skin looked yellow. Not the high yellah Momma called people with light skin, but the yellow that looked like

I was getting ready to die. But it didn't surprise me none, because I felt like couldn't nothing bring me back to life. I turned on the bath faucet mostly hot and sat at the edge of the tub just staring into the water. For the past few nights when I laid in bed I could hear Momma and Simeon in the kitchen without me. It was the first time they weren't fussing at each other. Both of them were quieter, most times all I could hear was the sounds of their forks hitting their plates. Momma was worried about what she thought she knew, and Simeon I suppose was worried about what I told him. I was wishing now I hadn't said anything about George Tremper. In one month, Simeon would be off to college and he never would have had to know anything about some white boy he couldn't do nothing about. And probably all he was thinking was that I was so stupid to get in that truck and become friends with Marny and it was all my fault anyhow.

I turned off the faucet, took off my nightgown, and got into the tub, feeling the water burn me as I sat down. I pulled up my legs and laid my head against my knees. Even with no one home it felt like about a hundred voices in my head all talking at once. But the loudest was my daddy's saying, *This don't seem safe.* Was this what my daddy meant? I didn't bother washing. Just sat until I could feel the water getting cold. In the cooling water, I closed my eyes, but it didn't stop the tears from coming, wishing I had listened to Simeon, to my daddy, anybody but me.

MARION

NEVER had no one I could tell something to and trust they'd keep it. But Simeon and Lamb been telling each other damn near everything since they were little, sometimes up half the night whispering. There was a time I'd get to wondering what they could tell each other they thought they couldn't tell me and then I thought about my own brothers, wishing I had what they did, and I left it alone. So when I sat at the kitchen table fretting about Lamb over dinner, wondering if this sickness was going to stay or pass, and asked Simeon if I should call on Dr. Prescott, I looked at him, hoping I could see in him one of the secrets he knew. But Simeon barely answered. Went right on eating. Simeon was always someone who could look me dead in my eye, tell me a lie, and not even blink. But tonight he was quiet. Told me not to bother with calling Dr. Prescott. "She'll be all right," he said. Never had a problem looking at me and telling me a lie before, but tonight I noticed, Simeon wasn't looking at me at all.

SIMEON

I couldn't wait much longer. Being home with Momma, with Lamb, thinking every day about George Tremper walking around Jackson like he owned it, was eating me up inside. Lamb could barely get out of bed. At night and sometimes early in the morning before the sun was even up, I'd go in and check on her and it looked like she hadn't moved since the day she told me what he did to her. He never choked the life out of her, I couldn't see no marks, but you could see Lamb wasn't going to be Lamb again. He killed her in his own way. Even Momma could see it.

"You think I need to have Dr. Prescott come and see about your sister?" she asked me one night. I could count on one hand the number of times Momma asked me what I thought about anything. I wasn't sure how to answer.

"Think she's going to be all right," I said, afraid to say more.

Momma waited, then said, "You and your sister a lot like me, never sick a day in your life. This ain't like Lamb." Momma shook her head.

I kept looking at my plate. Stabbing at my dinner with my fork and thinking the time was now. I got to go take care of George.

CHIME

SIMEON had me sitting up all day and night in bed thinking. Thinking I should get on over there and talk to Marion. Thinking it was my job to take care of this problem with that Tremper boy on my own. Thinking maybe Simeon was right about that gun. Thinking ain't no way I'm going back to Parchman. Thinking Lamb may be 'bout the only thing worth going back to Parchman for. All that thinking did was take me round in circles. There was a time my mind would have been made up before I was out the door. But I got more to lose now. Being on the outside, with Marion, Simeon, and Lamb, my family. I can't lose them over some white boy. Nah, I got to think careful. If Imma do this right, I got to think smarter even than Simeon.

SIMEON

MOMMA looked like Lazarus hisself had risen from the dead and come to the table for breakfast when Lamb walked into the kitchen.

"Lamb baby, you're up?" she said, rushing over to feel her forehead.

"Yup," Lamb said, sitting down. "Must have been Myrtle's pie."

"Thank you, Jesus," Momma said quiet, and I looked over at Lamb, not believing that was our momma thanking the Lord. Lamb didn't look at me.

"Simeon, it ain't like you to be this quiet. You ain't got nothing to say to your sister?" Momma said to me.

"I'm just beholding the Lord's miracle, Momma," I said, smiling again at Lamb. She barely smiled back. "Good to see you, sister," I said soft, just to her.

She looked back to Momma. "Can I have some toast?"

With Momma making toast I looked at Lamb, looking at her hands in her lap. I reached over and touched her arm. She jumped.

"Simeon, you working today?" Momma asked me. I pulled my hand back from Lamb.

"Yeah. I've gotta work late again," I told her.

"They don't got nobody else working there? Seeing your sister is feeling better"—she turned and smiled at Lamb—"I thought we'd have a little celebration dinner tonight."

"Oh, Momma, you don't have to do that," Lamb said. "I don't even know how much I can eat yet."

"Yeah, and I'm not sure what time I'm gonna get off. I only got a month before I leave and, well, you know…I need to have as much money as I can."

I didn't know what Momma hated more, me talking about my leaving or college. She was quiet for a minute.

"You don't have enough for that school yet?" she asked. I could hear the way her voice changed.

"School is all covered by the scholarship, but I'll need money for books, and traveling, some food. Of course, I'm hoping to get work there…." I could hear her breathe out heavy.

"So there ain't no schools near Jackson you could go to…?"

"Momma, we been through this before. I don't want to go to school in Mississippi. Wilberforce is a great school for Negroes. Besides, living in Ohio means I don't have to—"

"Yeah, I know, Simeon. You free from slavery," Momma said, shaking her head.

"Well, yes. There's that," I said.

Lamb stood up. "My head hurts," she said. "I'm going to go lie down."

Momma looked at me. Me and Momma don't agree on much but we both know that with the two of us fussing at each other, we aren't helping Lamb feel much better.

CHESTER

I waited all week for Lamb to come by my job. I told Velma to make other plans hoping Lamb would stop by my place after work. But she never showed. I ran over in my head the last time we talked. In the car when I drove her home, she kissed me on my cheek, thanked me. I couldn't lose my baby girl again. Funny I almost got used to being without her all these years, and now I didn't think my heart could ache this bad after just a week without seeing her, hearing her call me *Daddy* again.

I got in the car and drove past the house one more time, just like I'd been doing every day this week. I don't know what I was looking for exactly. Maybe wishing I'd see her on her way out and I could talk to her, but I didn't see nobody outside. Couple of days ago I drove past just as Marion was leaving for work. I'd seen her here and there through the years. We always nodded hello, never more than that. Marion always been one to keep herself up. Not fancy, but well kept. But this morning when I saw Marion leaving out the house, she looked more tired than I'd ever seen her. I knew then something wasn't right, I just didn't know what.

SIMEON

I emptied my satchel on my bed and pulled it on. Before I left for work, I stopped by Lamb's room. She was in bed, on her side staring at the wall.

"How you feeling?" I asked her. She didn't answer.

"I know you're tired of me and Momma's fussing sometimes," I told her.

She breathed in deep. "Sometimes?" she said, turning so she was lying on her back looking at the ceiling. "How 'bout all the time?"

"Okay, all the time," I laughed. "I'm sorry about that. Especially with everything you're dealing with."

"I'm fine, Simeon," she said low.

I walked over to her bed. "No you ain't fine, Lamb. And you probably never will be because of what George went and did to you." She put one hand over her eyes and started crying. I bent down to her, careful not to touch her. "You ain't got to worry about George no more," I whispered. "He's not going to hurt you again." I stood up, walked to the door.

"Simeon?"

When I turned Lamb was sitting up in bed, her hair sticking up every which way.

"You ain't gonna do something, are you? You can't—that would be stupid, Simeon. We got to leave well enough alone. Forget about those Trempers and get on with our lives." She looked scared now.

I smiled at her. "Go on back to sleep, Lamb. Don't I always make sure things work out for us?"

"But Sim—" she started.

"Well, I'm gonna do that again."

I closed the door behind me.

SIMEON

I took my time looking at the shelves of wedges and axes, sockets and cement. I don't care how many shop classes they made me take, I didn't think I'd ever know what half these things were for. Or why you needed five sizes for every single bolt and screw. There were times I thought about my daddy. Wondered what would make him leave and never come back. Wondered what our life would have been like if he'd stayed. Standing here now in this store made me bet I'd know most of what these things were if I had a daddy to show me instead of a momma who sewed and knew more about fabric and needles than hammers and nails. I made my way down another aisle till I found what I was looking for. At the counter the clerk barely looked at me as he was ringing me up.

"You need any nails, son?" he asked.

"Excuse me, sir?" I asked him, polite as I could.

"You don't need no nails?" he said again louder, looking up at me now.

"No sir, thank you sir, just this is all I need today." I pushed my money across the counter so I wouldn't have to put it in his hand.

He put it in a bag and handed it to me. Outside, I crumpled up the bag and threw it on the sidewalk. Slipped the hammer right into my satchel and headed on to work.

LAMB

My head was pounding so loud it made it hard to think straight. What was Simeon talking about? How could he make things work for us? I tried to remember how much I told him. I knew I told him about George's truck. But did I tell him anything else? Where George went to school? Where they lived? I had a bad feeling starting inside me that the smartest person I knew was about to do something only a fool would.

CHIME

THE only right thing to do was to tell Marion. She's their momma and she got to know. Knowing what to do set my head right. In the morning, I'd catch her on her way to work. Tell her what Simeon told me. But I wouldn't tell her the rest. About how I was going to make that boy pay for what he did to Lamb. She didn't need to know that. I'd take care of business and head out of town for a bit. Come back when things settled down. I know Simeon worried on his sister, but there ain't no sense in Lamb going through this without another woman to talk to. Marion is tough as a man, but she's all the woman Lamb has.

SIMEON

IT was a good thing it was busy at work because I would have had a hard time not thinking about George Tremper. How by the end of the day I was going to make him pay for what he did to Lamb. Not the way he should pay. But enough that I could feel good I did something. We're in church every single Sunday of the year, and I trust in the good Lord's providence, as Reverend Greer likes to say, but I'm gonna have to trust too that he's gonna right this wrong and do what I can't. I smiled thinking about George crashing his truck into a tree. Coming down with one of those bad cases of polio that would leave him so infirmed, he walked all stiff and slow like President Roosevelt. Maybe he…anyhow, I was gonna do all I could do to make his life a little less pleasant in the here and now.

I changed out of my work uniform, back into my clothes, and grabbed my satchel. I took my time because I needed the dark if I was going to be walking on the white side of town without any business there. Back at home, I'd already memorized the map of the neighborhood where the Trempers lived, and it was a fair walk. I was guessing three miles at least from downtown. I walked fast, so I'd be there easy in an hour, maybe less. Made me think of me and Lamb walking to school and her always complaining about me leaving her behind. Her short, chubby legs trying to keep up.

"You trying to be Jesse Owens or something, Simeon?" she'd ask me, out of breath. Course I never said anything about her legs being too short or too big to keep up. She would have bust out crying. But it made me smile to see her face red and sweaty those mornings, till I had to finally slow down.

"Good thing we brought lunch. Slow as you're walking, we gonna barely make it to school before last period," I'd tell her.

As much as I was aching to get to Ohio and Wilberforce and start a whole new life, leaving Jackson far behind, I couldn't imagine one without Lamb. She is so much a part of me. I've been dreaming and planning with her for so long, I wonder if I can dream without her by my side, telling me anything was possible.

I turned a corner and looked again at the street signs, trying to remember if I was going the right way. There weren't many cars on the street, and I had to look like I knew where I was going, like I belonged there. I wished now I kept the bag the hammer came in so I could pretend to be making a delivery, the only reason I should be in that white neighborhood. I didn't know what I'd say if someone stopped me and asked me where I was going. I knew I should have planned better, but I didn't have the time. This had to get done. Yup, this was the right way. I looked at my watch and could see I was making real good time. But then I starting thinking, suppose George wasn't even home and I came all this way for nothing? Would I have to come back again?

With the light getting dim, I had to walk right up on the street signs before I could read their names. The satchel started feeling heavy and there were street names I didn't know at all. I stopped and dug inside the satchel for the map I brought along. I heard a door open across the street and an old woman came onto her screened porch and sat down. She looked up and saw me standing on the corner and stood up fast. I smiled, nodded my head to look like I belonged. *Look relaxed*, I said to myself. I was showing I was a respectable Negro in her neighborhood for a reason. She frowned at me and went back inside.

I knew I needed to move quick before she went and told her husband or neighbors that a nigger was roaming the streets waiting to rob, rape, and murder them all. Somehow the idea made me laugh. Here was George just around the corner, trying to rape young girls, and his neighbors probably thought he was a fine, upstanding young man. I did a Jesse Owens walk over to the next block, looked at my map again while I was walking, and kept on until I found Alta Woods Boulevard and made a left turn onto Merigold Drive.

I heard a car coming and I stepped out of sight behind bushes and ducked down low. I could hear the car driving slow, stopping every now and again like it was looking for something. Or someone. As it was passing, I poked my head out and saw a big black car with two white men in the front seat. One had his arm hanging out the window and he was looking up and down the street. I knew then, they were looking for me.

LAMB

I waited until I heard the front door close. Momma always went straight to the kitchen to make a cup of coffee. She didn't hear me come in behind her.

"Momma," I said. I had to say it a second time before she turned around.

"I didn't hear you, Lamb. How you doing?" she said, taking out her coffee cup and setting it on the table.

"Momma...I think Simeon may be in trouble." Her face looked like it folded in two.

"Trouble? What kind of trouble?"

"Momma." I took a deep breath and sat down. "I gotta tell you something."

SIMEON

I found out quick, there wasn't no easy way to hammer soft. Especially when you ain't hammering to build but hammering to break. Trying to hide from those white men in the car and cutting through two backyards landed me right on the Trempers' street. Pinecrest Circle. I had to walk up one side and then down the other before I saw it. A blue Dodge pickup truck, sitting right in the driveway just like Lamb said.

But my mind started telling me all kinds of things. How did I know this was George's pickup truck? And just as soon as my brain started making me wonder what I was doing there, little Miss *Hi, I'm Marny* walked past the window. I wouldn't have even noticed if it wasn't for that bright red hair. *The good Lord's providence.* It was like he was telling me exactly where I was supposed to be.

I crouched down low and ran over to the driver side of the truck, pulled the door handle. *Creak.* It opened. I had to climb up a bit, but I was in. I eased the door shut behind me. I could smell him in there. Cigarettes. Leather. Gasoline. Spoiled. *Lamb.* I took out the hammer and got started. First with the knobs on the radio. *Tap tap.* Nah, that wasn't going to do it. I started banging harder till the knobs fell off in pieces.

I saw Lamb that night she came home. Heard her talking about his singing when he shoved his hands down her dress and I banged as hard as I could. *Crack.* Between the radio breaking and the loud hammering, I never even heard the passenger side door open.

MARION

I couldn't hear nothing Lamb was saying. After her telling me about that white boy I was watching her lips moving and seeing the water run down her face, but all I was doing was thinking, not listening. Thinking all these years of trying to keep her safe was for nothing. Trying to keep Simeon in line 'fore these white folks found a way to do it for him was for nothing. Turns out there ain't nothing a colored momma can do to keep her children safe. 'Cause here was my baby, my Lamb, in a truck with some cracker all on top of her pulling at her dress and panties.

And I knew exactly why Simeon was 'bout to give up everything he worked for to try to make it right. I ain't never been prouder of my boy. But I didn't want him sacrificing himself for that trash. Trash was just what he was. With trash for a daddy. Probably his momma too. I knew it the second I walked in Dr. Tremper's office. Called himself a doctor, like that made him respectable. But I could see in his eyes he was using that doctor name and letter from the school that gave it to him all prettied up in a frame to make him feel like something he wasn't. Liquor on his breath and looking at me and every other colored person in that office like he was better. Took Simeon to take that smile off his face when he spelled out his name proud.

Course it was trash that gone and did this to my baby. Thank you sweet Jesus he didn't finish what he started. I wouldn't be surprised if his daughter, Manny I think Lamb called her, had a hand in it too. Friends? I don't trust white folks far as I can throw 'em. But Lamb never learned that. If she had, we wouldn't be sitting here now mixed up in white folks' mess.

"What are we gonna do, Momma?" Lamb was asking me.

What are we gonna do? What else could we do but wait. And pray Simeon got as much sense as I hope he does.

SIMEON

"**WHAT** the hell you doing, boy!"

My arm jerked where his hands were pulling, and I turned to see Dr. Tremper's red face beside me.

"I—I—I—" I couldn't breathe.

His hands reached up to grab my neck. "You nig—" I didn't think his face could get any redder, but it did. I didn't understand how everything was happening so fast. How I didn't hear him opening the door of the truck. Where did he come from? He was screaming out loud now and it took me a minute to recognize the name. He was yelling for George.

"Get off me!" I kicked at him, and he squeezed my neck tighter.

"George! George!" he screamed. "Get out here!"

He let go of my neck with one hand and reached over to press down on the horn. Held it long. I could smell his breath on me. He pushed me back and my head hit the window. I slid down onto the seat. He was laying flat on me now. I couldn't move. I looked up at the roof of the car and for one second I wondered if this what Lamb felt like when George was on top of her breathing heavy. I could feel tears starting just like I bet she did.

I heard a door to a house open outside. Soon there would be two of them on me. My hand holding the hammer reached up and hit Dr. Tremper's head. Hard. He fell to the side. He looked at me first mad, then confused.

"Nig…ger," he said, staring right into my eyes. He fell sideways off of me, holding his head. I saw blood coming through his fingers. I let the hammer drop. I pushed him off of me and grabbed my satchel, hopping down out the truck. I saw someone rushing down the front steps. I didn't have time to see if it was George because I ran. Like Jesse Owens.

LAMB

MOMMA said there wasn't nothing we could do but wait. But how's waiting going to help Simeon? I sat with Momma in the kitchen, the two of us quiet at the table listening close to every sound outside, hoping it was Simeon's whistling coming down the street or Simeon's feet walking up to the house, till finally I got up and told her I was going to my room. Momma looked over at the clock and nodded her head but stayed sitting still.

I pulled on my sweater and sat on the edge of my bed waiting to hear her move from the kitchen. Hoping she'd at least go into the parlor or be so tired she'd go lie down in her room. Only thing I was going to wait on was for the right time to head out the back door and try to find out for myself if my brother was safe.

SIMEON

I didn't have time to think about which way was the right way to run, I just had to get away quick. I saw house lights on I didn't see before, and I wasn't sure if that was because of Dr. Tremper's screaming or because it was full-on dark now. I ran back across the street the way I came. Back through those two yards I crossed through, hoping no one happened to be looking out their window. I ran without stopping. Without thinking where I was going. I was sure the sound of my own feet slapping through leaves, mud, cement, dirt was going to lead those Trempers right to me, but every time I turned around, all I saw was the dark.

I tried to figure out which way was east. I knew that was the direction I should be headed. But first I had to keep moving to get out of this side of town. A back door opened, and a man stepped out onto his porch with a cigarette. I stopped short and then ran a few steps and crouched down behind a bush at the edge of the yard.

"Who's there?" he shouted. I heard him walk down the steps and into the yard.

"Who are you talking to?" his wife yelled from inside the house. I could hear their radio playing.

"Thought I heard—"

"Oh, you always think you're hearing something. C'mon now, the commercials are ending," she said. He flicked his cigarette. I waited till I heard the door slam behind him till I got up and kept on running. Over his fence and then the next. I had good practice jumping fences. I jumped the one in my own backyard all the time, trying to teach Lamb how easy it was. I needed to hurry to get anywhere away from this neighborhood, that black Buick, Dr. Tremper and George, and most likely now, the law. My satchel was banging up against my back as I ran and it got caught as I was climbing the last fence.

When my body was pulled backwards I was sure it was Dr. Tremper's hands pulling me back, reaching for my neck. I started to scream out, then stopped myself. It took me longer than I wanted to unhook my satchel from the fence because between the dark, my hands shaking, and now my crying, I could barely see where it was caught. *I'm a murderer.*

I could see Dr. Tremper's face over mine. He would have killed me without thinking if he could have just for breaking his son's radio. I was nothing to him I knew. I was just trying to get him off of me.

Up ahead I could see the lights of the hotel and beyond that was home. I should have felt safe. But I knew the second that hammer hit Dr. Tremper's head, I never would feel safe again.

CHIME

I went to sleep thinking about Simeon and woke up hearing his voice.

"Uncle Chime!" I heard knocking on my door. "Uncle Chime, it's me!"

I laid there in my bed thinking, one, I had to be dreaming because two, my landlady would never let Simeon up to my room making all that racket. But when the knocking didn't stop, I got up, opened the door to make sure I wasn't hearing things, and there he was. Looking like a drowned rat.

I pulled him in quick and closed the door behind him, but I knew right away that Simeon at my door meant that the plan I had before I went to bed wasn't going to be the plan I had now.

LAMB

I heard the kitchen chair scrape and the faucet turn on and knew Momma was washing out her coffee cup. She was going to bed. I turned out my lamp. I figured I would start first downtown at Simeon's job to see if he was there. Maybe he really was working late tonight. And if he wasn't there, I could check at the diner where he and his friend Kirk always met and tried to talk to girls. Simeon never seemed to have much luck, but Kirk always did. Kirk ran track for our high school and the girls always said he was handsome. He even tried to get Simeon to join the track team. He was sure fast enough, but Simeon wondered why he would waste his time running around a track when he had studying to do.

"Girls," Kirk told him.

Simeon said he wanted a lady who could appreciate an "intellectual." I'd seen Simeon around girls at school, and he either talked them half to death or didn't say much at all. I know it's selfish, but there are times I'm grateful he doesn't have a girlfriend, because it means he has more time to spend with me. I wasn't sure where I'd go if he wasn't at those two places. I heard the faucet stop running, and I stood up, listening close to hear Momma's bedroom door closing. Instead my bedroom door opened wide. Momma stood in the doorway looking at me in my sweater.

"I was coming to check in on you," she said. "Where do you think you're going?"

SIMEON

"**Uncle** Chime, you gotta help me—" I could barely breathe.

Uncle Chime was looking at me like he didn't know who I was.

"Uncle Chime, you hear me? I'm in trouble! I—I—I killed—"

"Boy, shut your mouth," he said close to my face, pushing me against a wall. "How did you get up here? Did my landlady see you?"

"Yeah. I told her something happened to my momma and I needed your help. She said to go right up."

"Anyone else see you?" he asked.

"Uncle Chime, what difference does that make? I'm trying to tell you—I need your help. I kill—"

"And I told you to shut your mouth." He looked around his room. Went to a corner and looked under some boxes. Then came back and pulled a suitcase from under his bed. "Talk soft while I pack," he said.

"Pack? Where are you going?" I asked him.

"If you ain't the dumbest—where am *I* going? Where are *we* going? We got to get out of here quick. Now what happened? You kill that white boy?"

"Not him. His daddy."

"His daddy?" Uncle Chime shook his head. He looked like he couldn't decide whether to laugh or whup me. He was packing his things in his suitcase but never looked at me, never raised his voice.

"Did you hear what I said?" I asked him. "I killed someone. I didn't mean to. I just went to—" I sat in the chair. I couldn't talk now. My throat was so dry, and my head was pounding.

"We ain't got time for all that," Uncle Chime said. "What's done is done. Grab my car keys." He pointed to the keys on top of some newspapers on the table.

Uncle Chime started pulling on clothes. "Imma tell you this," he said. "When I tell you to let me handle something, I mean let me handle it. You done got yourself in a mess. And if we're lucky, imma help you get out of it. Now get those keys and from here on out you listen to me."

I wiped my face and picked up the keys.

"But where—"

Uncle Chime shook his head. Put his finger to his lips. *No questions.*

He closed his suitcase and lifted it off the bed. Grabbed the sheets and blanket too. I followed him out the door and down the stairs. Quiet.

MARION

I waited, making sure she was sleeping good, then figured I'd head out, maybe see what Chime could find out. I almost had to laugh when I opened her door, seeing Lamb there. Thinking about Lamb out at night checking on Simeon. What was she gonna do? Lamb surprised me more today than she had since she was born. Friends with a white girl? That she been meeting every week in secret? She's 'bout the only person in this world I think was born good through and through.

But I was coming to find the ways I thought I knew her ain't what I thought at all. She's still good but she's got more of her own mind than I ever thought she did. And she's less afraid than I ever thought she could be. Maybe Lamb didn't need me and Simeon as much as I thought she did. Maybe she waited for the right time to let me know.

"We got to be patient, Lamb. Trust that he's gonna be okay." I told her to go on to bed, then I closed her door and turned in too.

SIMEON

WE made it out of the boarding house without his landlady seeing us. Then around the block where Uncle Chime kept his car. His car had seen better days. It was an old Chevrolet, but he always says it gets him where he needs to go. He keeps her clean, though. Shines her up every week. "She been good to me, better than most women I had," he always tells me.

While he opened the trunk first to put his suitcase in, I stood at the passenger side. Uncle Chime shook his head *No*. Pointed to the back seat.

"The back seat?" I asked him. I was wearing on Uncle Chime's nerves, I could tell, but he opened the back door and laid down the blanket he brought from his room on the floor of the back seat. I groaned but I laid down and he covered me with the sheets.

"Just till we get to the house, right?" I asked him. He didn't answer me. I didn't know how I was gonna tell Momma, or Lamb, what happened. They had to understand it was an accident. I'd never kill someone on purpose. I could hear Momma now yelling that she told me so. "Guess you ain't so high and mighty now," I supposed she'd say. And she'd be right, because here I was lying on a blanket in the back of Uncle Chime's car. Hiding. From the police, the Trempers, and anybody else who was looking to make me pay for what I did.

Uncle Chime was driving slower than I ever seen him drive before. He turned the radio on low and all I could think of was George and me and Lamb. Everything I ever wanted gone now because of a radio. The road turned bumpy and I could hear the gravel underneath.

"Where we going, Uncle Chime? This ain't the way to the house."

He turned down the radio. "You been saving up for that school you going to, right?" he asked me.

"Yes, of course. But what does that have to do—"

"I'm asking. You answering," he said. "That money at the house?"

"Yes."

"Your sister know where to find it?"

"Yes."

The car stopped and I heard him put it in park. "Good. Now you gonna stay here. And when I say stay here, that means your ass stays here. You don't move from under this blanket, you hear? I'll be back soon as I can."

Before I could ask another question, I heard the car door slam and Uncle Chime's feet walking away on the gravel.

LAMB

THE sound came from the back near the kitchen. Sounded like a *thump* but before I could even get out of bed, my door swung open and Momma came in, whispering, "Stay here, Lamb. Don't move."

I turned on my lamp and waited.

I heard some more scuffling and looked around for something heavy to pick up to follow Momma into the kitchen. I didn't know what I was supposed to do if someone came into our house to steal something. Go run for help I suppose, but what if Momma was hurt? Did I stay with her? All I had in my room were lamps and books, my purse. I grabbed my purse off the chair and walked quiet to the kitchen. In the almost dark I could see Momma standing in front of a man. Whispering. Crying.

Uncle Chime? He reached out to hold her and she slapped him.

"You did this, Chime. You did this. You got my boy killed."

"Simeon's dead?" I screamed. I ran into the room.

Both of them turned now and Momma moved quick to grab me. Uncle Chime's hand reached for my mouth to cover it. He leaned in. "Now I'm gonna need you to be very quiet, Chop. Your brother ain't dead. He's fine. He's with Uncle Chime. We just came to get some of his things." Momma nodded at me. At what Uncle Chime was saying. I could see even in the little bit of light her face was wet.

Uncle Chime kept talking. "Now your brother said he got some money here. Said you'd know where it was. You know where your brother keep that money he been saving up for school?" His hand was still over my mouth and I looked from him to Momma back to Uncle Chime. Shook my head. *Yes*.

"Okay, good. Now I need you to go on and get it real quick for your uncle Chime, okay?" He smiled at me like everything was all right and we weren't in the dark in the kitchen at night whispering about Simeon not being dead and talking about where he hid his college money.

Uncle Chime slowly let his hand off of my mouth but kept it above my lips, maybe making sure I was gonna stay quiet. I didn't say a word. Finally he dropped his hand to his side. Momma didn't let me go but walked with her arms around me to Simeon's room.

I turned to Momma. "Where is Simeon?" I asked her. "Is he okay?"

"Simeon is fine, baby," she said. She wiped her nose, then her face with the back of her hand. She took my face in both hands. "We just got to..." She rested her forehead against mine, and I could feel her body shaking hard. Sobbing. I wrapped my arms around her tight.

"Momma? Can we see him?" I asked into her chest, but all she said was "Get his money."

I went to his bureau and pulled out the second drawer and reached all the way to the back until I felt the metal box. I pulled it out and opened it. Sitting on top was Simeon's letter from Wilberforce and underneath were stacks of bills, some rolled up tight with rubber bands. Simeon liked to show me how much he'd saved, how much more he had to go. I heard Momma behind me getting his suitcase from the closet. She came beside me and started emptying his drawers into the suitcase.

"He need any of these books?" she asked. She stood at the foot of his bed, all made up neat with a pile of books thrown in the middle like he dumped them there in a hurry.

"I don't know," I said because nothing made any sense right now. Why were we talking about books when I didn't even know what happened or where Simeon was?

Uncle Chime was at the front door, looking through a small crack. "Y'all got everything?" he said, whispering to us without turning around.

"Mmmhmm," Momma said.

He followed us into the kitchen, and I handed him the box.

"I need to see my boy," Momma said.

"Now I done told you, Marion—"

"You don't tell me nothing Chime. I want to see my—"

"Right now he's safe. But I don't know how long it's gonna be before they figure out it was Simeon knocked ole Dr. Tremper on the head with a hammer and killed him. Maybe tonight. Maybe tomorrow. Maybe never. Now I can have him come in. Y'all can have a send-off feast. But if that lynch mob shows up while y'all getting second helpings and saying your goodbyes, there ain't gonna be much I can do 'cept pick off a few of 'em while they're carrying him out of here. That what you want, Marion? Or you want me to get this boy on up to that school in Ohio he been talking about since he damn near came out your womb? You decide."

So even though Uncle Chime told us we had to hurry, he pulled out a chair, leaned back, crossed his legs, and waited for Momma to decide.

MARION

WHAT was I choosing between? Loving my boy or watching him die? Having Chime sneak him off in the middle of the night or saying all the things I should have said but didn't? That I was proud. That I loved him. That I knew he was gonna be everything he wanted to be. That he'd grown into a rightful man. I had about as much choice as my daddy did when those white men came in the night. Live or die, they were asking him then. Same as Chime was asking me now. I didn't have no choice but to let my boy go.

"Tell Simeon..." Chime and Lamb looked over at me. "Tell Simeon to be good. Study hard in school." My heart was hurting so bad, I didn't say nothing I wanted. Nothing I should have. Just what I could.

LAMB

I couldn't say how long me and Momma sat together in the dark in the parlor after Uncle Chime left. Maybe we were wishing he'd change his mind and bring Simeon back to say goodbye. I wondered if I'd ever be able to sleep again worrying about him and Uncle Chime. Wondering when I'd see him. *Simeon killed Dr. Tremper?* Momma said Uncle Chime didn't tell the whole story, just the parts he thought mattered. Simeon got caught in George's truck. Hit Dr. Tremper with a hammer. Killed him. None of it made any sense to me. Why would Simeon be in George Tremper's truck? And as hard as it was thinking about Simeon being gone, I thought too about Marny. She lost her momma and now her daddy too. I laid my head on Momma's shoulder.

"You think Simeon's going to be okay?" I asked Momma again.

"God I hope so," she said, laying her head on top of mine. "We all gonna be okay, Lamb."

And then we heard the cars.

MARION

I sat up and Lamb's head fell off my shoulder.

"Momm—"

"Sshhh," I told her, running to the front window. She was right behind me. Lined up out in front of the house were all kinds of cars. White men standing outside. Some women too. Waiting. The street was quiet. No one came out to see what was happening. Every light was turned off. I took a deep breath. *Here they are.* They always came at night. Always in a crowd.

I turned to Lamb. Smiled. "Baby," I told her. She looked so tired. All I wanted was to sit at the table with a brush and a little bit of grease and get in her hair. I smoothed it down as she looked at me. So scared.

"Lamb—imma need you to do something for me. I'm going to need you to trust me and listen to me good, okay?"

She nodded her head. Her eyes were running over with tears. I wiped them away. "We don't have time for that now," I told her. "I need you to be strong for your momma tonight. For Simeon. I need you to go."

"Go? Go where?" Her eyes were big and round.

"I need you to go out that back door, Lamb, quiet as you can. Soon as you clear of this house, I need you to run. Run, Lamb, and don't come back here. Do you understand what I'm saying to you?"

"Momma, I'm not gonna leave you here alone—"

"Lamb." I took her face in my hands. "I know what these men are here for. They ain't gonna leave till they get it. Simeon's gone and safe. I need you safe too. Please, Lamb."

I said to her then what I didn't, couldn't say to Simeon.

"I love you, Lamb. You my light, baby. Make me proud to be your momma. *Run.*"

LAMB

RUN? How was I going to run and leave Momma behind with a crowd of angry white folks?

But I lied and told her I would. Soon as I told her, Momma ran to her bedroom, and I heard her throwing things on the floor. I stayed at the window watching. Right in front of the house was George Tremper's truck. He got out, talking and laughing with some of the men. Like they were getting ready to have a good time. The passenger door of his truck opened, and George ran around and helped out an older man. *Dr. Tremper? But Dr. Tremper's dead.*

A few of the men rushed over to Dr. Tremper, shook his hand. When he turned, I saw a bandage on his head. I ran to Momma's room.

"Momma—Dr. Tremper—he's not dead! He's out there. Simeon didn't kill him. He musta just hurt him. Look!" Momma didn't move.

"You gotta go now, Lamb!" she said. "Go."

"But Dr. Tremper's not dead." I thought maybe she didn't hear me.

"It don't make no difference if he's sick, dead, or alive. Simeon hit him, Lamb. Hit a white man. That's all that matters."

I grabbed her arms. "Momma. Maybe if you tell them it was an accident…"

"Lamb, you got to go now. I got to handle this my way." I looked at her face. Calm. Like she'd been waiting on this. She walked to the front again. Holding her arm close to her side.

"Momma? Is that a—"

"Now, Lamb. Now!"

I walked fast to the back door. Looking back at my momma. I heard the pounding at the front door and watched my momma standing there ready to fight an army of white men with just herself and a gun I never even knew she had.

SIMEON

SOON as Uncle Chime left, I threw off the sheets so I could breathe. All I could hear outside was the sound of cicadas. And from where I was lying all I could see through the window was the dark of night. Not a star in the sky tonight. Lying there with the windows rolled up tight, I could smell days-old sweat and just a little bit of a woman's cheap perfume.

I didn't know what Uncle Chime was planning but I could tell there was a long way between what he thought was best for me and what I wanted to do. What I wanted was to go home. To Momma. But mostly to Lamb. To sit at the kitchen table reading the paper and arguing with Momma over what seemed like nothing now or stay up late with Lamb talking about life outside of Jackson. I wanted one more Saturday night party where I could play a round of cards, cut up on the dance floor, and watch Uncle Chime throw his arm around women while he whispered in their ears. I hated more than anything not knowing what was going to happen to me. I spent my whole life knowing what was coming next and now I didn't know anything.

I heard the sound of gravel and what sounded like running. I pulled the sheets back over my head and laid still. The door opened and Uncle

Chime climbed back in. Started up the car and started driving. When we got back on smooth road was when I felt brave enough to ask.

"Where are we going?"

"You know what, nephew?" I could tell Uncle Chime was smiling. "I heard the women in the North are even finer than these southern gals we used to. You know anything about that?" he asked me, laughing.

I didn't know what Uncle Chime was talking about. "I wouldn't know," I said. "I've never been north."

Uncle Chime put his foot on the gas and sped up. "Well, I guess we both about to find out," he said.

MARION

THEY were already at the door pounding. I waited till I heard the back door close and tried to picture in my head how long it would take for Lamb to make her way across the backyard, past the tree, and over the fence. And then I waited a little bit more. I wished we had more time, but finally I opened the door. First thing I saw was the red hair. *Just like his sister.* Taller than me, and it took all I had not to spit in his face. *George Tremper.* The boy who hurt my Lamb. He leaned his arm against the doorframe and smiled.

A policeman was standing next to him. Big fat face with his bottom lip poked out, looking around me into the house.

"Your boy Simeon Clark?" he asked me.

"Yes, that's my boy," I told him.

"I'm gonna need him to come on out here and talk to me," he said. "There was an attempted murder over on Pinecrest tonight, and we got a witness claimed your boy did it."

"He ain't here," I said to him. "Left awhile ago."

"Well now, I'm gonna need you to tell me just where he's gone," the policeman said, crossing his arms.

"Get out my way," I heard from behind George, and Dr. Tremper pushed past the policeman and stood staring at me. "We know he's in there. Bring that nigger out here."

I smiled at him. Looked at the bandage on his head. "*Simeon* ain't here."

"We know who your boy is, and trust me we gonna see to that boy. Tonight."

George Tremper shouted over his daddy's head. "My sister Marion saw him running from our house. Said, 'I think I know that boy.' Course she didn't want to say, but I got it out of her. Got her to tell us right where y'all lived too. He damn near killed our daddy after he tore apart my truck. Thank God she came out when she did, he probably would have come in and ravaged her too."

Some men from the crowd behind him started shouting.

"Why would my boy be tearing up your truck?" I asked him, looking him dead in his eyes. "He ain't got no problem with you, do he?" George Tremper looked at his daddy.

"I don't give a good goddamn who he got a problem with. Since when do y'all niggers need a reason to go around messing with white folks' property or putting your hands on a white man? I remember your son talking big in my office. We can't have that. Y'all people got to learn your place."

Our place. "Your daughter think that too?"

Dr. Tremper opened his mouth and closed it. George shouted, "My sister ain't got the sense she was born with. We told her about y'all, but she didn't want to listen. Now she knows."

The crowd started shouting again. One of them yelled, "Get that nigger!" and I looked again at George. Looked in the eyes of the boy who hurt my baby. His eyes looked to the side. He was a coward, I could see. Just like his daddy.

"Funny thing my boy would go all the way 'cross town just to mess with your truck, isn't it?" I asked him. He tried to look away, but I wouldn't let him. I wanted him to see Lamb in me.

"We done talking here," Dr. Tremper said, pushing me back.

"Slow down now," I told him, raising up my gun. "This is my house, and I got a right to protect it."

"Put it down. Now!" the policeman said, reaching to his side.

"Hold on there, Auntie," Dr. Tremper said, stretching his hands out in front of him. His son looked at me now. They both took a step back. "We just want to talk to your boy is all. Get things straightened out." He looked over at the policeman.

"And I already told you he ain't here," I said slow and steady. Pointing the gun straight at Dr. Tremper's chest.

George Tremper turned to the crowd. Shouted at them, "She got a gun!"

Before I could say another word, they were on me.

LAMB

THE screen door banged behind me as I ran out the back door, down the steps, across the yard, past the pecan tree, and was just about at the fence when I remembered. *I can't climb a fence.*

It was Simeon who always helped me over it. When Simeon would get it in his head that we'd need to go exploring or head down behind the Chasten place to pick blueberries. "C'mon, Lamb, hook your foot right here. Now pull yourself up," he'd tell me from the other side, watching me sweating and begging him for help.

"I can't, Simeon."

"Here, watch me do it again," he'd say. "I put my left foot here like this. Now you got to swing your other leg over." I wondered why sometimes he even dragged me along, but he said being with me made it more fun, even if I was slow and couldn't hop a fence.

He could jump back and forth over that fence while I couldn't get over it once. Finally, he'd just give in and end up pulling me over into the tall grass on the other side. I was always afraid there'd be snakes hiding in the grass and bushes, but after not being able to climb the fence, I stayed quiet about being scared of snakes, thinking he'd for sure leave me behind next time.

"Why can't we just walk around, Simeon?" I'd ask, out of breath from all that pulling and leg swinging.

"Too far, and not as much fun," he'd say. But it was never fun for me.

And now I'd have to climb it because I sure couldn't go around to the front. There was barely enough moonlight so I could see where to put my foot just where Simeon told me. *Now swing my other leg over.* Just like with Simeon, it didn't work.

I tried again, pulling myself up as I swung my leg. I kept a picture of Simeon in my head even though seeing him there was making my eyes blurry with water.

"Now pull yourself up," I said to myself. I wasn't moving. Between the running and the fence climbing, sweat was pouring down my back. I jumped down and dried my hands on my dress. I rubbed my sore hands together and looked back at the house. *I can't do it.* I heard shouting from inside. *Momma.* I stood waiting. Wondering what to do. I looked around the yard for a place to hide but aside from the tree, there was nowhere.

I saw the back door swing open and a group of men dragging Momma out of the house. I grabbed hold of the fence, put my foot in, breathed in, pulled myself up as hard as I could, swung my other leg over, and jumped into the grass on the other side.

MARION

NEVER intended to do no harm to those men. I might have wanted to, but I wouldn't. Just wanted to show them I wasn't scared. Wasn't gonna let no one try and make me afraid in my own home whether they had ten, twenty, or one hundred men with 'em. What I needed besides was to give Lamb more time to run.

It had been a long time since I thought about Chester. But I thought now about the day the two of us first stepped into this house he bought us. How proud we were. How happy. Our children grew strong here because of him. I hoped somewhere, somehow he knew that.

LAMB

I sure wasn't thinking about snakes when I landed in that grass. I crawled on my hands and knees to the nearest bush, hiding behind it and hoping no one could hear me. But when I heard all the whooping and shouting, I knew no one could. I knew I should get up and go, keep moving. But thinking about all those men dragging Momma out of the house made me stay.

I crawled to another bush closer to the fence. Till finally I could see everything. *Was that fire?* They were all lined up around the tree. *Waiting.*

And then, there, there in the torchlight, I saw her. Pressed in close against the others. Her face red as a fever sweat. Hair bright as a flame. My friend. *Marny.*

When the men let her go, I heard branches snapping and watched the crowd move closer. Simeon was long gone now I suspect.

Far.

North.

Safe.

From this. From them. From all of it.

I searched again for her face but I could hardly tell one from the other in this crowd. Each one looked just like the next. Smiling through shiny white teeth like a pack of hungry dogs.

A branch cracked as loud as a gunshot and the crowd cheered. I looked up through the leaves at the dark. Not a star in the sky tonight. But the flickers of gold from the embers lit up the sky in what looked like fireflies. Pretty almost.

I wished then I had just kept running like Momma told me.

MARION

THEY held my arms while one of them white boys punched me again. "You gonna tell us where your boy's at?" I felt a tooth go loose in my mouth. Smiled big at them. *Go, Simeon.*

My eyes were swolled. But not too swolled to see they had torches lit now. Like a party.

"Somebody got to pay for what your boy went and did," I heard Dr. Tremper say. "Looks like it's gonna be you, Auntie." *Run, Lamb.*

They dragged me to the tree. *Chester's pecan tree.* Could hear the back of my dress rip. That tree had grown taller, stronger, since we moved here. Like Simeon and Lamb, our babies. George Tremper stood in front of me. His daddy handed him a rope.

LAMB

I ran now. Harder, faster than I ever ran in my life. Even though it felt like someone lit a fire to my throat I didn't stop. I wanted to scream for help. But who was gonna help me? What folks were going to get mixed up with a white lynch mob? At first I was running just to get away from what I saw. But the further I ran I realized I knew just where and who I was running to.

MARION

I heard branches snapping up high around me and the crowd moved closer. Simeon got to be long gone now.

Safe.

Soon she would be too. From this. From them. From all of it. The two of them, just like they wanted.

Each one in this crowd looked just like the next. Smiling up at me through shiny white teeth. Just like a pack of hungry dogs.

I looked up through the branches at the dark. Not a star in the sky tonight. But the flickers of gold from the embers lit up the sky in what looked like fireflies. Pretty almost.

SIMEON

I didn't know how long I'd been asleep, but it couldn't have been long because it was still dark when I woke up.

"Where are we?" I asked Uncle Chime.

"Still in the great state of Mississippi," Uncle Chime said.

I sat up and all I could see was the dark behind us and the road in front of us.

"C'mon, sit up front. We got a ways to Ohio, and imma need some company."

I crawled over the seat to the front and leaned my head back. Uncle Chime looked over at me. "Are Momma and Lamb gonna be okay?" I asked him.

"You ain't got to worry about your sister. One thing I know about Marion, she gonna make sure Chop is okay, so you can rest your mind there. I know they sure wish they could have said goodbye to you, but your momma was glad you are on your way to school. Said to tell you to study hard." His hand clapped down on my knee.

I sat staring at Uncle Chime from the side. His face looking at the road now. I waited for him to say more. He turned up the radio and started bobbing his head to the music. He said Lamb was going to be just fine. But he never said nothing about my momma.

CHESTER

SHE didn't knock but once and I was already at the door. Her hair was wild, dress dripping wet. The girl just about fell in my arms. I half carried, half dragged her into my apartment, and laid her careful as I could on my bed. Brought her some water and tried to sit her up to talk. Even when she could breathe right she wasn't talking.

"Lamb, talk to me, girl. What happened?" She shook her head.

"Is it your brother?"

Her face was still red. The smell of her filled my bedroom. It was more than sweat. It was sharp. She had soiled herself.

I'd been thinking about her every day this week, knowing in my heart something wasn't right. But short of going up to the front door and knocking, asking to talk to Lamb like her little white friend did, there wasn't nothing I could do. I saw now I was wrong to have waited for the trouble to come find me.

Felt like I should get her out of her clothes into something dry, but that didn't feel right, even if I was her daddy. "Velma left some women things here—you could probably fit... I'll give you some privacy." She moved her head a little bit. *No?* Instead of her head going from side to side, it was bobbing around so I didn't quite get what her meaning was. She took another sip of water. I got up to get her a washcloth. Figured maybe I could get her to wash up. That'd help her feel better. But she reached out and grabbed my arm.

"Momma," she said in a whisper.

I leaned close to her. I was trying to think of what a daddy was supposed to say. "You want me to go and get your momma?" I asked her.

She let out a cry I don't think I ever heard before and know I didn't ever want to hear again. First I couldn't get her words. Said to her, "Say it again, Lamb?"

She looked at me and said, clear as could be, "They…hung…her."

CHESTER

I thought she wasn't thinking right.

"Hung her?" I shouted so loud, she jumped back like I hit her. I could see in her eyes, the scared there. This had to have something to do with that white friend of hers I told her was going to be nothing but trouble. She was looking at the wall but looking at nothing at all. "Lamb, you gotta tell me what happened now, so I can help."

"Can't no one help now," she said soft. Still staring at nothing.

"Where's your brother? He at the house?"

She smiled just a little. "He's gone." Made my stomach sick seeing her smile like that. *She mean gone and strung up too or gone and run off?*

"Gone where, baby?" I reached out to touch her face. I could see scratches there, it looked like from branches. *What did they do to her?*

"With Uncle Chime." *Chime mixed up in this too?* No telling then what happened to that boy. None of this made any sense. I wasn't going to get nowhere with Lamb the way she was. She let me lay her back in the bed. Cover her with my bedspread. She closed her eyes, and I sat next to her on the edge of the bed so she'd know I wasn't going nowhere. Even after I could hear she was sound asleep I stayed. And I was still sitting there when the sun finally came up.

LAMB

SOMEONE'S hands were around my neck. Squeezing tighter. I opened my mouth to scream but I couldn't. I tried again.

"Lamb?" My daddy was looking down at me. "It's me. You okay. You were just dreaming is all," he said, rubbing my arm.

What is my daddy doing here? I turned over and could feel my dress sticking to my back. It was damp like Momma took it off the wash line too early. *Momma.*

"Daddy?" I sat up quick. "I gotta go see about Momma."

Daddy grabbed my arms. "You said some things last night didn't make much sense. About your momma. About her—being…"

I laid back and covered my face. *Momma.* I closed my eyes to all the pictures in my head from last night.

"You got to tell me what happened," Daddy said.

I didn't know if I told him in order or if what I said made sense to my daddy. He wiped my face and listened close. He didn't ask questions. He held his head in his hands and stood up and looked out the window when I told him the part about those men dragging Momma out of the house toward the tree. Then sat back down.

"I gotta go back to the house. To see—to see about Momma," I told my daddy. He turned and looked at me. Shook his head no.

"Can't let you do that, Lamb," he said.

"Let me?" I said to him, just about shouting now. "Let me? She's my momma. I have to go see about her. Maybe she's still—?"

"Your momma told you to run for two reasons, Lamb. One to save your life. The other was so you would never have to see what you did.... Me and your momma know what these people do when they mad. When they scared. When they in a crowd. Hell, when they ain't got nothing to do on a Saturday night. Ain't no maybes about it. You saw right. But you gonna stay here while I go handle things from here," he said, serious as I ever heard him talk to me.

"But—" I started.

"Now, Lamb, there ain't no way around this," he said. "I don't know if they're coming for you next."

"But what about Myrtle?" I asked him. "Shouldn't I go tell Myrtle?"

"Who the hell is Myrtle?" my daddy asked.

MYRTLE

I never knew Lamb had any idea where I lived. Everything with Marion was a secret. You couldn't ask her nothing about her past. Her momma and daddy. Her husband, Chester.

"Why you always looking back?" she asked me once. "Ain't none of that matter." Like anything that happened before today didn't mean nothing to her.

But she kept us secret too. Least to Lamb. Simeon knew all about us, Marion told me once. She never told me how. Just said, "There ain't much that boy don't know."

I told her, "The way you're acting makes us feel wrong, dirty, Marion. Love ain't like that."

"Not to you it ain't," she said. "And not in here. But out there…"

She never once said the word "love" to me. But I loved her enough for the two of us. I think she only had enough in her for Simeon and Lamb. *My babies,* she called them, big as they were. I wasn't never blessed to have children of my own, but there was a time, I was hoping I could be another mother to those two. If Marion would let me. She wouldn't.

But like I told Marion, can't nothing stop you from loving.

There was only one reason Lamb would be knocking on my door

and standing in my doorway too early in the morning. She didn't need to tell me nothing.

I pulled Lamb to me. "How?" I asked her. "How?"

What she told me made me fall to my knees. She knelt down with me. Looked like we were praying together there.

I held her in my arms and told her, "You got to go, Lamb. You can't stay here."

"But Momma…"

I took her head in my hands, just like I'd seen Marion do. Like I wanted to do so many times. "I'll see to Marion," I told her. "Make sure she's buried proper. You know I will, right?"

"I know," she whispered, tears falling from her eyes, and hugged me then. Hard. We were still on our knees. Still in the doorway. I wished Marion coulda seen us. And seen how her girl cared more about love than secrets.

LAMB

My daddy was standing outside the car with his hands in his pockets when I came downstairs. He walked over to me. Put his hand around my shoulders.

"Everything all right?" he asked low, looking up at Myrtle's window. I nodded yes.

When I looked up Myrtle was there watching us. My daddy nodded at her. I don't know what he thought about her and Momma. I told him as little as I could, partly because there wasn't much I knew. But I knew they loved each other. Probably in a way folks didn't think was right. Especially folks like Earvent and her momma. But I knew too that they were happy together. Happier I suppose than my momma was with my daddy.

Your momma didn't want no husband, my daddy said when I first went to visit him. My momma wanted to be loved, I knew now, she just didn't need a husband to do it. Myrtle suited her just fine. I raised my hand to the window, but Myrtle was gone.

"We got to go," Daddy said, walking fast to the driver side. But in the car, he didn't put in the keys. He turned and looked at me.

"I been thinking," he said. He cleared his throat. "'Bout what your momma would have wanted."

"What Momma would have wanted?" I asked him. *How would my daddy know what Momma would have wanted?*

"Now I can see on your face—listen here." Daddy leaned closer to me. "I know this. Your momma would've wanted you and your brother to be together. Safe. Mattered to her the two of you grew up taking care of each other. And now...now that she's gone..." He looked at me. His eyes were filled up.

I nodded. Reached out my hand to his. His hands were so rough and chapped and I remembered he worked at the lumberyard. Before that he was working a farm. I looked down and rubbed my hands over his. "Simeon's all the way in Ohio now," I said to him. "At school."

"So, that's what I wanted to talk to you about," Daddy said. "I spent my whole life in Mississippi. Was born here, figured I'd be buried here too. Back in Shubuta right 'longside my mamma and pappy." He smiled a little bit at that. Daddy looked like he was having a hard time saying what he wanted to say.

"Myrtle said she's gonna see to it that Momma is buried proper," I told him. "But I don't know where..." I could feel myself starting up crying again.

Daddy spoke up fast, like he had to get his words out quick. "I never figured on going north, but I want to take you on up to Ohio. To be with your brother. We'd all be together. As a family."

I looked long at my daddy. The car was getting warm with the windows rolled up. Wasn't no one on the street this early in the morning. "Leave Jackson? But you got your job here. Velma..."

"I didn't say it was gonna be easy," Daddy said. "But it gotta be done."

"Why can't I stay here? With you?" I asked him.

Daddy laughed to himself. Shook his head. "Here? You waiting for them to come for you next? You want to walk around this town seeing

George Tremper and his daddy? Watching the men who done this to your momma walking round free as a bird? They ain't never gonna have to pay. Only one paying is you."

What would Momma want? I asked myself sitting there in Daddy's car. I knew she wanted me to stay close to her. But I knew more than that, she wanted me to follow my own mind. Not hers and sure not Simeon's. To be the kind of woman she raised me to be, who could stand up for myself and say exactly what I wanted.

CHESTER

I drove slow as I could. But wasn't no putting off what needed to be done. I had to go and see what they did to Marion. Was a part of me wishing like Lamb, that maybe Marion was fine after all. They roughed her up some, but she was at the house, waiting on Lamb, mad as hell, looking for a fight. But I knew. Just like Lamb knew. And so I took my time, taking the long way to Barrett to the house I bought going on eighteen years ago.

Down the road from the house, I pulled over and parked. "Imma walk down to the house and go round back. You going to have to stay here, out of sight. You hear me?"

Lamb started to talk, but I stopped her.

"The way they did your momma ain't nothing you likely to forget. Go to sleep at night, it's all you gonna see of your momma till you older than me. That what you want?"

I knew I was talking hard, but it was the only way I could think to keep her in the car.

I opened the glove box, took out my pocketknife.

"What's that for?" she asked me.

"Stay in the car," I said again.

I walked slow up the road toward the house, looking back at the car to make sure Lamb stayed put and wondering if anyone still lived there I knew from when I bought the house. I passed by an old white house with peeling paint. Mrs. Grover had to be dead and buried by now, I thought when I passed her house. I walked faster and saw someone looking out the window. A woman across the street came out on the porch, her husband and children came too, and stood beside her. Watching me walk. Other neighbors came out onto the porch, watching me as I got to the house. One looked down at his shoes.

It was quiet. No cars, no people were in front of the house. I stopped and looked back again at my car, just a speck now at the end of the road, trying to see if Lamb had moved. The front door to the house was still open so I walked up onto the porch and in. I didn't take but two steps, and I could see in my mind how it must have gone. The men knocking at the door. Marion trying to hold them off while she got Lamb to run. And them bustin' in and dragging her out back. Looked like she must have put up a fight the way the furniture was broken up. I righted a chair, stood the table up, turned around, and went back out the front door, closed it behind me. I didn't want to see the house this way, torn through, soiled.

I walked down the steps and around to the back. I could smell smoke. Burning wood. I kicked an empty bottle out of the way and kept walking. Slow as I could.

I kept my eyes down, looking at my feet. Afraid I guess to look up. I walked into the yard. All the grass was torn up, stomped down. Torches were left behind still smoking. More bottles. *Like a party.* I thought about stopping to pick them up, but that wasn't what I was here for.

I could feel the knife in my pocket as I walked, banging against my leg. I'd had it since the war. Brought it back with me. Used it for things I didn't much like to think back on now but home in Shubuta, I used it to gut the fish I caught with my pappy. Here in Jackson—

I heard a sound behind me, and my hand reached for my knife same time as I turned. Like I was a soldier all over again.

"Look what they done did…"

An older man stood looking up past me, over my shoulder. At the tree behind me.

"Heard 'em out here half the night…" he said, shaking his head. "We all did. Wasn't nothing we could do."

"I know, I know…" I said.

"Lamb? The boy?" he asked.

"They fine," I told him.

"Thank you Jesus," he whispered. "You Marion's people?"

I nodded. "Her husband. Chester Clark."

His eyebrows went up.

"Long time ago," I said.

"You gonna need a ladder," he said, looking up again. "I'll get my boy to help."

"Appreciate the ladder, but this is something imma need to do on my own."

Another man came out. Stood beside the first. Looking up, shaking his head. I still couldn't turn.

"We'll go and get that ladder for you," the older man said. I nodded thanks.

Breathed in deep and thought of Marion's face on the front porch of her house the day I thought she was Turner's wife. Her standing before me in church on our wedding day. With her sewing machine on her lap leaving Shubuta. Holding first Simeon, then Lamb in her arms here in this house the day they were born. Could barely recollect now all the times we fussed and fought. Finally, I made myself turn to look at the pecan tree.

I saw her feet first, covered in mud. Scraped and bloody. And then I let my eyes make my way up her legs, past her torn-up dress to her face. *Marion.* The prettiest woman I ever seen. Her face now was so swolled her own momma and daddy wouldn't have known her. I spread my legs wide and put my hands on my knees to keep from falling over. Heard the men behind me coming back with the ladder and turned.

But it wasn't them.

"Lamb!"

She'd fallen to sitting and was on the ground staring up at her momma. Mouth wide open. Her head was laying to the side. Arms wide open reaching to her like she was asking for a hug.

"No!" I screamed. Running to her. "No." I reached down and grabbed her up in my arms quick like she was a newborn baby. Pushed her face in my chest, trying to hide her eyes. *Too late.* "I told you not to…"

I ran with her into the house. Her head banged against my chest like she couldn't hold it up. I ran past the busted-up chairs and turned-over furniture. I ran to the room I remembered was hers. Sat her up on the edge of her bed.

"Get your things together," I told her, out of breath. "Don't come outside. Don't go near the windows. Put your things in a suitcase. Anything you want to take with you to Ohio. That's all I want you thinking about now. Ohio and your brother."

She looked like she didn't hear me.

"Lamb?"

She shook her head up and down and I went back outside where the men were waiting now with the ladder. *How?* I grabbed it from them. *How could they do this?* Laid it up against the tree. Made sure it was steady. *To a woman?* Took out my knife and started climbing to cut the rope they used to hang my wife.

LAMB

WHAT do you pack when you're leaving behind your life? Momma didn't keep a whole lot of pictures, but she had one of her and Uncle Chime standing in front of their house in Shubuta. She looked almost the same. Uncle Chime was smiling big in short pants and boots, holding on to Momma's arm. And Momma was looking into the camera. Maybe squinting at the sun. Not smiling, but not frowning either, like she had somewhere else to be. I put that in first.

I knew now I was packing to take a piece of Momma with me because I wouldn't never be coming back to Jackson. I couldn't ever return to a place where someone who called herself my friend stood by, like she was at a parade, and watched while a crowd hung my momma from a tree. All those times she told me that our friendship was more than Negro and white, and I let myself believe it because I needed to. The truth of it was, hard as we tried to pretend, the differences between the two of us were as wide as the Mississippi River. How else could she stand there under a tree with a crowd of cheering white folks knowing me and knowing my momma done nothing but want her boy to live and breathe another day? I was sure that what I wanted was to leave Jackson, Marny, this house far behind. I was finally going to decide things for myself.

I packed as many dresses as I could fit and the only sweaters I had because Simeon told me how it got so cold in the North there was even snow nearly every day, all winter long, not just like we had every once in a while. That'd be something to see. How was I going to tell him about Momma? I was hoping Uncle Chime knew and already told him to save me from doing it. Or maybe that should be left to me? I wondered what Simeon was going to say about seeing Daddy. About seeing me with Daddy. I sat down in the chair, looking around at my room for the last time. In my nightstand were books I'd have to leave behind. Too many to bring. But I squeezed in a few of the smaller ones. I walked over to the bureau and took my hairbrush, comb, and barrettes. I could almost feel Momma's fingers in my hair. Under my schoolbag was the book, *A House Divided*, that Marny had given me. I picked it up, then set it back down on the dresser. I used that pretty ribbon she wrapped it with as a bookmark. How long had it been since I first met her in her daddy's office? On the bridge? Since she asked about my daddy and I went to see him at the lumberyard? Since I thought we could be friends? Because I thought that, my momma was dead.

I heard Daddy's boots coming up the back stairs, and I stayed in my room, waiting till he told me to come out. My daddy had been right about so many things. About us spending time together. About Marny's family being trouble. But he was wrong about me seeing my momma. The woman hanging in that tree, beaten bad, her clothes nearly ripped right off her, she wasn't who I would see when I closed my eyes at night. My momma was the woman who held my face and told me how I was her light. Told me she loved me. *Told me to run.* My momma was the woman who saved my life. And Simeon's too. That's who I would see when I closed my eyes at night. The woman hanging from our pecan tree was someone those white folks needed her to be to get out all their hate. But that wasn't *my* momma.

I heard my daddy breathing heavy, his boots walking slow. Step by step into Momma's room like he was marching. I heard the sound of her bed creaking. I waited, listening. He came out now, closed the door behind him.

"Lamb?" he called out.

I opened my door. He looked down at me and my suitcase.

"You all ready?"

I nodded. He took my suitcase from me. "This everything?"

We walked again out the back and down the stairs. Neither of us looked toward the tree.

"Daddy—" He turned, looking scared. "I forgot something—I'll be right back."

"Lamb—"

"I'll be right back—"

I ran in the house before he could stop me. I went to my room again and grabbed the book Marny gave me from the dresser. I closed my door behind me and looked at the closed door to Momma's room. I walked toward it.

"C'mon now, Lamb," I could hear Daddy calling.

I opened her door slow.

Momma. Daddy had laid her out in her bed. Her head was up on two pillows. He'd covered her with her prettiest quilt. The wedding quilt she made with her momma. It had all the colors she loved. Blue. Green. And I never noticed before but right in the middle was yellow. *The color of sunshine.* Daddy had covered most of her face with the quilt and looking at her I could almost pretend she was sleeping. *Peaceful.* "Goodbye, Momma," I said, and closed the door quiet, just as I heard Daddy step back inside the house. I closed the door to her room and met him at the back door.

"I forgot this book," I told him.

"Well, we got a long ride. Good you bringing along something to read," he said.

"Oh, it ain't for reading," I told him. Outside I walked over to the pecan tree and laid it there up against the trunk.

My daddy looked but didn't say nothing.

"I'm ready," I told him.

My daddy reached for my suitcase and we walked down the block, toward his car. Toward Ohio and Simeon. And away from Jackson, my home, and what I loved most, my momma.

EPILOGUE

MYRTLE

It was almost a year after she left that her letter came. I knew that just like me, she was thinking about Marion and the date that was coming round again. That letter sat staring at me from on top of my bureau near a week before I could open it. Reading her words, I knew, was going to be like opening up a cut that was just starting to heal. But one night, after I ate supper and was good and tired, I sat in my chair by the window with the letter on my lap, seeing Lamb's face next to Marion's. I opened the envelope and ran my hands over her pretty writing on the paper and heard Lamb's voice clear as day, like she was standing in the room with me. I wasn't never much of a letter writer. But if I was, I could fill a book with all I wanted to tell her.

I'd gathered bits and pieces from folks round town and knew the Trempers had their hand in what happened to Marion. That nasty doctor, who I told Marion wasn't no good, but she said she was tired of dragging Simeon miles away when there was a doctor just a walk down the street. She was always needing to do for herself, was more like it, and hated asking for help even if help meant having Chime drive her every now and again. I had to laugh to myself thinking about Marion and her stubborn self. I wanted to tell Lamb how her mother got back at ole Dr. Tremper in the end. I'd see a few folks trickling in and out of his sorry building, but it wasn't nothing like before Marion passed when he had to just about turn folks away. Looked like Dr. Tremper learned quick that colored folks will put up with a lot of foolishness from white folks when they have to, when they don't have no choice. Turns out when they do, they will drive, walk, or go without before they step foot in a place with a man whose idea of justice is a rope and a tree. I heard even that daughter of his left town, headed off to stay with her momma's people.

Truth is, I thought about leaving Jackson myself. I see Marion around every corner. I hear her voice at night in my ear and not a Saturday night goes by when I don't want to put on my prettiest dress and fix up my hair and make my way over to the house. But leaving here would be like leaving Marion behind.

And I know that just like Chime, I'm never going to be no northerner. I could have told you he wasn't going to last in Ohio. He was back in Jackson soon as the weather turned. He didn't come see me straight away. He waited on that. I had to hear from Edgar, his running buddy I used to see him with every now and again down at the Camelot.

"You heard from Chime?" he asked one day when he come into the store.

Most folks stopped asking after him weeks after he left, after Marion was buried. Figuring Chime was settled for good up north.

I didn't look up, kept on packing up the things he bought. "You know he's gone," I said, thinking maybe Edgar done gone soft in the head asking me something he already knew the answer to.

He leaned over to me. "Nah, he's back. Saw him last night. I was crossing the street and he nearly run me down. Didn't stop long enough to catch up good. Had a lady friend with him. Thought you knew, but from the looks of it, you didn't."

I looked up at him.

"I'll tell him to stop by," he said.

"You go on and do that," I told him.

He took his sack, left the store. I sat down hard. *What is Chime doing back in Jackson? And why didn't he come to see me?*

Time he made his way to my place I was good and mad and stood in the doorway telling him about himself. But it was Chime, with his excuses, flashing his gap-toothed smile at me, and next thing I knew I had stepped out the way to let him inside and he was sitting on my couch making me laugh about some foolishness up in Ohio.

"Suits Simeon just fine," he said. "But me? With all those ed-u-ca-ted folks?" He shook his head. "I told my nephew, 'They gonna run you out this school they find out I'm your family.'"

We laughed about all night. Till we started talking about Marion. About my laying her out. About the Trempers. Getting Simeon out of town. Lamb following behind with Chester.

Chime bent his head. "If I'da known they was gonna go on and do what they done…" And we sat quiet, the two of us, for a long time, thinking about that night and the days after.

Knowing Simeon and Lamb were safe was all that got him through, he told me. Was all Marion would have wanted. I told him Marion never told me much about Chester, that's how I knew he couldn't have been all that bad. She saved her cursing for the ones who deserved it, not for those who didn't. But she did tell me once he loved his children. Her too. She just couldn't love him back the way he needed.

And it made me think of all those years me and Marion spent together, but never really together as a family and never really being able to love the way we both needed.

But I couldn't write all that to Lamb.

In the end, I picked up my pen and scratched out my words to her, slow and neat,

Dear Lamb,

I sure appreciate you taking the time to write. Your momma would be proud of you both, doing all that you doing. It's no surprise Simeon is keeping himself busy. And you are going to make a fine nurse one day, Lamb, kind as you are.

Here's a little something so you don't forget me...

I wrote in the recipe for my pie she loved.

Maybe you can make it for your daddy. I miss you too. Please write again soon.

Signed it,

Love, Myrtle

I took Lamb's letter with me when I went to see Marion on the first Sunday, like I do every month. I sat down in the hard dirt, picking at the weeds that had grown up around her marker, and smoothed the dirt back down. The church saw to Marion's headstone and that reverend came out and prayed so powerful, folks who barely knew Marion's name cried like they lost their own mommas.

"Marion," I started, wiping my face dry. If I tried hard enough, I could remember the Marion before. Pretty and brown. Before they got to her. Hurt her so bad I barely knew her face when I went to her. Chester had laid her out in her bed. Covered her with her prettiest quilt. The one she told me she made with her momma. The folks down at People's Funeral Home came and took her away, quiet as can be, like they do. I wondered if that must be something they learn, to be quiet, like a ghost, spiriting loved ones away, almost before you even know they gone.

"Your babies are getting on good," I told her. "Looks like you are gonna have yourself a doctor *and* a nurse."

I reached in my purse and took out Lamb's letter that I'd read over and over again till the paper was wrinkled. Laid it out on the smoothed-down dirt and read it out loud...

Dear Miss Myrtle,

I'm sorry it's been so long since you have heard from me. It was so hard seeing you on that last day and telling you all that had happened. Daddy said we had to get out quick and I know now he was right. I never got a chance to thank you for making sure Momma got a proper burial. Daddy says one day when the time is right, he'll need to head back to Jackson to settle his affairs, most likely sell the house, and when he does we can all say a proper goodbye to Momma then. I keep the picture I took with me of her and Uncle Chime by my bedside waiting for that day.

Not a day goes by when I don't think about what those men did to Momma. She told me and Simeon once that when it comes to what white folks do to Negroes, the law looks the other way. But I watched the law looking right at her, making her pay when the only law she broke was to see her children safe. As hard as I've prayed I know I'll never find it in my heart to forgive. But I am hoping that one day Momma will forgive me and Simeon for bringing those men to her door and tearing us all apart. It was all we could do to stop Simeon from hopping the next train back to

Jackson. Daddy told him that after all Momma sacrificed to get him north, he couldn't waste it fighting a war he was never going to win. I try to remember that on the hardest days. All the ways me and Simeon can make sure her sacrifice was worth it.

I sure wish you could have seen Simeon's face when he saw me and Daddy show up in Ohio. I don't think I'd ever seen Simeon with nothing to say, but there he was staring at me and Daddy with his mouth wide open and not a thing coming out of it. It was a sight to see. I've been praying and every day we're together we all feel a little more like family.

I know Momma would be proud I started college as a nursing student at Central State University, not far from where Simeon is in college at Wilberforce University. Daddy found us a nice place near Simeon's school. Simeon lives on campus in a dormitory. Daddy found a job at another lumberyard not too far from Wilberforce. I thought it would be hard starting at a new school and meeting new people, but everybody's been real good to us. There's a part of this town that reminds me a little bit of Jackson. I think even Momma might have liked it here. It could be the way the folks are kind and don't mind speaking to strangers. Not at all like I thought northerners would be. Daddy found us a church home at Holy Trinity Church. I say us, but I don't think Daddy was much for churchgoing, but since I joined the choir, he doesn't seem to mind going to service. The pastor there is nothing like Reverend Greer, but the choir is just fine and last Sunday, I sang a solo and I could almost see Momma sitting in the pew smiling up at me with Simeon laughing right along beside her.

By the way, Simeon sends his love too. He's so busy with school and his clubs there are weeks when I barely see him. But it's nice

*knowing he's close by (and can still help me with my studies if I
need it—ha, ha).*

*That's all I have for now, but I promise to write again soon.
Please keep an eye on Uncle Chime for me and make sure he is
behaving himself. Without Momma there, who knows what trouble he'll get into.*

I miss you.

With all my love,

Lamb

I folded the letter up. Let myself see Marion smiling at all Lamb
wrote. I was hoping it wouldn't be too long before Lamb found out that
if there was any forgiving that needed to be done it wasn't from Marion. She was going to have to learn to forgive herself in her own time.
But it seemed to me, the people that need the most forgiving usually
ain't the ones asking.

"You ain't got to worry no more," I said to Marion. "They are going
to see each other through, just like you wanted."

I stood and brushed the dirt off my dress as I headed on home.

The way to right wrongs is to turn the light of truth upon them.

—Ida B. Wells

AUTHOR'S NOTE

There's not much I know about the real-life Lamb Whittle, for whom this novel and its title character are named, other than that her name was one among a partial list of female lynching victims in Rachel Marie-Crane Williams's book *Elegy of Mary Turner: An Illustrated Account of a Lynching*. But seeing the name Lamb in the context of a lynching made me wonder about the innocence the name implied for its namesake. I tried to imagine the life of Lamb Whittle up to its horrific end. How old was she? Where was she from? Who were her people? What were the details of her murder? Sadly, my research uncovered no further details of her life or the circumstances surrounding her lynching. And the same held true for many of the other female victims she was listed alongside. It was as if they'd simply never existed. But they did exist. They lived and breathed and left an indelible imprint on this earth.

I came to Williams's book as part of my research after a trip to the Legacy Museum and Memorial, often referred to as the Lynching Museum, in Montgomery, Alabama, in the summer of 2018.

I visited to deepen my understanding of one of the most painful chapters in the history of the United States. The heart-wrenching stories of Black men were what brought me there to record and bear witness to all of the victims of white mob injustice. But with the men's stories were those of female lynching victims, whose stories have often gone untold. I discovered that unlike Black men, who were most often the target of mob violence, wrongly accused of a host of crimes, women were often lynched in retribution, in retaliation, in vengeance, or as an afterthought. The numerous female victims were mothers and daughters. Some were wives. Some were pregnant. Most often the "crime" that led to their lynching was simply that they were related to a male suspect. And so, as is often the case when conducting research, while I went to learn about one particular facet of history, my heart led me to another. There at the Legacy Museum and the National Memorial for Peace and Justice, I knew I had in some way to memorialize these women in a story.

Between 1877 and 1950, the Equal Justice Initiative recorded more than 4,400 lynchings in the United States. Of those, the U.S. National Archives estimates that approximately 173 women were lynched between 1837 and 1946. Lamb Whittle was one of the many documented Black female victims of lynching whose stories were never recorded, but in my research, I uncovered the accounts of so many others. Among them was Cordelia Stevenson of Columbus, Mississippi, who was lynched in 1915 after a white mob accused her son of burning down a barn and was unable to locate him.

In addition to Lamb, many of the other names of characters in this novel are derived in part from the real names of lynching victims:

Marion Howard

Chime Riley

Milly **Thompson**

Mrs. **Brisco**

Laura Wood

Cora

Hayes **Turner**

Lloyd **Clay**

While this is a work of fiction, many of the scenes depicted are based on factual accounts by people who were subjected to the intimidation tactics of the South's Jim Crow laws and practices. Lynchings were not the only tool whites used to slow the economic and educational advancement of Blacks. Obscure laws and ordinances, such as the prohibition against Blacks wearing military uniform for longer than three days, were put in place to ensure that Blacks remained disadvantaged and disenfranchised in the communities in which they lived.

Simeon's encounter with Dr. Tremper about the spelling of his name is based on an actual account in which a young boy named Ulysses was sentenced to hard labor on a chain gang for providing the correct spelling of his name to a police officer.

In 1918, the Shubuta Bridge, dubbed the "Hanging Bridge," was the site of a quadruple lynching of brothers Major and Andrew Clark and sisters Maggie and Alma Howze, both pregnant, all of whom were accused of the murder of Dr. E. L. Johnson. The incident received national media attention and prompted an investigation by the NAACP. Secretary Walter White traveled to Shubuta with a private detective to request further inquiry into the case. Mississippi governor Theodor Bilbo denied the NAACP request, telling the organization to "go to hell." None of the perpetrators were ever brought to justice. The NAACP used the Shubuta incident in their publisher report "Thirty Years of Lynching: 1889–1918."

In the late 1800s, journalist Ida B. Wells used *Free Speech and Headlight,* the Memphis, Tennessee, newspaper of which she was an editor and co-owner, to begin the country's first antilynching campaign. Her editorials pointed out the hypocrisy and misrepresentation of the lynching narrative perpetrated by whites and mainstream media outlets, who often portrayed Black males as violent aggressors and sexual predators.

To the contrary, no offense was considered too minor to warrant lynching, including vagrancy, personal debt, laughing at the wrong time, union organizing, using boastful language, refusing to accept an employment offer from a white person, and being too successful.

One young man was lynched when he accidentally brushed up against a white girl while running to catch a train. An elderly man who was slow to remove his hat when a group of white men spoke to him was hanged alongside his dog.

Ida B. Wells called for Blacks to organize, boycott, and migrate to other areas to form their own communities where they would be free to advance themselves and live without fear. As a result of her editorials, the *Free Speech* offices and presses were destroyed and Wells became the target of death threats. In 1894, she published *The Red Record*, a statistical record of lynchings she had collected while traveling the country, researching and documenting lynchings throughout the South. Lynching has been considered one of the main causes of the Great Migration, during which, between 1917 and 1970, nearly six million Blacks left the South and moved to northern states.

Only seven states—Arizona, Idaho, Maine, Nevada, South Dakota, Vermont, and Wisconsin—have no reported lynchings. The state of Mississippi had more than 581 between the years of 1882 and 1968, the largest number of any state.

Despite a massive campaign by the NAACP, attempts to pass anti-lynching legislation failed repeatedly, beginning with its initial introduction in 1900.

Congressman Bobby Rush of Illinois introduced the Emmett Till Antilynching Act in 2021. Nearly sixty-seven years after the infamous lynching of fourteen-year-old Emmett Till in Money, Mississippi, in 1955, the bill was finally passed on March 2, 2022.

ACKNOWLEDGMENTS

It was my visit to the Equal Justice Initiative's Legacy Museum and the National Memorial for Peace and Justice that began me on this journey of documenting the lives of female victims of lynching, but it continued with countless others who offered their stories, unwavering support, advice, expertise and guidance. The number of people it took to bring this book to life is remarkable. For each answer I found during the research process, several more questions arose. But it was my time in Jackson, Mississippi, at the Museum of Mississippi History, the Mississippi Civil Rights Museum, and the Mississippi Department of Archives & History, where the incredible librarians helped me sort through countless documents and archival newspapers, that helped to shape this book.

Jessica Russell and Rachel Lott at the Eudora Welty House & Garden offered extensive resources and patiently led this visiting Northerner to neighborhood pecan trees (along with the *correct* pronunciation of *pi-KAHN*) to photograph for reference. My engaging chat with Forrest Galey, Special Projects Officer at the Eudora Welty Collection, offered me an additional Jacksonian perspective well beyond the Welty photo collection she oversees and I used as a historic reference. At the Big Apple Inn on Farish Street, a local and historic Black-owned institution, where I ate pig ear and fried bologna sandwiches, I met Plas

Lindsey, who shared stories of his family's history and the Black communities in Jackson.

Thanks always to my editor, Mary Cash, who when I tentatively told her my idea of wanting to write the story of female victims of lynching asked how soon I could start, knowing this was a story that urgently needed to be told. Her implicit trust in my storytelling voice has given me the confidence to expand from picture books to middle grade, and now to my very first young adult novel. Page by page, draft by draft, weekends included, Mary was a true partner on this journey. Thank you to my powerhouse agent, Rosemary Stimola of Stimola Literary Studio, whose honesty, guidance, and friendship encouraged me to tell the story of this tragic moment in our nation's history. And thank you, as always, to the wonderful team at Holiday House Publishers who grab ahold of each story and enthusiastically share them with readers far and wide, and to Dara Sharif for her editorial feedback. My brilliant assistant, Mya Rose Bailey, whose insight and research help have transformed my writing life.

My mother-in-law, Margaret Williams, and aunts Marie Jacobs, Frances Williams and Gladys Harris, whose honest portraits of their lives as girls growing up in the South, shared with me at a kitchen table in Paterson, New Jersey, gave me the fortitude I needed to carry on. For Nava Atlas for pointing me towards Ida B. Wells.

Thank you to Ida Thompson for hunting down information on segregated doctor's offices, Vito Parrinello for his period car expertise, and Eduardo Vann and Marlene and James "J.E." Williams, whom I turn to time and again for advice on scripture and spirituals. My friend and critique partner Ann Burg and my fabulous and fearless writing groups for their invaluable input. My sister Linda Cline, the keeper of our family history, sent every relevant article she came across, and was always a keen and ready ear during each stage of this story.

My children, Jaime, Maya, Malcolm and Leila, who listen and cheer in equal measure. I began writing so they could know their history, and each day they give me hope for our future. My husband, James, who was a tireless traveling companion on each one of my research trips and whose patience, feedback and support breathed life into this book and me.

Finally, research can be a long and tedious process, but I am so thankful to the authors whose riveting storytelling and detailed research gave voice to the unheard with dignity and compassion and provided the foundation for this book: *The Blood of Emmett Till* by Timothy Tyson; *Without Sanctuary: Lynching Photography in America* by James Allen, Hilton Als, Congressman John Lewis, and Leon F. Litwack; *Elegy for Mary Turner: An Illustrated Account of a Lynching* by Rachel Marie-Crane Williams; *Hanging Bridge: Racial Violence and America's Civil Rights Century* by Jason Morgan Ward; *Eudora Welty Photographs* by University Press of Mississippi; *Trouble in Mind: Black Southerners in the Age of Jim Crow* by Leon Litwack.

Lesa Cline-Ransome